keep the ends loose

keep the ends loose

Molly D. Campbell

This is a work of fiction. Names, characters, places and incidents are either products of the author's imagination or are used fictitiously. Any resemblance to actual events, locales, organizations, or persons living or dead, is entirely coincidental and beyond the intent of either the author or the publisher.

Studio Digital CT, LLC
P.O. Box 4331
Stamford, CT 06907

Copyright © 2014 by Molly Campbell
Cover design by Barbara Aronica-Buck

Story Plant Paperback ISBN: 978-1-61188-204-9
Fiction Studio Books E-book ISBN: 978-1-936558-54-4

Visit our website at www.TheStoryPlant.com

All rights reserved, which includes the right to reproduce this book or portions thereof in any form whatsoever except as provided by U.S. Copyright Law. For information, address The Story Plant.

First Story Plant Printing: February 2015
Printed in the United States of America
0 9 8 7 6 5 4 3 2 1

To my grandson, Charlie

Chapter One

Have you ever heard of a guy named Proust? He was an insanely famous writer. Get this: he wrote about his boring life. I figure that if Proust could do it, so can I. So let me tell you about my Aunt Iris.

Iris Fletcher is my aunt on my mother's side. My mother, Winnie, is absolutely *nothing* like her sister. Here is my mother: busy, bossy, and in everybody's business. My mother, Winnie Heath, is about five foot three and weighs two hundred pounds. She's chunky. I don't know why, but even though she has never been thin, men love her. It might be because she has bright blue eyes and eyelashes that stick out a mile. But the rest of her is kind of ordinary. She has wiry, dark brown curls that spiral around her face. Plus, she has skin so soft that I like to pet her arms. And her boobs never fell. Winnie is quick to smile, with teeth straight from the braces Grandma insisted on getting for her. And I have to say that Grandma was right: Winnie has a real winner of a smile. She will never need those whitening strips. Winnie has a cheerful face, and her eyes wrinkle when she smiles. All in all, she is satisfactory. But she is a legend in the Heath family.

They say that a girl who acts as if she is God's gift to men becomes one. For sure, that has to be the case with my mom. She had a whole lot of boyfriends back in the day—when she was young, before she married my dad. She was chubby then, too. Didn't matter. She had her pick. She picked Roy Heath to be my dad (well, her husband first) because she says she knew he would be a "good provider." He has been. By the way, Mom quit being a heartbreaker when she got married. Men still like her, though. Go figure.

My dad, Roy Heath, is a pharmacist. He owns Heath Pharmacy and Assorteds. He added the "Assorteds" because he knew what all the big chains were doing. They were taking over everything, becoming the "Pharmacy as General Store," he said. "Trying to push all the little guys out of business." So Dad started selling bread, eggs, milk, and motor oil, to keep the "big boys" from stealing his business and his store. So we stayed open. And the "big boys" never really got a foothold in our little town. And we still do just fine, thanks to Roy.

I said this was a story about my Aunt Iris. It kind of is. And it kind of isn't. Let me just say this: without Aunt Iris, I wouldn't be telling you this. So I have to set up the comparison/contrast between her and the rest of the family. You see, she is *completely different* from the rest of us.

As I was saying, my dad, Roy Heath, is a visionary. He does a lot of reading, and then he thinks about it. We take about ten different newspapers. That is, we did, until all the newspapers started going out of business. Then Dad took to reading stuff on the Internet. Now he's thinking about the sorry state of the world, with all the global warming, terrorism, our sicko economy, and things. You know how everything big in the world always filters down to all of us in middle America. So Roy thinks about all of this and makes plans for the future. I don't know what he'll come up with, but I bet it will be something good that will make money. That's just the way he rolls.

I am fifteen. Oh, my name is Miranda. Can you believe it? Dad liked it. Mom said it sounded way too sophisticated, so they call me Mandy. What do I look like? Ordinary: Brown hair. Brown/black eyes. Three freckles on my nose.

Anyway, I'm in junior high school (this town is so backward they don't even call it middle school), and I hate every minute of it. I think it is because I live a lot inside my head. I have read all the books in our living room bookcase and a shit ton from the library, and I think I would prefer life in another era. This one is way too complicated. Mom says that I'm an "old soul." I think she's saying I'm immature, but in a nice way. I don't think old souls can be immature. We just choose to float around somewhere in between Jane Austen and Harry Potter, instead of some dystopian place where you have to cook up some meth in order to afford medical treatment. I also hate zombies. Oh, yeah. I am extremely smart for my age. Even so, I would classify myself as a throwback. Ok. So I am a late blooming, smart, old soul. Anyway, this year coming up, I'm going to be a sophomore. This is classified at Framington High as officially "high school."

Ugh. As soon as I graduate, I am going to leave this forlorn cement-block town forever and move to New York or Toronto and have a career. I like business. I'm pretty good at math. My English teacher, Mrs. Hardin, says I am excellent at writing. Writing *is* fun, this is truth.

I am not into sex. Not that I don't have hormones. It's just that I have all kinds of aspirations. So I have no time for all that porno texting, sending nude selfies, and throwing myself at what Mom calls "intercourse." I have to focus on what's going on in my brain. Boys don't seem to like me much anyway, even though I am not chubby like my mom. I just don't have "the gift." That's what Mom calls her talent with men. She says you're born with it, chubby or no.

It doesn't really bother me about the boys, at least not right now. To me, living in a big city and working in a glass skyscraper with your own office sounds fantastic. I know I have to get a skill. Don't get me wrong, I know you don't just get an office because you *want* one. So I will go to college. I am sure that when I get there, I will pick a major that will result in my having an office with windows on two sides. I might not want an office, actually. I may end up being a writer. Writers get to stay home at their laptops and wear sweats all day. Maybe I will consider that. But really, I am not kidding myself here. Yes, I have aspirations. Yes, I want to get out of this town. And yes, I am a throwback who is mainly scared shitless of sex. There you have it.

Okay. Now for my brother—I know, we Heaths all sound like candy bars, to start with. But Adam Heath? Believe me, he is the furthest thing from sweet. Adam Heath swears like Satan, uses dip behind my parents' backs, and he has body odor that he tries to hide with the clinical strength deodorant that he gets for free at the store. What does he look like? He has eyes the color of the water in swimming pools, you know? That is a plus. A minus? He has hair the color of copper. It is *curly*, on top of that. Typical ginger kid: sullen or angry—take your pick. However, he's about six feet tall, and even though I feel kind of incestuous saying this, he has that triangle body shape from his shoulders to that narrow waist that girls find sexy. Adam rarely speaks in actual words—preferring grunts and "Yes" or "No" answers—but when he uses it, his voice sounds like black velvet. And he has hooded eyes. But good Lord—I have told him that if he *ever* hopes to get married, he has to start washing. He insists that he washes, and that "you just have a sensitive nose, you asshole." I told you, he sucks.

My brother just graduated from Framington High. Next year he is going to the community college, whether he likes it or not. He has made it clear to Dad that he does *not* want to be a pharmacist. He thinks he wants to learn about taxidermy. Either that or forest management. He's kind of outdoorsy. This is good, keeping in mind how he smells. But realistic? Of course not. Who stuffs animals anymore? He is bullshitting Mom and Dad. Plus, I think the forests are almost all gone, due to all the idiots in the world cutting them down and not replanting them. Global warming! And nobody supports hunting and killing just to stuff heads and hang them up over the fireplace these days. Well, most people with good taste and sensibility don't go big game hunting any more. Anyway, I don't think he has any future at all. Mom says that this is nonsense and that he will take a little time finding himself. Truth is, he *finds himself* just fine at night when he surfs the Internet for porn, but she doesn't know that. Or she is choosing to ignore it. Adam is an asshole. Just the other night, he blew snot in my direction when I was sitting at the kitchen table, eating toast. I was infuriated and called him a cocksucker. Of course, I know that Adam is hetero and isn't interested in sucking his or anybody else's cock. So of course Adam felt free to inform me that I am an idiot. So I called him a prick. As far as I am concerned, any and all genital terminology applies to Adam.

But there's a real problem with the whole college thing. See, Roy Heath has his heart set on Adam joining the family business. And like I said, Adam has made it clear that he has no intention of being a pharmacist. Dad/Roy doesn't even consider me. In his mind, I am way too much of a "scatterbrain" (Dad's word) to want to go to pharmacy school. He thinks I will get married to some man who will sweep me off to some exotic place like Indianapolis, where the commute to the pharmacy won't work at all. So Dad has given Adam an ultimatum: either go to college, get a pharmacy degree (which, by the way, is almost like being a doctor), or Dad won't pay for *any* education at all.

Mom/Winnie, who is more practical, sees this as a major problem. Adam says that he can get a scholarship to go to taxidermy school or something. Again with the taxidermy. I think he says that just to infuriate Winnie and Roy. As if anybody is actually buying the taxidermy thing. *Come on.* Or, Adam says, he'll work his way through forestry school. Or he'll go to work full time at the pharmacy in the fall. Hah. Winnie knows Adam the way I do. She doesn't have a pharmaceutical fantasy like Roy does. She knows that Adam will never count a pill in a lab coat, *no chance.* So she's been squirreling away money like mad, hoping that she can at least fund part of Adam's college experience. Even if it's stuffing dead things with sphagnum moss, or whatever they use when they mount those disgusting moose heads. Oh, God. *Squirreling.* Unintended pun.

You see, our family is just the typical American situation-comedy variety. Nothing interesting. Nothing outrageous. Not even a gay couple anywhere.

Aunt Iris is my mom's older sister. Aunt Iris is my mom's complete opposite. Remember, Mom is short and stubby? Well, Iris is statuesque. Tall, willowy, and graceful. Iris has long, taffy-colored hair that falls around her in waves. She always looks as if she just stepped out of a poem. Her skin is like fine china. Okay, I got that from a book. But really, she's never had a pimple in her whole life, I bet. Her eyes are blue, but not like my mom's. Iris's eyes are a kind of light and watery blue. Sort of like the water in aquariums, you know? And her voice is her best asset, in my opinion. When Iris talks, it's a combination of talking and purring. I swear. Aunt Iris is absolutely *deadly* over the phone. She sounds like one of those old-fashioned movie queens, only with a slight cold. Iris has long, elegant fingers and arms. She wears three gold rings on each hand. One of them is her wedding ring.

I think Aunt Iris is pretty. But most people say she is bland. Isn't that wild? Her sister is short and fat but beautiful, and even though Iris has it all over my mother with her wonderful figure and graceful ways, she is sort of boring. Iris puts her caramelly hair up in a French twist sometimes, but usually she wears it loose, with a headband holding it back from her high forehead. Her eyebrows frame her pale blue eyes with high arches that make her look just a little surprised all the time. Iris has a Grecian nose. And she has lips that nearly pout as much as Angelina Jolie's. Behind those eyes, I have to admit, it's a little vacant in there. Like Iris has left the building. I know, I'm tearing her down, but I am devoted to her, actually. But I'm compelled to be truthful.

Winnie crackles. She has enough energy bursting out of her pores to light up a small city. Winnie is totally competent. She could probably change a tire while texting. Sometimes she moves so fast it seems like she can be in two places at once. So if you were to compare Iris to Winnie, it would be like comparing an Afghan hound wearing a silk scarf as a collar to a little pug running down the street with a stolen hot dog in her mouth.

Here is what I know about Aunt Iris:

Iris was born two years before my mother. When she was born, it was kind of hard on Grandma, who swore she didn't want any more pregnancies, on account of the pain. They say that the pain you have in childbirth is easily forgotten, or else there wouldn't be the population explosion we have now. And that's exactly what happened, because two years later, out popped Winifred. Iris always loved her sister. They didn't fight or anything. Apparently, my mother claimed that the dollhouse Grandpa made for Iris on her seventh birthday was "for both of us!" and Iris didn't even argue. You see what I'm saying: Iris doesn't have much of a back bone. In her defense, though, living with Winnie would push anybody onto the path of least resistance.

Iris plays the piano. She went to some kind of music college—maybe it was Ohio State or something. When she was there, she met Frank Fletcher. Frank Fletcher. It sounds to me like something you get after you eat a lot of fiber: "Oh, boy. I'm going to pay for *that* with a Frank Fletcher . . ." Anyway, this Frank played the saxophone. Yeah. He was some kind of lounge musician: a jazz man. Now what Frank saw in Iris is beyond me. Actually, I am telling this story about Frank secondhand; it comes from my mom, who actually met the guy. She says that Frank Fletcher was scary handsome, with romantic auburn hair (I picture some aging Rolling Stone type), muscular arms, and piercing blue-green eyes. He wore black clothes. I guess that was the height back then. Apparently he was pretty sexy. I hate to think of women my mom's age getting all hot and bothered back then. Gross. But I guess Frank Fletcher was suave and charismatic, but with a cockiness that drew women like a magnet.

Anyway. Frank just swept Aunt Iris right off her feet. I guess they even had an affair. So Aunt Iris wasn't a willowy *virgin*. Mom says that Grandma and Grandpa were very alarmed. Musicians always get a bad rap. So they yanked Iris out of music school, but it was too late: she and Fletcher were *married*. Okay, a little bit happens in this story.

Iris came home, but she was wearing a wedding ring. Frank was out on the road, playing gigs. He's a character straight out of a book, right? Not Proust, though. Too long ago. Maybe a movie hero, more like Rob Lowe or maybe George Clooney—one of those cool old guys from my parents' generation. Their generation was full of iconic heroes—mystery and swagger. Anyway, Frank was gone a lot, and Iris started teaching piano lessons at home, just for something to do, I guess. Or for money, or maybe both. She must have earned some money, because she moved out of my grandparents' house and into her own little one across town. More about that later.

Things went on for a while. Frank Fletcher came back a few times, but then he faded out of the picture, I guess. It's kind of interesting that they didn't get divorced. Iris Fletcher just kept on wearing her wedding ring and teaching piano. I think she gave up sex altogether to focus on her music. So the wedding ring kept men at a distance.

Here's the whole part about Aunt Iris. All of the Frank Fletcher stuff happened years ago. For all we know, he died somewhere. He never sent Aunt Iris any money at all. Iris must have been a real budgeter, because she managed okay with her piano lessons. That and the fact that she ate dinner at either our house or Grandma and Grandpa's a lot. Plus she got an allowance from Grandpa. But she wasn't living like a queen, I will tell you.

Then about three years ago, everything changed. Grandma had a stroke. She lived a little while but she couldn't talk, and we all know she hated living after that. So she just gave it up and died. It was kind of awesome that she just quit eating and drinking and willed herself out of here. I was proud of her courage in making that decision. But then Grandpa just gave up, too. He told us that life without Grandma felt like he was numb all over. You know where this is going: Grandpa died eight months after Grandma.

Aunt Iris inherited a fortune from her parents. That really sounds good. But it isn't actually true. I put it in for color. No, Iris inherited enough money to live on for a long time. Keep in mind her lifestyle: bare bones. So

Iris was happy. She at least seemed happy to the family. Maybe because we didn't want to think about her being alone, sexually frustrated, and rattling around in her tiny house. In reality, she was a recluse with a part-time job.

Iris calls her house a bungalow. It isn't really. To me, it is more like a little red-brick box with a black roof. There isn't a front porch or anything. Don't bungalows have to have porches? Don't start thinking British village cottages, either. It's a little square house, that's it. It has a lot of charm to it, don't get me wrong. In the middle of the front is the bottle blue front door. On each side of the door is a skinny window. They have a name for them, but I am not an architect. Just imagine an ordinary, run of the mill place, and then pretty it up in your mind. That's Iris's house.

Grandpa died when I was twelve. So that means Iris became a recluse about two and a half years ago. During that time, she decorated her house, like I said. Okay, a few more specifics, but really, you should be using your imagination: She got it painted inside, in really pretty, pale colors. I like the kitchen the best because she painted it pale yellow and refinished the wide-plank oak floorboards. She got a square maple table with Windsor chairs for the breakfast nook—which, of course, has a bay window with yellow gingham curtains. She got a new stainless steel stove, a new icebox (we call them that in our family), and these really fancy countertops that are black with little speckles of silver in them. She had them put her new farmhouse sink under the window facing the side yard, so she can look out on the ash trees and her lilac bush. She keeps a fake geranium on the windowsill, but it's made of silk and looks totally real. It doesn't have a smell, so Aunt Iris has a plug-in thing that smells like a cross between lily of the valley flowers and vanilla. Her kitchen is heaven, I tell you. I regress when I am over there. Like right back to third grade, when all I cared about was getting hugs and eating junk.

What does she do all the time, now that she is a recluse? Well, Iris loves playing the piano, like I said. It sits right in the middle of her little living room, across from the fireplace. She plays and burns a fire in the winter, and, boy, is it nice in there. I go over a lot when it's cold. I like to sit on her new sofa (oh, yeah, she got some furniture, too) with the blue-and-beige stripes. It has down cushions. I sink right in. The fire in the fireplace crackles and pops and Aunt Iris plays sonatas or something. All I know is that it's so relaxing, I feel like I'm just as safe and happy as if I were on Aunt Iris's lap. Yeah. Third grade.

During the spring and summers, she gardens out back. Again, you really need to use your imagination, because I'm no Rembrandt, but suffice it to say that she has flower beds with only white-and-pink flowers. She bought a fountain that's more like a birdbath—water squirts out of a sparrow's beak. He's kind of perched on the side of it. Two wrought iron chairs and a little round table are out there. She got those out of our garage; we never sit outside because Winnie hates bugs. Anyway, with the flowers and the water noises, it's really peaceful. And Iris has hummingbirds. Flying jewels. Hummingbirds are so fast that I can't even see their wings beating in the sun. They look like big bees that roar. Aunt Iris says that they fly all over the world. Just think. Those tiny, be-sparkled birds have been more places than I will probably ever go.

Being a recluse has agreed with Aunt Iris. She is still willowy, but not quite as much as she used to be. Now I would call her "graceful and calm." She smiles to herself, and sometimes she hums a sonata. She isn't plump as a potato like my Mom. More like a filled-out version of a ballerina. It may be because now that she has a lot of time on her hands, she makes scones. Man, are they delicious! If you get a hot scone and put butter, whipped cream, and jam on it, it's better than chocolate cake, in my opinion. It crunches with just a touch of sweetness, and with the melting butter and strawberry jam, it makes my mouth burst with happiness. I go over there whenever she makes them. Mom says that Iris is getting to look more like her these days. Oh, boy. Chunky. But on Aunt Iris, the added weight looks good, like I said. She has bigger boobs now. And her cheeks are redder. And eating scones has either turned her hair darker or she is using a Revlon product from Heath's Pharmacy and Assorteds. Her hair now looks like chocolate caramels. She sure smiles more. Aunt Iris has white teeth. Probably from the toothpaste with extra-whitening power that she gets from the pharmacy.

But I have a feeling that Aunt Iris's days of being a hermit might be numbered. Because ... a *man*. His name is Don Horley. Remember those countertops? Well, Mr. Horley is the owner and installer at Horley's Kitchens and Baths. Yep. You guessed it. He sold Iris those fancy black countertops. She says that he painted such a beautiful verbal picture of just how the kitchen would glow with the glossy black and little sparkly bits. A beautiful verbal picture illustrated with rippling biceps and male pheromones. And maybe some aftershave.

When the day came to have the counters installed, Mr. Horley showed up with the crew. This isn't ordinarily the case. I know this because that's what Aunt Iris said. He came with the crew and stayed *all day,* sweating right along with the men and getting everything put in just so. I won't put words into her mouth, but I guess Don Horley looks quite sexual in a tank top. Even though he's something like fifty-five years old. But I get it—a hot man is a hot man at any age. Anyway, Aunt Iris talked to me about Mr. Horley just about non-stop for the next two weeks.

Okay. Forget Proust. Things are starting to sizzle around here. First of all, Aunt Iris *took off her wedding ring*. I guess it kind of freaked out Don Horley, kissing a married woman. You heard me. And Aunt Iris is walking around with stars in her eyes. That kind of freaks *me* out, thinking of old people having sex. Don't say it. I know—I need to get *over* my fear of sex. Adam would say "fear of fucking," but I try to keep the F-bomb out of my vocabulary. Mostly.

What's worse, my mom sat me down for a conversation.

"Mandy, Iris is in love." We were sitting at the kitchen table in the middle of the afternoon last Saturday. It was June the first. Just to give you a time frame.

"I know. She's all glowy, and I think she's wearing makeup. Has Dad noticed her upping her shopping habits at the store?"

I guess I have to start filling you in on some details. We live in Framington, like I mentioned, which is a medium-sized town. Kind of north of Columbus. In Ohio. Nobody important ever lived or died here. It looks like any other boring town in Ohio: squatty buildings, not much more than a main street and five intersections. One grocery. My dad's store. And, of course, Walmart is just *drooling* to buy Jasper Plevin's farm outside of town and move in. Like I said, typical. We have policemen, but they do things like write tickets. *Absolutely nothing exciting ever happens here.* So this conversation with my mom was starting to get me nervous. Because I know Winnie Heath. Those blue eyes don't blaze without a reason.

"So she can't get married." Mom started to drum her fingers on the tabletop. When I didn't respond, she drummed harder. "Well, Mandy?"

"Well, what?" I tried to act noncommittal. Like this wasn't the most earthshaking lead-in to a conversation I had ever experienced.

"We have to *do* something about it." She stared right at me, her eyes like lasers.

"What do you mean, *do* something? Mom, you sound like somebody on TV. What can we do?"

Winnie Heath transformed before my very eyes. Instead of the chubby little charmer, she morphed into a stocky private investigator. Just like that. You won't believe what happened.

I will always remember that exact moment. There we were, in our kitchen: big and square, with black-and-white linoleum. We sat at the red Formica-topped table (Mom is very vintage), and the sun was pouring in from the window over the chipped old farm sink (again, vintage: Mom is a flea marketer extraordinaire). As a matter of fact, the sun was kind of blaring into my eyes and making a big bright stripe down the middle of the table where Mom drummed her fingernails like castanets or something.

Here we were, having what I thought was just a regular afternoon. Mom had put out a plate of my favorite molasses cookies. Sidebar: these cookies are *to die for*. They are big, soft, and chewy. Just a little bit spicy and full of raisins. She sprinkles granulated sugar on top before she bakes them, so they are both soft *and* crunchy. I must learn to make them before I leave home.

I thought we'd just be kind of chewing and chatting, you know? Happy teen with her favorite sugary fix, passing the time with her mother. But then Mom hit me with Frank Fletcher and Don Horley and Aunt Iris.

"Mom, Mom, Mom! Back up! I grant you, Aunt Iris seems to have a thing going with Don Horley. Who wouldn't? For an old guy, he is pretty ripped, and bald men with muscles are very nice. But this is none of our business."

Winnie straightened up in her chair and adjusted her apron (the one with the cherries and red rickrack on it. You know, vintage). She gave me what I'd have to describe as a very steely look.

"Mandy, your Aunt Iris isn't getting any younger. This whole thing about being happy living all alone in a gilded cottage is something out of one of her British WWII novels. It's not enough."

I had to squint at her through the sun blast. I shifted to get out of the main swath of the sun ray. Mom was staring off into space with her eyebrows bunched up like two small, annoyed caterpillars. She got this look very seldom, so I was getting more uncomfortable as Winnie grew agitated.

"Mom, why on earth is this such a big deal for you? It's not like you've been concerned with your sister's love life in the past. Who knows if she's serious about this Horley guy? Has Aunt Iris said she loves him or something?"

Mom slapped her hands down on the tabletop. I have to admit, I jumped.

"Mandy. Let me try to explain this to you. At age fifteen, you think there's an eternity in front of you. You have a million possibilities. You still get to choose what you want to do in life. You get to go to college. You will have lots of boyfriends. And adventures."

She swiped a few cookie crumbs off the table and onto the floor. This was ominous. Winnie Heath is a sanitary woman. Our floors have not one single dust speck on them. Clorox is her middle name. So for her to idly spray crumbs onto the floor was jolting, to say the least.

Not even giving the crumby floor by her feet a glance, she went on.

"Iris is a mature woman who has never had happiness! She was abandoned by Frank Fletcher and now she pretends to love her isolated life. So she has a very nice little house. Yes, she and I have had fun going antiquing and filling it with pretty things. But Mandy, honey, living in cute surroundings and giving piano lessons is *not* what life is all about! Iris deserves to have happiness and fulfillment. You don't get that from a piano! To answer your question—yes, she has told me that Don Horley is an *exciting* man."

This was too much information, and it kind of made my skin crawl. I don't want to even consider sex between people over the age of twenty-five. Just not something I want to picture. But back to Iris, the piano, and her love life:

"What on earth can *we* do?" I knew I had to ask, even though I didn't want to. Mom had me playing right into her hands (I know, a pun, but it was just too easy).

Mom pounded her fist on the table like a judge with a gavel.

"We have to find out where Frank Fletcher is. If he's alive. If he is, then we have to convince him to let Iris divorce him, so she can get married if she wants to. If he's dead, then that will be the end of it, and Iris will be free. This is important, whether Iris loves Don Horley or not. Because she needs to cut the ties to Frank and to the past. She needs to be able to move on!" Those man-killer blue eyes were blazing.

I put my head in my hands. The inside of my forehead felt like there was a rock band warming up in it. Visions of me and Mom on stakeouts, Googling and reading old newspapers in musty libraries came to mind. I thought about those Sherlock Holmes books in the attic. Good grief. But I was trapped by Winnie Heath, the dynamo with the cherry-festooned apron.

"Okay, okay. Let's not get crazy. Let's start by looking for him on the Internet."

Mom and I were now partners, for God's sake.

Chapter Two

Let me backtrack a little bit. I told you about my father, Roy Heath. But I have to fill you in. He looks a little marshmallowy around the edges. He has kind, black eyes with very faint crows' feet. He has a sunny smile and a nice, warm and dry handshake. I wouldn't say that he is completely bald, but those whitish yellow hairs are getting sparser. He's what most people would call a sweetheart. My dad is a patient man. He has to wait on people in the pharmacy all day, and he has to listen to them very carefully. No one gives pharmacists the credit they deserve, in my opinion. They spend much more time with people than doctors do with their patients. And pharmacists have to sort out the tangled web of medications that a lot of people are prescribed, often by multiple doctors who don't know what the other doctors are doing. So Roy Heath can save lives. I am serious. The man is a freaking hero.

Roy Heath is a combination listener, medical wizard, and problem-solver. In his job, he has to understand people. I'm telling you this, because he thinks he understands my mother. This is no mean feat for a mild-mannered pharmacist. Winnie Heath is completely complicated.

When she told him about our plan to find Frank Fletcher in order to give my Aunt Iris new meaning in her life, my dad listened to the whole story. He nodded a few times in the middle of it and cleared his throat some—Dad does have a nervous throat-clearing habit. We were sitting in the break room at the store. Mom was there that day, running the register in the front, because Cheryl Packer, the usual checkout clerk, was out sick or something. Cheryl is not at all dependable. Mom fills in for her a lot because Roy doesn't fire people. Anyway, we had had mac and cheese, and we were getting ready to go back to work.

Here is the break room at the store: It's the size of a large closet. Really. It's brownish. There aren't any windows, so it can get claustrophobic. There are fluorescent lights on the ceiling, and a table with six chairs. For some reason, it is "faux painted" to look like marble. I guess that's so that when you are in there, you don't notice how dinky it is. We have a counter with a microwave, a sink, and a little fridge underneath. That's all there's room for.

So we were in there, the three of us. I was washing the lunch plates, and Mom and Dad were at the table. When Mom finished with her story of the need to track down Frank Fletcher, Dad cleared his throat for the like, ninth time. He looked kind of sweaty all of a sudden.

"Winnie, this all sounds very noble. Have you asked Iris if she even wants you to do this?" He picked up a placemat and started to fan himself.

The pause was the size of an elephant.

"Well, no. I don't see any reason to tell her about this. We haven't gotten started yet. What if we don't find Frank? I think we should keep this to ourselves until we know something."

My dad looked incredulous. Here's what incredulous looks like on my father: He runs his fingers through his wispy, whitish-yellow hair until it stands out on the top like two horns. His normally pink complexion gets mottled, so it looks as if he's smeared raspberry jam on his cheeks like blush from the Revlon aisle. His normally button-black eyes open up like a zoom lens. And he wrings his hands a little.

"Winnie! You can't go around digging up missing persons like it's a hobby! This is your sister's life we're talking about! This isn't your business! What's more, it isn't like you to want to involve yourself in Iris's life this way. Winnie, we mustn't play God. We aren't the cast members of some television detective show, you know. Good heavens, all kinds of unsavory things can happen when you dig around in people's histories. Have you thought of the *implications* that trying to find Frank Fletcher might have?"

I put the dishtowel on the counter. "Dad, I've been down that road already. Mom says that Aunt Iris isn't getting any younger, and somebody has to open up her possibilities for her. Mom, tell Dad."

Mom sighed. Rather dramatically, I thought. But she also twitched her mouth a little. Kind of like a nervous tic thing. Weird.

"Roy, I put it to Mandy this way: When you're young, you have your life ahead of you. You have choices. You have adventure. You have time. But Iris has only the end of her life to look forward to. How is she spending it? Holed up in her little house, playing the piano. Suddenly, Don Horley shows up. There is romance in her life. But you and I both know that if she isn't free to marry him, Don Horley might get tired of being her 'date.' I don't think he has any idea that Iris is still married. She took off her wedding ring a few weeks ago."

Dad smacked his forehead.

"That proves my point! This is turning into a soap opera! Winnie, this can of worms has to remain closed. Or at least, it should be Iris that decides if she wants to open it, not you. It's a private can of worms!" Granted, he was hopelessly tangled in his metaphor, but Dad was getting wound up.

"Winnie, I am an understanding and patient man." (Told you.) "But I have to put my foot down on this one. You can't go around meddling in your sister's *and* this family's life like this. It could be disastrous. I think you know what I mean?" He cleared his throat, this time ominously, more like a growl. And he gave Mom a piercing look. Kind of scary.

Mom stood up and began to pace. As much as a chubby woman can pace in a break room the size of a teensy cubicle with a table in the center of it. She paced for what seemed like five minutes, but it was probably thirty seconds. Then she put her hands on the back of her chair and leaned in and fixed Dad with her baby blues.

"Okay. You're right, Roy. It is a wild goose chase, and it isn't any of my business. You and Mandy are right. I'll leave things be."

Dad smiled, beatifically. He *is* a real angel, that man. He seemed extremely relieved. He brushed a stray noodle off the sleeve of his lab coat and got up. Sighed. My dad never sighs.

"That's the end of that. It has to be, Winnie, and you know it." He paused as a look of vast relief (kind of the look he gets after farting, for God's sake) settled over his face. "Now! Got to get back to pushing pills." (His favorite line.) "Mandy, when you finish straightening the stock room, you can go on home. Winnie, back to work." He blew me a kiss and left the break room.

"So now this is an undercover operation, right?" I asked Mom. She saluted.

I am of two minds about this detective thing. First of all, I'm fifteen, and I am in full possession of my technical faculties. So asking me to look for somebody on the Internet is right up my alley. Let's face it, who *doesn't* want to be adventurous and find a missing person? Well, not actually a missing person, but you know what I mean. On the other hand, I've been thinking a lot about life lately. You know. The fork in the road, or the path not taken, and stuff like that. What if what Mom wants us to do really fucks up somebody's life?

I've read books and seen documentaries about stuff like this. A person makes a decision to do something that he or she thinks will be right and good. But the ripple effect kicks in and things happen as a result that knock people's socks off for miles around. Like that news story about the teacher who (gag me) had sex with her twelve-year-old student and lost her family, got sent to jail, had babies with the twelve-year-old, and all kinds of unsavory garbage. People all over the place were scandalized and destroyed. All because this teacher for some reason wanted sex with a kid.

Aunt Iris is happy. I know this, because I'm at her house more than anybody. She loves her piano. She cooks delicious things to eat. We have lively discussions about things. When we sit out in her backyard in the warm weather, with the pink-and-white blossoms foaming all around us, Aunt Iris seems to throw off a kind of glowing aura.

I tried to draw her out on her feelings about Don Horley when I was over at her house the evening that Mom lied to Dad about giving up on the idea of searching for Frank Fletcher. You know, the night of the showdown in the break room.

We were side by side on the piano bench, playing chopsticks and laughing. It was getting a little hotter outside, since June was almost over, so Iris had all the windows open. We could hear the beating of a lawn mower down the block, and there was a light breeze that puffed our hair off the backs of our necks as we were clowning around, banging on the ivories.

"Aunt Iris, do you want to have Don Horley as your significant other?" I asked—we had kind of run down after laughing so hard. She was still sort of chuckling, under her breath.

"What?" She stopped smiling all of a sudden. Her long fingers rested on the keys, and she turned to look out the window. I counted ten freckles on the side of her powdery neck. "I'm not sure."

She didn't look sure, either. She took her hands off the keys, and began to rub her palms together. She closed her eyes. It looked to me like she was having a REM-cycle dream; her eyeballs started shifting under the lids real fast for a few seconds. Then she opened them really wide, and looked at me very seriously. "Significant other? Honey, I had one of those. We both know that there wasn't a happy ending to that story."

So I tried again. I patted her back, to reassure her that it was okay to spill her guts. "But you really seem to like Don Horley. You two go out together all the time. He smells sexy, and he is one of those bald men who can really carry it off. What I mean is, don't you want to be his girlfriend, or whatever you call it when you aren't really a girl? That's why I said significant other. Don't you want to get serious with him?"

Aunt Iris just looked at me with those water-blue eyes and smiled. Then she shrugged and started to play some Mozart. This was not exactly what I was hoping for. See, so far in my life, everything had been pretty clear-cut. I knew right from wrong: Getting good grades and eating vegetables is good, even when you hate math and Brussels sprouts. Underage drinking leads to traffic deaths. Smoking pot is a gateway to hell. Sexual intercourse is for mature people, not teens (yeah, right). Things like that.

But all of a sudden, my mother was delving into her sister's love life and past. My father didn't want her to do it, but she was oblivious to *that*. Winnie Heath was on a *mission*, and I couldn't figure out why she wanted to do it. When I thought that a simple question to Aunt Iris would make it all crystal clear, all I got was an, "I'm not sure." The lawn mower stopped droning, and I heard Mr. Jordan from down the block calling his dog.

"Prowler! Here, Prowler! Come on, boy!"

Iris smiled. "Ironic, isn't it? He names his dog Prowler and then gets mad when the dog does just that . . ."

Okay, so *this* is what is totally ironic. Winnie and I were about to embark on the huge secret mission to uncover some guy who ran away from being married to Aunt Iris, so she could unmarry him in order to marry Don Horley, and Iris wasn't even sure that she liked the guy that much! And I was roped in to the entire thing by Winnie Heath, the former-man-killer-turned-antiseptic-housewife-turned-detective. Forget Proust altogether. We had moved directly into Sherlock Holmes territory.

This is as good a place as any to tell you a little more about me. I am kind of a cross between my mom and dad. I'm five foot seven, I have dark brown hair. I wish I had Winnie's startling blue eyes, but I have eyes like the pharmacist: brown-black as pitch and deeply mysterious. Probably not, but I like to think so. I am not overweight at all, but I'm certainly not like Winnie in the man department. I have to admit that I have lusted after a few guys, but as I mentioned, I push that stuff down. Denial. I am sure that pretty soon, I won't be able to keep myself from getting horny, but for right now it is easier to stay out of the whole sexual arena. Yeah, yeah—I am an intellectual—I focus on what is playing inside my head. But what it really boils down to is this: Honestly and deep down I am scared shitless of womanhood. I think sometimes that I am the only fifteen-year-old girl on earth that is in no rush to be a woman, and that worries me, too.

I have friends at school and everything, but there's really only one girl that I am besties with. Her name is Barley (you heard me; it's a nickname) Crowder, and I love her to death. Barley is nothing like me in the looks department. She is gorgeous. She has a small waist, C cups, and hair so shining and streaky blonde that it's almost unbelievable it isn't a dye job. Because it *is* a dye job: she uses that Sun-In boxed stuff. She isn't tall enough to be a supermodel, but she says that by the time she's old enough to run away to Los Angeles or Milan or something, maybe they'll be favoring shorter models in magazines. Oh, yeah. She has green eyes the color of parrot feathers. And Barley Crowder is astute. She has an inquiring mind, and she can keep her mouth shut. Barley has life experience. But even so, she likes being with me. My lack of any kind of worldliness must charm her or something.

Anyway, with all of this sleuthing starting up, I needed a sounding board, and Barley was the one. There was no way to keep this whole thing under wraps completely. So I asked Barley to walk over to the library with me. I brought some of Mom's molasses cookies with me for fortification and we sat down on a shady wrought-iron bench under some listless maple trees to chomp and chat. It was hot enough to make us sweat, and there wasn't much of a breeze.

Of course, Barley looked very crisp in her madras Bermudas and Ralph Lauren sleeveless. Today she was coordinated in yellows and blues. I had sweat rings under the arms of my Gap T-shirt (they were three for fifteen dollars; not something Winnie could pass up), and so the sweat rings under my pits looked black; the rest of the tee was cerulean, and my shorts were bunching a little in the crotch. Plus, I was not at all sure that cerulean even looked good with the dark denim shorts, even before sweat rings. Barley and I: high contrast friends.

History: I became best friends with Barbara (Barley) Crowder in the third grade. It happened one winter day, at Hightower Elementary. Our schools here in Framington? *Ancient.* The windows in the classrooms never actually closed all the way, and the wind just whipped in under the warped brown wormy wood sashes in the cold weather. All the girls had to wear tights under their pants to keep warm. But I, very susceptible to icy drafts and also stress, developed *hiccups*. Coldness hiccups. Stress hiccups. It follows that I got hiccups about a million times that winter. And in any other season when things got dicey. So I hicced frequently.

Two things about hiccups: They make you breathless. It sucks. If you have them for a long time, the other kids make you a laughingstock. Truth. So who came to my rescue in a big way? None other than Barley Crowder, the most beautiful girl in third grade! She started having sympathy hiccups. Imagine, me in my double layer of red tights under my jeans and a Cincinnati Reds sweatshirt, spasming up a storm and trying to be as inconspicuous as possible, mortified right up to the roots of my basic brown hair. All of a sudden, this stylish girl in blonde French braids and a Lacoste twinset begins hiccing right along with me. Friends for life.

"Okay, what is this secret thing you want to talk about and have to do outside where the walls don't have ears?" Barley asked, brushing some crumbs off her glossed lips.

I told her the whole story. It took about a half hour. By the time I was finished, the shade had moved from under the maples, off the bench. We were even hotter. The sweat was trickling down not only my pits, but it had pretty much turned me from Gap á la cerulean blue to plain sopping wet all over. We got up and started strolling home, me flapping the front of my shirt like Winnie having a hot flash, and Barley striding along like a runway model.

Barley had some interesting comments.

"First of all, we can get started on this right away. You can come over to my house and we can search the Internet. I'm good at getting into Internet black holes. This may be a snap. We might just find Frank in one afternoon. I think this will be way easy. Your mom probably won't have to lift a finger to help out her sister."

Barley squinted fashionably. "Here's my question to you, Mandy. Just how close is Winnie to Iris, anyway? This whole secret mission to help free Iris to pursue true love with this Horley guy sounds a little forced to me. Does your Mom have an ulterior motive, maybe?"

"Winnie? The supersleuth wannabe? Naw. I think she's having some kind of midlife crisis, and she thinks this is just the ticket to bring excitement and intrigue into her life. She is married to the most boring man on the planet, remember. Don't get me wrong. My dad's a prince. But he wears a lab coat, fills prescriptions, and reads seed catalogs in his spare time. It's a no-brainer. Mom's looking for adventure. Since our family doesn't have any safaris scheduled, Winnie needs stimulation."

This was good enough for Barley. She nodded and said, "Ohhh, right." Then she thrust her left shoulder forward to make her neck look swan-like, and kept on swishing down the sidewalk like it was the Armani showroom or something.

Speaking of seed catalogs? A seed of doubt had just been planted in *my* mind.

Barley and I got to work on the Internet research. Really, in this day and age, it's a wonder anybody gets away with anything because it's pretty hard to disappear in the world of Google and Facebook. Mom was trying not to seem overly interested but, by the following weekend, she could not hold herself in any longer. I was in my room, sitting on the bed. In my room, you mostly have to sit on the bed, because my desk chair is buried under five pairs of jeans, a couple of sweatshirts, and my backpack. My room is big and square. It actually has two big, rectangular sized windows—one right behind my queen-sized bed and one over the desk.

Winnie got all excited when I turned thirteen, and she redecorated my room so it would look more grown up. She let me pick the paint color (buttery yellow), the duvet set, and curtains (matchy-matchy 1960s vintage blue-green-yellow paisley), and she "antiqued" my desk, chair, and dresser a creamy blue. I think Mom was hoping against hope that if I had a beautiful bedroom, I'd come to my senses, smell the coffee, and start tidying up after myself. By week two, post-remodel, when my new room looked like what Mom calls a pigsty, it was all over for Winnie's dreams of my neatness redemption. Anyway, Mom came into my room and tried not to wince at the general casual atmosphere I called home.

"Mandy, have you and Barley been working on the Iris project?" (I forgot to tell you, Mom named it that so Frank Fletcher's name wouldn't come up at inopportune times, like during dinner, when Dad would start asking questions.) She brushed aside a few books and my cell phone, removed an empty cereal bowl and set it on my nightstand (also antiqued that creamy robin's egg blue), and sat down with a little pluffing noise. She pierced me with that bright blue gaze.

I nodded. "Yes. As a matter of fact, we're uncovering some leads. We decided to start with Ohio and see what we could find locally first. Barley isn't done, but so far, there are at least four Frank Fletchers in the state. Barley wants to investigate a little bit more by looking for him on Twitter and Facebook and stuff and you have to use name variations and things like home towns. She's finishing up phase one this afternoon. We planned to give you a report tomorrow."

My God, you'd have thought I pricked her with a pin. She gasped, and her hand flew up to her mouth.

"Mom, are you sure this is the right thing to do? I mean, Aunt Iris *is* a complete grown-up. If she wanted to find Frank Fletcher to divorce him, she could do it herself. I don't really get it."

Winnie exhaled as if she'd been holding her breath. The air popped out of her chest the way it does when you're trying to stop the hiccups (I know from experience, remember). Her hand went from her mouth to her neck, and she massaged her minorly double chin for a few seconds before answering.

"Mandy, I have my reasons. You don't know the whole story. Frank Fletcher almost ruined your Aunt Iris's life when he left her. He stirred up a whole cauldron of trouble in the family, and that's a fact. I want to find him so that we can wipe him out of our lives completely. We *all* need to put the Frank Fletcher episode behind us. To move on."

With that, she stood up, nearly losing her balance as she sidestepped to avoid walking on my pile of clean laundry, which I totally planned to put away ASAP. She shot me a hateful glance before turning to leave my room. In the doorway, she stopped to give me a parting shot.

"It's complicated. You're on a need-to-know basis. But I'm certainly so thankful to you and Barley for helping me out on this. You have to have faith that I know what I'm doing. And for heaven's sake, can you do *something* about this mess? It looks like a whore's closet and smells like the inside of a boot!"

Her answer? Totally unconvincing. By the way, I'm sure that Winnie Heath has never seen a whore, much less her closet. She doesn't go around smelling boots, either.

Here's what I knew so far. Frank Fletcher might be living in Dayton. Two were listed in the Dayton phone book. There was one Frank in Columbus, and Barley said she found one Frank Fletcher from Ohio on Facebook but she wasn't sure if he would accept her friend request.

My social studies teacher told us that most people who move away from home remain within a five hundred-mile radius of their birthplace. We were doing a unit on demographics, and it stuck in my mind because I felt sorry for all those losers who never seem to go anywhere. Maybe Frank was one of those "leave, but leave locally" people. This was our hope, because school would be starting in late August, so we only had a month and a half to solve this whole Frank thing. As long as he was one of the Franks we'd uncovered in Ohio so far, I figured we could track him down before Barley and I became sophomores. Because really, sophomores have better things to focus on than some decades-old love story gone wrong.

I also worried about what would happen if we figured out which of the Franks was still Aunt Iris's husband. I know Winnie Heath like the back of my hand. She would race right out, get in the car, and drive right over to this Frank's house and confront him. There were a couple of problems with this: First of all, I was totally worried about what a confrontation between my mother and Frank Fletcher might mean. Who *was* this guy, really? What was "the cauldron of trouble" that Winnie says he stirred up, anyway?

Barley and I didn't have our licenses yet, so Winnie would have to drive. However, my intrepid mother has always refused to drive on the highway. It makes her nervous and gives her headaches. This meant but one thing: if we wanted to go tracking down Frank Fletcher all over the highways and byways of Ohio, guess who would have to drive us? You got it: MY STINKING BROTHER, Adam! Okay—honestly, he only stunk after he came home from playing basketball or from track. But when he smelled bad, it was like being hit in the nose with maggoty road kill. I swear.

And worse was the fact that Barley had fallen in love with Adam Heath when she was eight and Adam was eleven. Sheesh. So you can imagine what a road trip with this crew would be like: a maniacal mother, a lemon-scented girlfriend in Guess jeans and a tight tank top, me with my antennae on high alert for anything suspicious, and one brother drenched in testosterone and deodorant. Oh, yeah. Good times.

Dinner that evening was interesting. Mom made her famous pot roast. It is the most delicious thing: She puts in onions and carrots and some water. Sounds totally like nothing. I tell you, the aroma of those roasting onions gets your mouth watering all afternoon long. She puts in potatoes toward the end. It comes out all glazed and tender and her gravy would make Martha Stewart jealous. Dad's favorite. We always have green beans with brown butter on the side. Have you had brown butter? It is so nutalicious, I could eat it mixed with Brussels sprouts and think they were fab.

Anyway, we were devouring the roast and Dad asked us what we had planned for tomorrow. Sidebar: Roy Heath is one father who always asks a question really wanting to know the answer. No lip service for him. Roy is tried and true. For instance, when I was eight and in the Indian Guides, Roy was our tribe leader. He threw himself into it! We had a pow-wow in our backyard. Roy got permission from the city to have a real campfire, and we passed the *peace pipe*. Honest to God, Roy got a corncob pipe, filled it with dried corn silk that he'd saved from when we had it on the cob at dinner, and he let us each have one puff. It was horrible, kind of like inhaling a burning building. But how cool was that? Dad is a real pal.

Adam, who by this time knew he was in on the plot whether he wanted to be or not, shifted in his seat. He said nothing, but he's totally monosyllabic anyway. I tried to act casual, but I looked at Mom. We all waited.

"The kids are trying to bring me into the twenty-first century," Winnie said. "Barley's coming over tomorrow, and we're Googling. Or they're going to have me Google. I think they're tired of having to do the leg work when I ask them if George Clooney is married yet." She smiled triumphantly. Really, Mom was no good at subterfuge because we all knew that she read *People* magazine at the store every week, and George Clooney's personal life was no mystery to her.

Dad always humors Mom. He loves her with his whole heart. I have heard him tell her that "I spend my entire life trying to make you happy." So even though I bet he thought her plan was kind of fishy, he smiled in that trusting way that he has and said, "Sounds fun. You and the kids will have a blast." I hate it when he says things like "have a blast" and "nifty." But Roy tries, and we all love him for it.

Stupid Adam. He eats like a Neanderthal and, with his mouth full and spewing potato crumbs, he said, "Is Aunt Iris coming over, too?"

The can of worms. It always gets opened, doesn't it?

"Why? Does Iris want to learn to Google? She doesn't even have a computer, does she?" Dad asked innocently.

Mom jumped all over it. "No, no, but everybody is getting those super smart iPhones. I think Iris is considering one. I know I'm going to get one. We have to keep up! Everybody Googles. We're going to get a technology lesson, right? My gosh, if you don't keep up with things, life passes you by. I think some of her piano students have those phones. So Iris might get one. They have cameras in them. Iris might want to start taking pictures of the garden, and things like that..."

She was babbling. I had to do something to throw Dad—who by this time was looking dubious—off the track.

"Aunt Iris isn't coming over! Adam is pulling your leg, Mom. Barley and I are going to show Mom how to find stuff like WebMD on the computer, and we think there's a Physician's Desk Reference site that Mom could show customers if they want to learn more about drug interactions. Dad, you get busy in the back, and so many customers have silly questions—we thought that might be helpful to you. Mom is hopeless on the computer; we'll throw in a Google lesson, too. She needs all the help she can get."

Mom let out a sigh of relief that would have blown out all the candles on a hundred-year-old's birthday cake. She beamed. "That's right. I'm hopeless."

I kicked Adam in the shins under the table. He winced, but with another mouthful of buttery beans, he couldn't say anything in response, which was a blessing because he probably would have blurted out Frank Fletcher's name or something.

Really, this whole thing was getting ridiculous.

After we had strawberry pie (Mom makes it with cream cheese on the bottom and tops it with real whipped cream. It is absolutely delectable, and Dad and

Adam ate two pieces each, which took their minds off the previous conversation), Dad and Adam left to watch TV, and I helped Winnie clear the table.

"Mom. You're going to have to start keeping your mouth shut. Let me handle this whole subject with Dad. And my God, you have to tell Adam to shut up too. He never listens to me."

Mom was wiping down the counters with something antibacterial. She paused to slump against the vintage wood-grained Formica. The wind was leaving her sails, I could tell. I used the opportunity for more probing.

"Mom, what is this whole Frank thing really about? You're so obviously bullshitting Dad. He's getting suspicious. Why are we doing this? You don't even really know Don Horley. And the whole 'saving' Aunt Iris thing seems shady."

Winnie put down her dishcloth. She looked even more deflated, like a balloon three days after the birthday party. I know. The birthday metaphor is getting old.

"Mandy, sit down."

I pulled out a chair and planted my ass. This better be good. Mom sat down opposite me and folded her hands on the table. I swear, it must have looked like we were setting up to arm wrestle.

"There's a good reason why I want to find Frank Fletcher. It's a very long and complex story, which I don't feel I can tell you right now." She got a faraway look in her eyes, kind of like she was having a flashback. It was creepy. Then she refocused those ocean-blue eyes and gave me a look. "Mandy, Iris and I were both tangled up with Frank. That's all I can say right now, because if we don't find him, I need you to be able to forget this whole episode. If I tell you any more, you won't be able to."

Shit.

I have always spent a lot of time with Aunt Iris. She and I have a bond between us. For instance, ever since I was little, I've had sleepovers with Iris. We liked to get all twisted up in percale and talk about life. Sometimes we'd play B is for Botticelli. One time I guessed J. K. Rowling after two questions My best score.

What I most remember is one night when I was ten. It was October, and the day had been kind of crispy cold, the kind of sweatshirt day that begs for a long walk and then muffins with dinner. Muffins to kill for—Iris is gifted in the muffin department. We were on the bed in Iris's room, it was the gloaming (I love that word), and we had lavender candles wafting. It was the kind of atmosphere that begs for deep discussions. Soul-baring ones. So I started out. "Aunt Iris, what is it like to get boobs? I'm worried mine are going to start soon, and I don't know what to expect. Barley has a bra already. She said her chest hurts. I didn't know boobs hurt."

Iris gently pushed my hair back off my face. I loved that. "Honey, it may be a little bit tender at first. You know, when the daffodils first push through the turf, it takes some gumption to poke through. It's the same with breasts. That first bit of growth might be a shock to your system, then everything adjusts. Don't worry. Barley has a little bit of the Sarah Bernhardt in her."

After she explained who the hell Sarah Bernhardt was, I asked, "Is it more fun to be a grown-up than a child? 'Cause I am not exactly loving this childhood business."

"Mandy, life is a jumble of contradictions. It takes a strong will and analytical mind to stay on top of things. Growing up is a swirl of the very best moments of your life combined with some of the worst. You'll never be happier in your life than you will be in your youth. But you'll also be relieved to get older because you are never more miserable than when you are young." She laid her head back on the pillow, ice-blue eyes glistening. The air was crowded with lavender and shadows. I wished in that moment that Aunt Iris were my mother.

You see, Aunt Iris is deep, where my mother is wide. I love them both, but sometimes I wonder if Winnie has emotions any more complex than irritation with dust and annoyance at Dad for putting his plate in the sink instead of the dishwasher. I know. I said Aunt Iris was bland. Take it from me, you can be both bland and deep.

Winnie is a doer. She covers a lot of ground, every single day. The world needs doers. Iris is what the novelists call a dreamer, and it's no wonder she has a past, a romantically musical missing husband and now a lover with extremely tight shirts and muscles. Winnie just can't measure up in the romance department. Winnie is a short story. I think Aunt Iris is a poem. A poem that isn't necessarily full of passion and fire, more of a peaceful poem—like one about musical notes and flower petals.

Anyway, after the boob discussion, when it was really dark outside and the candles flickered off the walls, Iris turned on the radio. She loves classical music and we listened to Mozart or Handel or somebody. I have no idea—all classical music sounds crescendoey and alike to me. It was so atmospheric. Really. We lay there listening, and Iris held my hand. Once again, the only time my mom did that was crossing the street. Anyway, we held hands and Iris started humming along to the music. Her voice was haunting, I tell you. It gave me goose bumps.

"Aunt Iris," I whispered. "Tell me a secret and I'll tell you one."

She shut her eyes. I thought she didn't hear me, but just as I was about to re-whisper, the humming stopped, and Iris said slowly, "I once gave up everything for the man I loved."

It sounded so much like a romance novel! I sat up in bed and got too eager, I guess. "Tell me about it, Aunt Iris! What did you give up? For Frank Fletcher? The man you loved? You mean you let him get away? What happened?"

It must have been like breaking glass to her ears, because Iris squinted as if she were getting a migraine or something. The entire mood shifted from lavender blue, blissful shadowy sharings to plain old nighttime. "Oh, Mandy! Shush! I've said too much already. Good heavens, look at the time! We have to clean up the dinner dishes and see what's on TV."

I felt my chest. My boobs hurt.

Chapter Three

So. Sunday afternoon. The big secret meeting. In my bedroom. Barley was at my desk, her laptop in front of her. She put her Diet Coke directly on the desk, completely ignoring the coaster Mom put there. Mom, annoyed as hell I'm sure, sat on the bed in her L.L.Bean no-iron linen blouse with tiny blue-and-green flowers. Of course, her elastic-waisted jersey slacks (that's what she calls pants—*slacks*) were a matching shade of blue. And she smoothed out the comforter before the meeting, arranged the shams, and Swiffered the room. Predictable.

Adam, who was in attendance against his will, sat cross-legged on the floor, with clean jeans on (Winnie's insistence) and he smelled kind of like a combo of Clorox (Winnie is forced to bleach absolutely everything Adam wears), sweat, and Axe. I noticed he had *shaved*. Oh, did I mention that Adam has red, curly hair? Redheads almost never have to shave much. Their beards are not exactly dark enough to create a five-o'clock shadow. Hey, they're lucky to get a midnight shadow, for Christ's sake.

Adam shaves once a week or something. Dad says that Adam should be glad that he doesn't need to do it more often, because shaving is literally a pain in the neck. Anyway, there were about a million little razor cuts on the A-man's face. It must be Barley, because since when did Adam spend any time on his looks? Hormones!

I was wearing my black leggings, an old Denison T-shirt of Roy's, and my Nikes. I don't know, I guess I felt that I might just need to *run* out of there or something. The atmosphere wasn't exactly *mellow*, if you know what I mean. I felt the need to pace a little bit. So I circled the room until Mom gave me the stink eye. I sat on the bed.

Mom got things rolling. "Okay, kids. We don't have all day. Barley, tell us what you and Mandy have discovered."

Barley swung around to face the group. She looked like Hermione Granger—for heaven's sake, she was wearing a white shirt with a collar and she had a *tie* on. Blue-and-gold horizontals. I think it was her dad's. Only Barley! She always looked the part. We waited expectantly.

"I think we need to keep our search as narrow as possible, to avoid spreading ourselves too thin. So, as you know, I began in Ohio."

Winnie began to vibrate, I swear.

"Mandy and I found four Frank Fletchers in Ohio. One is in Columbus—more in a second. Two are in Dayton. We think we should investigate the Dayton ones because Mandy looked them up in the yellow pages and one of them teaches music lessons. The other one is listed on Facebook as having music as a hobby. I 'friended' him, but he hasn't respond yet."

Mom stood up. I think she was about to burst. Her chest was heaving. (Okay, I read that in a book. But she was breathing hard.) "What about the one in Columbus and the other one?"

"The Columbus one calls himself Francis Fletcher. That's how he's listed on Google. The info on him lists his occupation as fashion designer. I think he might be gay. I've moved him to the bottom of the list. The other one is dead. I found an obit online that says he died six months ago."

Mom *pumphed* down onto the bed. "Okay. I guess Dayton it is. Let's plan a trip before school starts. Adam, you'll drive. Mandy and Barley, find out where these Franks live."

Barley's eyes snapped on like a flashlight and she sucked in her breath really fast. "Aren't we going to just *call* them? Why not use the phone?" I think the whole craziness of this had eluded Barley so far. Now it hit her like a ton of bricks. I had told her that this was going to be an all-out operation, but I don't think she ever really believed me. Not until she saw the bull-doggedness in my mother's face at that moment.

"This is something that requires face-to-face resolution. I want to talk with Frank Fletcher." Mom surveyed the room. "We have just a few months until Halloween, and I need to get this resolved before then."

You see, Winnie needs all her energy to plan the haunted house on our front lawn. At Heath's, we have the best selection of trick-or-treat candy in town. Winnie Heath loves going all out for holidays. For example, at Christmas, let's just say that having a Christmas tree in every room of the house is the *beginning* for my mom. We all knew where she was coming from. A to B. That's Winnie. Make a list, check it off, and move on.

So here we were in my bedroom at three on Sunday afternoon. Barley's green eyes blared right out of her head. She tugged at her tie, trying to come to grips with both tracking down a man like they do on TV, and spending three-and-a-half hours in a car with my brother. Like I said: Hormones.

Adam looked sullen. Was I the only one who noticed that he'd just picked his nose? He absolutely hated this whole idea, but he knew Winnie had him by the balls. He sat there like a doomed man about to be executed.

Well, I'm sure *some* doomed men have been known to pick their noses. Let's be real. I felt like I wanted to throw up. What in God's name were those poor Frank Fletchers in for? What if neither one was the right Frank? How would a visit from this particular goon squad change their lives? What would their wives do to them? Really, it boggled my pubescent brain.

Not ol' whirlwind Winnie! She had a tribe! We were her slaves! She stood up, her flowered bosom full forward and triumphant. She planted her hands on her chubby hips and summed it up: "We'll go next Sunday. I think we should leave here around ten a.m. That will get us into Dayton just after church. Everybody's home on Sunday afternoons. Plus, Dad always goes in on Sundays to check inventory. I'll tell him we're going school shopping at the mall all day. Barley, you and Mandy need to find the two Fletcher addresses on Google maps or however that works. Adam, you'll be driving my car. Everyone, be here ready to go next Sunday morning at 9:30 a.m."

Frank Fletchers of Dayton, WATCH OUT.

So it was all set. The more I thought about this caper, the more I felt like there were bats flying around in my stomach. I was terribly worried. What if this turned out to be one of those "from that moment on, their lives were never the same" kind of things? I sat there, on my rumpled but cozy bed, in my Winnie-decorated room, nice and secure. It smelled like molasses cookies (there were four on my pillow) and Pledge in there. My room was secure and everybody loved me at that moment. You know that "teen angst"? There wasn't ever any of that in my bedroom. Just peace and paisley.

I contemplated the worst. What if the Frank Fletcher in Dayton turned everything all around? Why was Mom so wound up about this? And here poor old Aunt Iris was, just puttering around in her new kitchen, polishing the sparkly black countertops, and probably lusting after Don Horley in his tight shirts. Why would Winnie want to stir everything up in one big dysfunctional soup kettle? (Pardon the metaphor, but, after all, those black countertops kind of begged for it.)

I had a theory: I wondered if maybe Mom wanted to kill Frank Fletcher for some reason. He had been hanging around in her brain, jangling her already pingy nerves, ever since he left Aunt Iris. And Aunt Iris was, unfortunately—as I have already told you— kind of flaccid. She must have just wilted on the vine when he left her.

Yeah. Here it *was*. Winnie, unlike Iris, must have wanted to bust Frank's head. Whatever he'd done to hurt Aunt Iris preyed on Winnie. She was, after all, a control freak. Winnie was a pit bull. I know, I said she was a pug before, but now I am amping her up to pit bull status. Winnie Heath, in her permanent-press blouses and elastic-waist slacks,was a gangster. I bet she was plotting how she wanted to kill Frank right now! She had made us into her homies, and now we were embarking on a road trip of death!

I fell backwards onto my paisley sham. My own theory scared the crap out of me.

So I called Barley. No satisfaction there. She was actually *looking forward* to Sunday! She didn't hold with my murder theory.

"Your mom is not going to murder anybody. That's ridiculous. First of all, she wouldn't know how to. She doesn't have a gun or anything. And she certainly can't beat a man to death. Winnie is strong and all that, but come on!"

I realized I was gnawing on my lip. There was a spot of blood on my cell. "Barley. You idiot. My Mom has access to *narcotics,* for Pete's sake! She owns a pharmacy! She could kill the whole town if she wanted to!"

Barley sighed at the other end. "Mandy, chill out. This is not an episode of *CSI.* Winnie would never use us to help her murder somebody. We'd be accessories. She wouldn't want to put you, Adam, me, and herself in jail. Who would take care of Roy?"

"What do you think she's chasing all over the state of Ohio for? Some sort of happy reunion? To give Frank a hug and catch him up on all the family news? Come on, Barley! This is big!"

I heard her munching on something. Side bar: Barley was a high-level professional snacker. She specialized in cheese-flavored things. Her top-rated snack at the moment was oven-baked Cheetos. However, she didn't like the orange-fingertip look they left behind, so she was trying out a few alternatives: cheese-infused pretzels, cheddar Corn Nuts, and other cheesy stuff. I wasn't surprised that she was combining this serious conversation with cheddar research.

Barley swallowed and cleared her throat. "Okay, I grant you, it's not run-of-the-mill to recruit your own children to track down your sister's ex. But you know Winnie. She's what, pushing fifty? You said it yourself. Her life is kind of boring. Winnie doesn't do boring very well. This is her way of spicing things up. You know, menopausal madness?"

I took a huge chunk out of my lip and winced. I reached for a Kleenex and held it to my lip. I hate the salty red taste of blood. "I've changed my mind. This whole thing is totally fishy. It's got 'shit storm' written all over it. We have to stop this junket. Nip it in the bud. Menopause or not. I just have a bad feeling about the whole thing." Good God. The Kleenex was soaked. I pressed harder.

"What does Adam think?" Barley always wanted to drag Adam into things.

"I haven't asked him. He's an idiot."

"He isn't an idiot." She gulped. Diet Coke is my guess. "You hate him because he's your brother. But he isn't dumb at all. Talk to him about this. If he buys into your murder-and- mayhem theory, which I doubt he will—because it's ludicrous—then we can talk. Call me back."

Adam came home about an hour later, sweaty from playing pick-up basketball with his friends. Stinky, as usual. I entered his man cave. It was horrible. Adam's room had gray walls. He'd convinced Mom that they'd look masculine and hide dirt. Chalk one up for him. His floor was carpeted in sweat socks and dirty underwear. He never closed his dresser drawers, which had virtually nothing in them because it was all on the floor. Posters of naked girls and basketball stars were on the wall over his bed. Disgusting. The bedsheets? Gray, too. This, because he changed them (Winnie gave up on chambermaid duties in there long ago) once every two years, whether they needed it or not. I would call the odor in here "eau d'athlete's foot." The testosterone hideaway. You could have grown mushrooms in there.

Anyway, Adam was sitting on his bed, looking at porn (probably) on his laptop, because he slammed it shut when I entered.

"What do you want?" He sneered. He always sneered at me.

I swept a pair of boxers, one sock, and what looked like a banana peel off the bed and sat down, but very gingerly. "We have to talk about this whole Mom thing and the Dayton trip. Why do you think she's trying to track down this Frank guy?"

He wiped the sneer off. He put his laptop on a stack of *Sports Illustrateds* on the bottom of the bed. It slid off and clunked onto the floor, but Adam didn't seem to care. He looked at me and scratched his sweaty forehead, squinting thoughtfully through his freckles. "I think Mom might have a crush on this Fletch guy."

OMG.

Adam smiled. "And Mand, you lip biter," (I touched my lip with my tongue—hurty and tasting like gore) "haven't you noticed how excited Mom is about all this? Lost love and stuff."

This was tragic. "Lost love? My God, you turd! What if it's true? What about Dad? What if they get divorced? What in hell are we doing?"

I noticed the sweat rings on Adam's shirt. His arms looked sculpted as he flexed his biceps. He was clenching and unclenching each hand into a fist, first the right, then the left. He shut his eyes and ran his hands through that ginger mess he calls hair. I guess thinking was an effort.

"Mand, what choice do we have? Mom's engineered this whole thing. Thank God she's making us come along. We can at least do damage control."

"Oh, yeah. Like you, me, and Barley are skilled human relations consultants. Like we can make a few wise comments and Mom will see the error of her ways, give up on her idea of either killing or seducing this Frank, and we'll all have a nice lunch with sundaes for dessert then drive home."

Adam opened his eyes. "Look at the evidence. Okay. Here's what we know: Mom says Aunt Iris wants to get married to this Don Horley guy. We don't know him very well. Hell, Aunt Iris doesn't know him that well—he installed her kitchen what, three months ago? She doesn't refer to him as her boyfriend or anything. Second, it seems to me like Mom jumped all over this Fletch thing like white on rice. Since when has Mom been so into protecting Iris, anyway? And third, Mom is *loving* this whole trip idea.

"You don't get all excited about murdering somebody, have meetings about it, and plan to take a road trip to do it. Mom isn't a premeditated killer sociopath. If Mom killed anybody, it would be a crime of passion—like if she found out we put plates in the dishwasher without rinsing them or something, she might hit us over the head with a frying pan."

First of all, I was completely floored that Adam knew words like "premeditated" and "sociopath." It took a few seconds for that to sink in. Then I realized that he was making sense. Jeez, now I had two things banging around impossibly in my head: the fact that Winnie was nuts, and that my brother may be in possession of human intelligence. I was reeling.

"So what do we do, you man of wisdom? I remind you again that the three of us are aged fifteen, fifteen-and-a-half, and eighteen. How are we going to do damage control? What about Dad? And Iris, for that matter?"

Adam stopped clenching and leaned toward me, his mouth in a menacing grin. "We have to think of something. Because this is way complicated." He leaned back, triumphant.

Reconsidering the human intelligence thing, I pinched his hairy thigh. He yelped. I got up to leave, stumbling over a Chuck Taylor. In the doorway, I shot him the evil eye.

"Right-o. Start thinking. I'll talk to Barley about this. Three—wait, two-and-a-half heads are better than one. We *have* to come up with something!" I pretended to fart in his direction (sometimes you have to sink to their level) and left the room. Then I turned around and went back in. "FLETCH? Oh, my God, Adam. Now he sounds like some sort of STD!"

But Adam was right. This *was* complicated. I'd never thought parents had any complications. Adults? One-dimensional. At least this was what I had always believed. *You know, they are a mom and a dad. They have wrinkles and get hemorrhoids. They go to work and fix dinner. They yell at you for being messy and getting bad grades. They don't have sex or anything anymore, because that is just disgusting. Young people? So much going on! Five-dimensional! We have lives that are deep, murky, and exciting. We youth have angst! We go backpacking in Europe and have lots of sexual partners. We get high and have incredibly interesting job opportunities.* All the good movies are about young people and their adventures. As far as I was concerned, life ended at adulthood.

I realized that I had to rethink. My whole worldview was in the dumpster: Winnie Heath had secrets, and *she* was an adult. My mom was embroiled in some sort of romantic escapade, and she might end up in jail or divorced. My dad was a potential casualty of this; my aunt was the focus of it all and had no idea. I was involved up to my neck. Barley, too. And to top it all off, I just discovered that my stinky brother wasn't completely stupid. Headache.

Let me interrupt this with more about Roy Heath. My dad is a cross between a genius and a stuffed animal. He has a sweetness that makes people trust him instantly. Roy Heath is the kind of pharmacist who can look at a customer and instantly tell that she's lying when he asks her if she's constipated. He knows drug reactions like the back of his hand. He reads trade magazines about Cialis and Paroxetine for recreation. Well, that and seed catalogs. You see, Roy Heath is a genius at work and a dreamer at home.

My dad is my cushion. Literally. He's not plump or anything, but hugging Roy is very calming. Roy has kind eyes. They have little crows' feet at the corners. He treats us all like we are just the biggest and best surprise he ever got. Every time he sees us, he beams.

He chuckles when I call him "Roy." If my English teacher asked me to write a definition of my dad, I'd have to say this: "My dad is the kind of person who gives above and beyond. My dad is Santa without the boots, beard, and red suit."

Okay.

I just couldn't make the trip on Sunday without sending out a few feelers in Roy's direction. I was not comfortable without trying to get more intel from his side of things. We needed to shed as much light on all sides of this situation before we motored down to Dayton for a day of fun and Frank.

So on Monday, when all the senior citizens had come into the pharmacy before it got dark, and the store was empty during what we smirkingly call "rush hour," I bought Dad a Diet Pepsi and asked if we could have a talk while he put stickers on the prescription bottles. As mindless a task as there could be in a drugstore, really.

I plunged right in. "Hey, Dad. How did you and Winnie meet?" (He always smiled when I called Mom by her first name. I think he thought I was going through a phase.)

He took a sip of his Pepsi and closed his eyes, sloshing the bubbles around in his mouth. He was kind of a hedonist, in a geeky way. After he swallowed and sighed in satisfaction, he burped a little then opened his eyes. He seemed to forget the question, but then refocused. "Your mom? Oh, we met when I was going to pharmacy school. After Denison. Iris and I were students at Ohio State." He coughed.

"I knew your Aunt Iris first. That was around the time when Frank came into the picture. I think we met one night at a bar where Frank was playing, and I happened to be there with some friends. Your mom was in Columbus visiting Iris. So I met your mom with Iris at the bar. You know, your mom and Iris were both young and gorgeous. Iris looked like Julia Roberts a little, and your mother reminded me of a dark haired and slightly chubby Madonna. You know, fast, and so bossy! But sexy, too." (I was nearly shitting myself here.) "Winnie was on the floor, dancing all night. She even got me to fast dance with her. This was in the what, early eighties? But I still loved Elvis, even though he was long gone. I preferred the old classic rock . . ." He seemed lost in the memory.

I wanted to get him back on track, even though memory lane with Elvis sounded interesting. "Did you fall for Mom right away? Or did you date for a long time?"

Roy's eyes got kind of cloudy. He sniffed and put down his Pepsi. He peeled off two more labels and stuck them on pill bottles before looking up. "Mandy, back then, it was right at the cusp of so many things. We smoked weed—and other drugs were popular. I know, you don't want to hear this, but you asked. People didn't have cell phones, not quite. Computers were around, but not like today. We weren't hooked on technology. It was the beginning of the technology revolution, but I still played Atari. Then Pac-Man. But rock and roll was our world of excitement. Punks. Piercings. People weren't exclusive. There was a lot of passion and frenzy, sexually and socially. You know, I was born just after the baby boom ended. The Vietnam War was still going on when I was born in '68. My generation was at the very beginning of the Internet and cyber-everything. There was so much history that occurred: Kennedy and Martin Luther King assassinated, Chernobyl—the world was waking up to the implication of what we were doing to the ozone layer. And when I was a teenager, AIDS hit us. That changed life for everybody. But honey, I still remember when people used *phone booths!*"

OMG. I never even thought about this! My parents straddled the border of old and new. They were the ones sitting around inventing computer code and realizing that the planet was in danger, but at the same time, they didn't even have iPads! My parents' generation was overwhelmed with upheaval—the Challenger exploded, John Lennon was shot, Tiananmen Square. Stuff that we have covered in Social Studies. There was terrorism, the beginning of the Islamic jihad. I looked this up on Wikipedia—my parents lived in an absolute avalanche of modern history! No wonder people my parents' age just want to sit in their recliners and watch TV on weekends. They're all probably a little post-traumatic! My head felt like there were squirrels running around inside. But wait—*Mom.*

"Hold on. Dad. What are you saying? Did you hang out with both Mom *and* Iris? Oh, my God, did you *date* Mom and Iris?"

He coughed again, and there was a *big* pause. "Mandy, the past is the past. Let's leave it there." He sighed and knocked a bunch of bottles off the counter. It wasn't an accident. He bent over and began to pick them up, avoiding my eyes and effectively breaking the mood.

My stomach flipped over.

Saturday, Barley and I went to the pool. The Framington civic pool is where everybody hangs out. The whole family can join all summer for thirty dollars. The pool is nice and big, with one end roped-off for serious lap swimmers. We never went there. Our favorite spot was on the concrete patio by the snack window, where we could always buy orange popsicles when we got parched. We loved to bake ourselves, even though we had to use SPF 500 or so to avoid skin cancer. We were lying on our stomachs, and the warmth was seeping into every pore. They say sweating pulls out all the toxins in your system, so we were nearly toxin-free.

I turned my head so that I could see right into Barley's eyes. They were at half-mast, due to the sun, but still shatteringly green. "Barley, what if tomorrow is a shit show?"

She peered at me, sweating. "We have to be prepared for the worst. I think we should use the three hours in the car to pump your mom for as much info as possible. Make her spill her guts. Between the three of us, we ought to be able to force the real reason for all of this out of her. She can't escape the car."

God. "Okay. But what will we do with this information? We'll be going to Dayton, to meet up with this Frank guy—if we have the right Frank Fletcher. Or as Adam calls him, *Fletch*. Ugh. What good will getting the truth three hours before the meet-up do?"

Barley considered while wiping sweat from between her boobs with her hand. "For one thing, we shouldn't let Winnie be alone with this Fletch person. Whatever comes down, there will be three of us there to throw ourselves between him and Winnie, if it turns violent or something."

This was getting to be way too much for me. Like my life was turning into a Lifetime Movie of the Week. "I think we should just refuse to go tomorrow. This is getting scarier and scarier. Let's *not* do this."

Barley rolled over and sat up. She put on her Ray-Bans (white with purple trim). She took a deep breath.

"It's too late for that. Your mother is unstoppable. What we have to do is restrain her from doing anything stupid. We don't even know if the Franks in Dayton are the right ones. Let's hope they aren't; then we can stop looking. And pretend that we exhausted all leads, and the Frank-Fletch case is closed."

"But how do we stop her from doing something crazy? Pretend to go into convulsions?"

Barley took me way too literally sometimes. "Great idea! We need a signal. If I pretend to sneeze, then you start seizing!"

I sat up and hit her on the back of her head with my water bottle. "You're an idiot! I wasn't serious! And if I were, d'you think I'd need *a signal* to know when things begin to get out of hand? Geez, B!" We both shook our heads.

"Well," Barley said. "What else can we do? Have Adam karate chop somebody? Call 911? You know, we might just be overthinking this whole thing. Your mom said she wants to tell Frank to let your aunt get a divorce. Remember? Maybe that's all there is to this. The murder and mayhem stuff might just be your imagination working overtime, Mand. Right? Really."

I nodded. "Agreed."

But I didn't buy Mom's motivation for this trip for one minute. I felt the boom of doom lowering. (I know. The boom of doom!) Barley laid back down, this time on her back. I followed suit. No pun intended. We shut our eyes against the blare of the sun. I tried deep breathing to slow down what must have been soaring blood pressure.

"Change of subject." Barley popped her gum. "We're going to be sophomores. What do you think it will be like? You know, going from being top dogs to being on the bottom rung again? Do you think the seniors will haze us or anything?"

We both worried about high school. Our school went from first through ninth. This last year was a blast. We had our own yearbook for ninth grade, and Barley and I were the photo editors. This was the most sought-after position. We had it nailed, because Barley was a genius with her cell camera, plus she knew how to use a Nikon. She took a photography class last summer, and she even learned how to develop her own pictures. See, if you're going to be a supermodel, you need to know what's happening on both sides of the lens.

Barley got to be president of the photo club; Mrs. Parsons appointed her. Mrs. Parsons is the social studies teacher, but she used to be, in her words, a "cub photographer" for Cleveland's *The Plain Dealer* or something. Anyway, ninth grade was so fun. Now we faced humiliation in high school.

"Mand, you know that next year you have to start wearing lipstick to school. And you have to wash your hair every night. No sweat pants. Nail polish."

I knew this time was coming. I hated to think about it. Some people like Barley and my Mom just *had* it. They knew how to merchandise themselves to the general public. I absolutely hated this. I didn't *want* to sell myself. But having a thing of beauty as your best friend kind of thrusts you into the spotlight, so to speak. I knew I had gotten away with being a slouch in the beauty department so far just by hanging around with Barley, but I realized that when high school happened, things would change. I'd have to start with the "woman" business. Holy crap.

See, here's the thing: I was smart enough to see things coming, and I knew that womanhood, love, and fornication were inevitable. But I wished I had a little more time to be a girl. (Sometimes I take my dolls out of my closet where I store them and just wish I could play with them again.) I hate having to shave my legs and use mascara. At night, sometimes I sing "Old MacDonald" to myself for old times' sake.

It seems to me that in the olden days, when people rode in horse-drawn carriages and things were all atmospheric, girls got to stay young a lot longer. There weren't things like *Seventeen* magazine and rap music. Sex didn't happen before you were married. Hell, I bet *kissing* didn't even happen before you were married.

Nowadays, there are beauty pageants for toddlers and sexting. I feel pushed and pressured. I resent this. I'm not ready for the next era of my life. I prefer being a kid. I remember when Winnie told me that many of her friends said things like "high school is the best time of your life." She said that was pure hogwash—high school stunk for her. It was full of mean girls calling her "fatso." And boy, oh boy, are there a bunch of bullies at Framington High. God. What I'll be in for gives me a headache. Barley will certainly be a boon, but I'll be on my own, in reality. And I love sweatpants and T-shirts.

I guess I'm confessing that I'm scared shitless of moving on. What if this has been the best time of my life? What if the rest of my life will suck in comparison to right now? What if Dad and Mom get divorced over this Frank thing? What if Adam becomes a drug addict? What if I never even have one boyfriend? What if I'm still a virgin when I'm thirty? What if I look back on my life and realize that nothing really happened in it? What if I never have a kid? What if I have a kid but he/she hates me? What if I get horrible pimples all of a sudden? What if Barley drops me for the popular girls? What if I somehow *get* a boyfriend and then get pregnant? What if I have a shitty career? What if I don't even have a career, but end up working as a checkout person at a grocery store or worse?

I think I need some sort of medication to get me through high school.

Sunday morning. Bright and early. My alarm went off at 8:00 a.m. I struggled out of bed and into the shower. As the water beat down, I said a little prayer for strength. I dried myself, put on cut-offs and my good luck T-shirt (the Beatles on *Abbey Road*), and went downstairs.

Startlingly, Adam was already at the table, chomping Cheerios. He looked his usual rumpled self in Levis and a Mumford & Sons concert shirt. Dad was having coffee. He was looking over the Sunday paper. Mom leaned over him as she put his eggs down. "Honey, when are you leaving for the store?"

Dad kissed her on the cheek (OMG, I just love him, and my heart was breaking).

"Around nine. What are you up to today?"

This was her opening. Winnie whirled around to grab the coffee pot, so her back was to the rest of us. Clever—the eyes always give away a lie. "I'm insisting on taking the kids to the mall for school clothes. I swear, Adam grows an inch a day, and Mandy has to start to step it up in the wardrobe department. Barley makes her look like a hobo. Just look at what she's wearing!" She busied herself wiping the Formica—another wise ploy, because I could see her hand was shaking a little. Dearest Roy bought the whole thing. Of course, why wouldn't he? Winnie has never given him any reason to mistrust her. *Until now.*

So we continued the charade. I tried to eat my eggs, but they stuck in my throat. I had to chug some orange juice to keep from spewing them down my front. Adam maintained a stony silence. Nothing new there.

Dad finished his coffee and the paper. "Have fun, you all. Mandy, get some pretty clothes. Your mom is right. You should try to be more feminine. You can get free nail polish at the store, remember." My God, the world revolves around *nail polish*. He swished the sports page over to Adam, got up, kissed Mom on the cheek and me on the head, and walked out to the garage, completely innocent and happy. For maybe the last morning of his life.

Mom sprang into action. "Okay, I've packed sandwiches for the road. I have a cooler with drinks." (What, did she think we were driving to *Oregon* or something?) "When is Barley coming?"

"Mom, cool it." Adam pressed his hands together in the Namaste sign. "She's coming over in about ten minutes."

This is the way Winnie is. Whenever she's challenged or nervous, she chugs right into action, cleaning something, cooking something, or organizing something. No matter that we would probably be in Dayton before lunch. Winnie has to keep busy at all times. Hence, ham sandwiches, potato salad, Diet Coke and regular strength Coke, all on ice. She had the cooler loaded, and it was sitting by the garage door in all its icy splendor.

"Mom, you look like you're going to church or something. We're going to track down a guy and ask him for a divorce, not going to a wedding!" Winnie was wearing a crisp (is there any other kind of blouse? I guess I don't need to tell you this) white blouse with a Peter Pan collar. Sidebar: I have *never* seen a picture of Peter Pan wearing that kind of collar. Over it was a very new summery white cotton cardigan with roses and pink pearl buttons. And a kind of A-line navy skirt number. Winnie had been to Target.

"Oh, shush." She buttoned the top button of her cardigan. I wrinkled my nose at her. She unbuttoned it. "Just because you like to look like homeless children, even when we're doing important family business, there's no reason why I should sink to your level." I guess she told *me*!

Adam looked up at the rooster clock on the wall above the refrigerator. "Quarter after." Then he just started staring into space. What a load Adam is.

"Put the cooler in the car, you idiot!" I pinched the back of his arm, right near his armpit. That's the sweet spot. It really hurts if you just get a little bit of skin. Adam pulled himself out of the chair, said "Shit, Mand!" and shuffled off to the garage to load the unnecessary lunch.

By the way. Mom bought her car all by herself. She's very proud of this fact. One day, she decided that her Ford Taurus was too boring or something. So she got it washed, drove it to the dealership and arranged a great trade-in deal on a brand new Ford Explorer. Burgundy with tan leather seats and that cool back-up camera. Mom was raised to be frugal, so she didn't opt for all the bells and whistles like that GPS woman or a TV in the backseat or anything. But it did come with satellite radio and AC vents in the back. It was a sweet ride, I tell you. Winnie bragged that she told the salesman "not to bother with that sales manager run-around. It's *this* deal or no deal."

Adam was going to get to drive "the ride," as he called it. One bright spot in an otherwise miserable operation. One tiny bright spot.

When Adam came back into the kitchen, Barley was with him.

Barley apparently got Mom's "wardrobing for manhunts" memo, because she was decked out in a hot pink Boden crossover tee, white leggings, and gladiator sandals. She had on hoop earrings that Beyoncé would die for. I think Adam approved, because he was walking behind her with his eyes glued to her ass. What a creep.

"Hi everybody! It's a great day for a road trip! Are we excited?" Barley asked. "We have two locations to visit: 450 Fairlawn is in Kettering, 312 Ash Avenue is in Oakwood. I have them both in my GPS. We're good to go." Barley grinned, like all the girls in the adventure movies who just know that there's action ahead, maybe even some car chases. Barley looked more and more like Emma Stone every day.

Sizzling with her usual energy, Mom did a final wipe down of the counters that you'd need a slow-motion video to track and hung the dishrag on the faucet. "Let's stop all of this fooling around and get out of here." With that, she grabbed me by the elbow, shoved Adam and Barley toward the garage, and we marched out.

Picture this. We were somewhere on I-75, heading south to Armageddon in Dayton. There wasn't much traffic. Adam was observing the speed limit, because Mom insisted on using cruise control (Adam control). Barley was up front, navigating. I was in the backseat with Mom, who was twisting her hair and sweating, despite the air conditioning blasting us and the prescription strength antiperspirant that she gets free from the store. She made a good choice with the white blouse and cardigan, because neither shows sweat rings, which she probably had all the way down to her waist. I'm starting to think I may have a future in the motion picture industry the way things are going.

Here is the scene from the movie:

> *Barley is blithely singing along to the Sirius 80s Pop Hits channel, which is the only one the three of us could agree on. Adam, because he really doesn't care and because Barley and I think that Mom needs to be rooted in the good old days, before people like Lana Del Rey spilled their guts all over the airwaves. We need her to be calm.*

Winnie and I are sitting in the backseat with the cooler between us, using it as an arm rest. So far, I have tried to pass the time looking for out-of-state license plates, but I just can't hold it in any longer.

"Mom. What's the real reason we're doing this?"

Mom is suddenly very still. "I am doing this for the family. I am." She leans back on the headrest. Boy, does she look tired all of a sudden. You know how people can turn from normally colored to white as a sheet in a nanosecond? Mom is like that.

"Mom." I don't know what else to say. "I think we should just go back home and forget all of this."

"Are you crazy?" Adam, who up to this point has said nothing other than, "Hey, I could use a sandwich" ten minutes after we left, chooses this moment to weigh in. "Mom needs resolution. We are going to get it. Besides, I'm not available after today—I have baseball practice from now on." He makes a fist on the steering wheel. Good God.

Barley turns around and smiles at us. "Mrs. Heath, we will be with you all the way on this, whatever happens. We have your back."

Winnie, who probably has no idea what "having your back" even means, smiles

> wanly at Barley, reaches forward to pat her on the shoulder, and then closes her eyes. I guess the real reason we are doing this will just have to play out. I, for one, like a little forewarning. Not going to happen. Fade to black. Consider renaming all the characters; after all—this is a movie scene.

The rest of the trip consisted of three potty stops (I have a small bladder, and it gets worse when I'm nervous), one wrong exit that almost ended us up in Indianapolis, and stony silence on Mom's part.

But we got to Dayton.

Barley took over at this point. The Googler. "We have two Franks. One lives in . . ." (she looked at her phone) "a suburb called Kettering. He's the one I tried to friend on Facebook. He didn't friend me back. So we have nothing on him. The other one lives in another suburb called Oakwood. I put them both in my GPS. Which one do you want to go to first?"

Adam, who was revealing his intellect more and more, much to my chagrin, said, "Okay, we're getting off on the next exit, which says Kettering. Tell me how to get to the Kettering Fletch's house."

Mom leaned forward, her eyes all slitty. I guess she'd never heard Adam's pet name for this guy, and I guess *Fletch* sounded as bad to her at first as it did to me. She winced a little. But you know, once you hear *Fletch* it's kind of hard to go back to *Frank*. I'm just sayin'.

Dayton is a really nice city. It actually has a skyline, which we don't have in Framington. I can fill you in on everything about Dayton. We had to study it in the Ohio unit in social studies. I had to memorize that Dayton is the sixth largest city in Ohio. Can you believe it? I still know this.

It's the birthplace of aviation, because Orville and Wilbur grew up here and had a bike shop, which another city stole. And they get mad in Dayton about Kitty Hawk claiming to be where flight was invented. There's a big Air Force base in Dayton: Wright Patterson. When I was in fourth grade, Roy took me and Adam there. I didn't want to go, because who cares about a huge building full of airplanes? But actually, it was very interesting.

Charles Kettering is the guy they named Kettering after. He was some sort of bigwig at National Cash Register. He and some guy named Patterson. Oh, *Wright* Patterson. Yeah. But there was something really interesting about Dayton that I remember. They had a secret place where they invented something to do with the bomb that they dropped on Japan during the war. It was in somebody's yard in Oakwood. And Oakwood is on our list! Kind of exciting.

Dayton used to have a lot of manufacturing, but now it's all gone. Like it is everywhere else in the US. So the people in Dayton must be mad about that. But there's the University of Dayton, where they like to party a lot on Saint Patrick's Day (that's always in the news in Framington, I think Framington wants to party down) and they have this cool baseball team, the Dragons. I bet Adam would love to play for the Dragons. He thinks he's a gifted pitcher.

Oh, they also have this great big glass arts center named after a heart doctor, Dr. Schuster, who gave a lot of money to build it. I've wanted to go there ever since I saw a picture of it in the Framington paper. There are palm trees inside. Wow.

We pulled off onto the surface streets. So this is where the Wright Brothers lived. Lots of big trees. And why Ohioans love Tudor houses was a mystery to me, but this Kettering place was full of them. And sidewalks. Lots of those. We passed kids on scooters, men in shorts mowing lawns. We rolled down the windows and turned off the AC, because Dad has a rule that when you're driving under fifty miles an hour, having AC makes the car tired or something. We saw a young, fit woman on Rollerblades being pulled by a shiny black Labrador. As they passed us, some other dogs in backyards started barking. Sidebar: I have always craved a dog, but Winnie ruled that they shed too much, and "Who would walk the darn thing? *Me.*"

It smelled very nice in Dayton. Kind of like a mixture of cut grass and Sunday dinners cooking. The sun beat down on porches and detached garages. All the houses looked old. I guess Kettering was built around World War II or so. People had picket fences.

Barley barked directions. "Turn right on Addison. It's about four blocks, then you go left onto Wright Boulevard. It's a hard left one block later onto Fairlawn. It is 450 Fairlawn. It will be on your left."

This was it. Mom, clenched, looked fiercely out the window. We passed some really adorable bungalows that I think Iris would have liked. One was dark brick with hunter green trim and geraniums in window boxes. So cute. I wondered if they had a piano in there.

As we went along, the houses got smaller, and the grass in the yards wasn't as green. Addison was lined with tiny Cape Cods, complete with window shutters and brick stoops. I counted one yard swan, three American flags, and two motorcycles. The neighborhood was becoming increasingly blue collar. Winnie mumbled something about it "not looking good."

Fairlawn. Mom suddenly shrieked, "ADAM! STOP FOR A MINUTE!"

He pulled over so fast that Barley nearly crashed into the dashboard. Damn!

Mom pressed her hands over her face. We weren't sure if she was crying or trying to faint or something. Barley, always perky and helpful, said, "Mrs. Heath, are you okay? Do you want some gum?" Perky. Not so helpful. Mom shrugged.

I pushed her arm off the cooler and reached into the icy depths for a Coke. When I pulled off the tab, some of it spilled on my arm. "Here, Mom. Take a swig of this. You need some fast sugar energy."

She didn't move. I realized that I needed some energy, too. So I took a swig. I've always loved the cold fizziness as it rips down my throat. Adam twisted around, took it from me, and gulped some down, then handed it to Barley, who took a dainty sip. Mom, who by this time had dropped her hands and was watching us incredulously as we drank *her* Coke, snatched the can from Barley's manicured grip. "You kids are the limit, you know?" And she glugged the remainder down like a parched dockworker or something.

We waited for the sugar to kick in and for Winnie to get her nerve back. A breeze stirred. Funny what you notice in times of stress. I wonder if people who are being robbed notice that the mugger has callouses on his hands or if you get thirsty while you're falling off a forty-story building. The mind is a complete mystery, isn't it?

Suddenly, Winnie handed me the empty can, bobbed her head with mucho determination and said, "Let's do this thing." Adam revved up the Explorer and, checking the side-view mirrors as he knew he should with Mom in the car, he headed for 450 Fairlawn.

Fairlawn had seen better days, let me put it that way. The houses on this street looked as if they wanted to be adopted. The houses were tiny and most were missing paint in spots. This was very obvious, because most were either bright blue with brown patches, yellowish and drab with light outlines where shutters used to be, or dreary, dirty white with rusty dark areas where the paint had just flaked off, I guess. It was depressing, and Winnie looked a little shocky, despite the Coke infusion.

"Here it is, 450. Oh, look," Barley whispered as she rolled up the window. We all followed suit. She pointed to a man mowing the front yard with an old-fashioned bladed push mower.

Snapshot: The guy was hugely fat, like three hundred pounds. He was wearing shiny black athletic shorts big enough for an entire basketball team. Black socks and black Crocs. His hair, either brown or black—we couldn't tell because he was entirely sweaty—was dripping wet. He had a cigarette hanging out of his mouth. If this was Frank Fletcher, I would vomit in my mouth.

Mom nearly shouted "No, that isn't him! I can tell from the hair! Thank the Lord! Now let's get out of here!"

Barley held up her hands. "We can't just leave! That isn't Frank, okay, but what if that's a neighbor or cousin or something? We have to ask. We've come all this way and we can't just *assume* that we can check 450 off the list, because..."

"BECAUSE OH MY GOD, ASSUME MAKES AN ASS OUT OF YOU AND ME!" Adam was such a load.

Mom nodded. "Mandy, you go up there and ask that man if he knows Frank Fletcher, and if so, find out where he is."

"Why am I elected?" I knew the answer before she even had to say it.

"Because Adam might punch somebody." Right.

Barley popped in a piece of Juicy Fruit, carefully crumpling the wrapper and depositing it in the empty can of Coke. Very slowly and deliberately. "Okay. I'll go." She pulled down the visor and checked her makeup.

"My God, Barley, are you planning on asking the guy for a *date*? Get a move on, we have places to go and people to see!" She shot me a filthy look, but got out of the car and slammed the door harder than necessary.

We watched her straighten her shoulders and take a few steps toward the guy with the mower. She hesitated and looked beseechingly back at us. Winnie waved her plump arm at Barley, motioning her toward the house. Barley groaned visibly and resolutely marched up the walk to Fat Man. The man stopped mowing, probably in amazement at the teenaged vision approaching him. I bet he thought maybe there was a God after all: gliding up his sidewalk was a green-eyed blonde *supermodel* with a killer tan, wearing hot pink. He wiped his face with his shirt. Yeah, *that* made him presentable.

Barley shook his hand. You heard me. Apparently that is manhunt etiquette. They had a brief conversation, then Barley nodded her shiny head at him, turned, and almost ran to the car. Fat Man looked after her wistfully. It was probably one of the most memorable days of his life. Barley scrambled into the car. "Onward, Adam!" *End of Scene in Movie.* (Hollywood screenwriter— more and more obviously my destiny.) Winnie nearly fell on me as Adam swerved the car. "What did he say?"

"He said he's not Frank Fletcher. He thought there might have been a Frank Fletcher who lived in his house a few years back. This Frank shared the house with his mother. That's all he knows. By the way, I am not doing that again. He had BO that nearly knocked me down. You're lucky I didn't faint." With that, Barley went back to the GPS on her phone. "Adam, you have to get on Route 48 and go north. Take the next left."

Winnie sat back with a grunt. She looked a little pale. It was this next Fletch or no Fletch at all. Whatever Mom had in mind, she knew this was her only chance. I could see the wheels turning behind those beacon-blue eyes of hers. Because there weren't going to be any more road trips. This whole thing was just way too ridiculous. Today had to be the perfect storm, or else. Winnie was shooting her entire wad today. Okay. Enough with the metaphors and comparisons.

Adam pulled onto Route 48, also called Far Hills Avenue. It was a wide four-lane road. We went past some shopping centers and then entered a kind of ritzy neighborhood called Oakwood. Lots of species of trees (I barely know an oak from a maple, but still) that were basking in the sun. There was a library on the left, and we passed what looked to me like a mammoth Tudor house. Good Lord, the kids here went to a high school that looked like some sort of English mansion.

Barley told Adam to turn right on Ash Avenue. We drove past three children on Rollerblades, whizzing along the sidewalk without helmets. I guess Oakwood mothers are kind of careless about safety. The houses along the way were surrounded by beautiful flower beds and had porches with furniture and pillows from Pottery Barn. This was not a neighborhood, it was a movie set (or maybe I'm just preoccupied with movie scripts at the moment).

"Slow down, slow down, it's coming up! On the left! Number 312, there it is!" Barley pointed the GPS at a light green clapboard house with darker green shutters. They had little cutouts of pine trees on them. It was topped by a black textured roof, the expensive kind. The house had a red brick foundation and a big porch with white railings. Ferns hung from either side of the steps leading to the shiny black front door. A white painted porch swing hung on the right side; on the left was a wrought iron table with two chairs.

All the furniture had cleverly coordinating cushions in bright colored paisley, flowered, or striped. Obviously an interior decorator was involved. Potted pink geraniums were placed around to look casual. An antique iron boot scraper in the shape of a frog holding a scrub brush. I know. But every detail is etched in my mind. The house numbers 312 were shiny brass, and they were fastened over an equally shiny brass mailbox to the right of the door.

The house looked like the kind that they have in family shows on television: You know? The upper middle-class house with the soccer mom and the lawyer dad. The annoying son with pimples and braces and the cheerleader daughter who is the actual soccer whiz. Which complicates everything for the son for the rest of his unconfident life. This was that kind of house. The house that *Fletch* lived in?

We parked across the street. Birds were singing. There was an occasional bark of what was probably a designer dog. A tiny breeze rustled the leaves of the oak-maple-ash whatever trees were lining the grassy lawns. It wasn't really as hot as it would get later on in the afternoon. It was a perfect Sunday summer day in Ohio. We all turned to look at Mom.

"This time, you three stay in the car. I'm going up there alone." It was more of a command than a statement. Winnie didn't look like she would be taking any prisoners.

Adam, who continued to amaze me (where was all of this substance coming from, all of a sudden?), shook his head violently. "*No,* Mom. What are you thinking? We've done all this detective work *for* you, you've dragged us into this *with* you, we are *all* sitting in this car right now, AND WE ARE ALL GOING IN."

Mom looked as shocked as Barley and I. She surveyed us, one at a time. Then she leaned back against her headrest and closed her eyes. For an eternity. We looked at one another, and Barley raised her eyebrows at Adam. I drummed my fingers as obviously as possible on the armrest. Adam cleared his throat. Nothing. So he did it again.

"Okay, kids. We will all go. But this may be a terrible thing that I'm doing. I have thought about it every day for years, you have to believe me. I'm doing what I think is the right thing. But it may be terrible, terrible."

Okay, at that point, we wanted to frisk her for a gun. But we followed her out of the car and onto the porch steps, in single file. Barley first, then me, then Adam, and Winnie pushing us forward from the rear. We held our breath as Barley rang the doorbell. We heard it ding-donging inside the house. Then footsteps. I about dropped dead right there, I can tell you. The door was opened by a woman.

This woman looked like a Gypsy. She was, I would say, oldish—like nearly forty or something. But her hair was raven black, and it kind of curled its way down to below her shoulders. She had beautiful, deep black eyes. Her face was long, and her cheekbones were to die for. She had on bright red lipstick. Big silver hoops stuck out of her curls, and her finger and toenails were black shellac. What seemed like hundreds of bangle bracelets jangled on her brown arms. She wore a white tank top and black leggings. This woman looked exactly like some kind of runway model.

Gypsy smiled at us inquiringly. Barley began, "Excuse us, but we are looking . . ."

Winnie shoved her way forward at that point and took over. "My name is Winifred Heath. I live in Framington, Ohio. I am looking for my brother-in-law, Frank Fletcher. He is, or was, a musician. Saxophone. Is this his house?" After she said all of that, which let's face it, was probably a shock to this woman, Winnie must have remembered her manners. She held out her hand to shake the Gypsy's. Awkward.

I felt the need to fill in a bit more. "I am Mandy Heath, this is my brother Adam, and this is Barley Crowder, my friend. We apologize for the intrusion. By any chance does Mr. Fletcher live here? The musician?"

Ms. Project Runway got a slightly glassy look in her eyes but replied, "Yes, my fiancé plays the saxophone with the Dayton Philharmonic. May I ask why you are looking for him?"

Winnie took a deep breath. "It's very complicated. Is Frank home? I would really like to talk to him in person. It's a family matter."

If I were this woman, I'd have slammed the door shut in our faces. Like, this was surreal. But she said, "Just a minute. I'll ask Frank. I'll be right back." Then she did shut the door, but in a polite way.

"Oh, my God," Barley whispered. Adam looked like he wanted to dissolve into the concrete and be done with it. I had to pee.

When the door reopened, it was us who had the shock. Well, me, Barley, and Adam, anyway. Because standing beside the Gypsy woman was *Adam*. I mean, down to the last freckle, just about. The man was Adam, only old. Tall, curly red hair, the same athletic build, hooded and sexy aquamarine eyes, and everything; I am not shitting you.

I couldn't believe my eyes. Apparently, neither could Frank/Fletch/Adam. Those sexy eyes nearly popped out of his head. "What is going on? *Winnie?*"

Mom said, "We need to come in. I have a lot to say." (Understatement of all time.)

The Gypsy stepped aside and motioned us to follow her into the living room, which I didn't notice much because at this point I was in shock. But it gave the same general impression as the porch. Colorful, comfortable. Barley and Adam stumbled over themselves but managed to get to a sofa, where they kind of fell downward.

I, by this time, had Mom's arm in a death grip. We both remained standing.

The Gypsy introduced herself. "I am Marianne Gardner. I'm Frank's fiancée. Frank, who are these people?" She said *people*, but she meant Adam.

Frank-Fletch-Adam seemed completely dumbfounded as well. "Marianne, I don't know what's going on. Winnie, what the hell is this?"

Marianne, who seemed to be the only one with brain cells that were still firing, moved chairs around so that everyone could sit down. So there we were, assembled in this stylish living room, waiting for the bombshell to drop.

"May I offer anyone a drink? Coke? Iced tea?"

This brought me back to myself. "Before we start whatever this is, may I use your bathroom?" I really was about to burst.

The powder room had wallpaper like green marble. It had a tiny corner sink and frothy curtains in the long, rectangular window. Wood floors painted dark green. A little frog on the edge of the sink holding a bar of guest soap. Marianne liked frogs, apparently. I washed my hands and dashed a little cold water on my face. I took stock in the mirror. My face looked a little hollow. Hell. We should never have let Winnie talk us into this. There was a knock on the door.

"Hurry up!" Barley hissed. "Your mom is going to explode, and Adam may burst into tears any minute!"

I opened the door and dragged Barley into the powder room. We were packed in there like sardines. "My God, Barley! Adam and this Fletch guy are *twins*!"

We hugged. We were both shaking. "We have to get back in there. Come on, Mand."

So trying not to fall over our own shaking feet, we stumbled back into the living room and took our places. Barley and I sat on the sofa with Adam, who by this time was sweating bullets. There were two dark blue leather wingback chairs opposite the sofa, and the Fletch guy and the Gypsy were in them, looking like someone had dropped them into the chairs from a great height. Everybody looked at Mom, who was standing in front of the fireplace, wringing her hands, her fierce little face drawn up with fortitude. The story began.

"I wanted to come here today by myself," she started, "but that wasn't possible. My husband, Roy, doesn't know about this. My sister, Iris, doesn't know about this, either. But I decided I couldn't keep it to myself, and so I included my children, Adam and Miranda. Barley is a good friend of the family."

She was getting lost in the introduction. "Mom, get to the point." Winnie faltered, looked at me, and then nodded. She smoothed her skirt and gathered her thoughts. Then she fired her first shot.

"Frank, does your girlfriend" (Marianne winced) "know that you are still married?"

Marianne whirled to face him. "*What?*"

Frank, who knew he was in major trouble, shook his head weakly. "I thought Iris got it annulled. She said she was going to. I assumed she did. The last time I saw her, she said she would. We didn't have kids or a house. I thought it was a formality. We didn't have anything to divide. It was dissolved, the marriage. I mean, I've never heard otherwise, so I just assumed. Life goes on. Why wouldn't Iris have done it? Why didn't she do it?"

"I don't *know* why, Frank. But you of all people know that this is a very complicated situation. This is why I'm here today. I can no longer live with our lives all tied up in knots like this."

Marianne interrupted. Of course she was bewildered. We were all completely lost. "Okay, we need to start from the beginning. Frank, who is Iris? Who the *hell* is Iris? What knots? Talk, Frank, *now*."

I felt sorry for the guy. Here he was, having a great Sunday, probably reading the *New York Times* and eating donuts and suddenly his past shows up at his door and everything implodes. Frank looked like he was shrinking into himself gradually, like an orange left out on the counter too long. He shut his eyes for a long time.

"This was all way back in the past. Almost twenty years. I was in Columbus, playing in a bar on State Street. A lot of college kids hung out there. I met Iris and, you know, we began to hang around together. One thing led to another, I guess."

Marianne spluttered. "Frank, don't be vague. For God's sake, spit it out. The truth!"

I was really starting to admire this Gypsy.

He continued. "Okay. I dated Iris. She was beautiful. She played the piano—was studying it. She was in music education. She wanted to be a public school music teacher. But she liked jazz, and she came to the bar most weekends to hear us play. We hit it off."

Mom took over from there. "Yes, they hit it off! She fell head over heels for you, Frank. She would have followed you anywhere! But you had no intentions of settling down, did you? No, you had visions of being the next Dave Brubeck!"

I found out later that this Dave Brubeck guy didn't play the sax, but that was irrelevant here. Winnie pushed on. "When she got pregnant, you wanted to run off, didn't you?"

What??? Adam looked like he'd been stabbed in the gut. Barley's eyes got as big as dinner plates. I felt as if there were cockroaches running around in my throat.

But Fletch? He said nothing; just studied his hands. Probably trying to stay intact for another second or two. All the while knowing that a huge, horrible thing was about to rip him into a million bloody pieces.

"My father had a talk with you. And you and Iris got married. Daddy made sure you did the right thing. Huh! But you didn't hang around much, did you?"

He shook his head. Defeat personified.

"Then Iris lost the baby. You didn't even seem to care. You came back to town only one more time. And that was to seduce *me*, wasn't it?"

Sidebar: As this drama was unfolding before our very eyes, I wondered if this was one of those movie moments that we would never forget. *Oh, my God in Heaven.* My heart skipped about twenty beats. I felt sick. But also a little excited. This *was* like a movie, except we were all in it. *My destiny as a screenwriter was once again slapping me in the face.*

"Yes, I'm no saint. I was young and impressionable. You came back to town to 'wrap things up' with Iris. To tell her you couldn't stick around. But you told me you needed my help, my advice. We met at Kyle's Keyboard downtown. Just for *a drink.* Boy, did I believe your sob story. You were misunderstood. Iris wanted to keep you from pursuing your *dream.* You knew you could make it big. I listened and drank more than I should have. You just talked your way into my pants, didn't you, Frank?"

She stopped. I think she'd shocked herself. Winnie never talks like that. But we could see the wrath in her eyes. She looked like a furious small terrier (I know—too much with the dog references, but if the comparison works). Meanwhile, Barley, Adam, and I were gasping a little bit ourselves.

"Winnie. It wasn't like that. We were both drunk. Both *adults.*"

She sprang to her feet. "Both adults? I was a small town girl, and I knew from nothing! You were suave and knew how to influence women! I had never even dated anybody but Roy!"

OMG. Dad. I had forgotten all about poor dad. Shit, this was awful.

"What happened? You, the fertile bastard that you were, got *me* pregnant too! But of course, you didn't stick around long enough to find out. You left the way you did all those other times. But you didn't come back again. You didn't leave an address. You vanished into thin air. You left Roy to pick up the pieces." This speech was so passionate that Mom had a little spit around her lips. Jesus.

Frank put his head into his hands. Marianne looked lost. Winnie strode around the living room like a woman possessed. Barley and I held hands. Adam shivered.

"What happened, Frank? Roy married me. He loved me. He still loves me. I told him about you. I couldn't lie to him. Roy told me that he 'always wanted a family.' So we got married, and we had Adam. We told everybody he was premature."

Adam jolted forward. He stared at Frank. "SHIT! THIS IS MY DAD? MOM! MY GOD, MOM!" Adam scrambled off the sofa, knocked into the coffee table, sending Marianne's carefully chosen accessories in all directions, and flew out of there. We heard the door slam after him. I mean, really—Adam didn't notice the resemblance until that revelation? My God, maybe he *was* an idiot after all.

I started to go and get him, but Mom said, "Mandy, sit down! Let Adam go. I want to finish this. I have to say the rest of what I came to say."

Barley reached for my hand and pulled me back down onto the sofa. I felt like I couldn't breathe deeply enough to survive. Barley put her arm around my shoulders. This was a moment that would live in infamy. I know. I've heard that somewhere. But it fit this situation to a T.

"Frank, you owe this family a lot. You have caused more heartache and trouble than you will ever know. I came here today knowing that my children may never forgive me for doing this. Frank, you have to make things right. You have to divorce Iris so she can get on with her life. You owe Adam. Your biological son. I want you to pay for his college education. It's the least you can do."

This wasn't like a movie—I take it back. It was a soap opera. They say that the reason people love soap operas so much is that they're like real life. I always thought that was hogwash. But here we all sat, right smack dab in the middle of *The Young and the Restless*.

Recap. Iris dated Frank. Roy (apparently, I would have to look into this further) dated Iris and Mom both. Roy loved Mom. Iris loved Frank. Frank loved himself. Both Mom and Iris got pregnant by Frank. Iris lost her baby. Adam was Mom's. *Shit show.*

Then what, you ask? It got worse.

First off, Marianne. She went over to Frank where he sat, head in hands. Standing over him, she just up and smacked him on the head. Hard. He ducked down like the beaten dog he was at that moment. Marianne turned to the three of us. "He'll do whatever he needs to do. You can count on that." Then something went off behind her eyes. Like there was a flashlight in there. She blazed out at Mom. It takes a lot to set Winnie back, but boy oh boy, that look backed Mom right down into the chair.

"If you think that you can march into our house and toss our lives around, you have another think coming. You look like a pretty strong woman, Mrs. Heath. I find it hard to picture you as an innocent young thing at the mercy of a young, redheaded saxophone player. As a matter of fact, I find it hard to believe that *anybody* could seduce you."

Mom looked like somebody had just pricked her with a pin.

"As a matter of fact, you look more like someone who has been around the block a few times." This Marianne was as fierce as a Gypsy, all right. Her eyes snapped like firecrackers. Her silver hoops swung as she looked from Mom to Frank. "Why did you come here? To get rid of your own guilt at having Frank's child? To get money for him? To avenge your sister? Fine. You've done all that. Now you can go back to Farmville or wherever you came from. And you can feel righteous. Does that about wrap things up? Because I am very tired of looking at all of you."

Frank looked up, still kind of dazed. I guess he realized that the party was over. He somehow managed to stand up and he grabbed Marianne by the bangle bracelets for support (his bones did seem like they were made of rubber) and said, "Winnie, I have to have some time to process all of this. It isn't every day that a man finds out that he is a father. I need time. But I promise I'll stay in touch. Leave me your email address and phone number. I'm sorry. I'm sorry."

He kept kind of mumbling to himself; Marianne peeled his hand off the bangles and shot him a poisonous look. She made it very clear that we were all *done* here with one dark look. Marianne indicated we should get up (we were sort of *paralyzed*) then marched us to the door, out onto the porch, and into the bright Sunday sun.

"Drive safely. If I were you, I wouldn't let that boy behind the wheel." Marianne pointed to where Adam leaned against the driver's side of the Explorer, looking shocky. With that, she went into her Pottery Barn house and slammed the door.

Stunned is the word for all of us. Stunned and mortified. Well, maybe Winnie wasn't mortified. We filed down the steps and crossed the lawn, which, by the way, was manicured within an inch. This whole suburb was like that: buffed, puffed, and pretty as a picture. I couldn't wait to get out of there.

When we got to the car, Mom reached out to Adam, who did indeed have tears on his cheeks. A first. He wrenched away from her and got into the backseat. Stony. Barley kind of took over at that point. She ushered Winnie into the driver's seat then went around and got in the shotgun position (oh, man—no pun, thank God). "Don't worry, Mrs. Heath. I'll tell you exactly how to get home. There won't be much traffic" (she looked at her watch) "because it's four o'clock. No worries."

Winnie, who was as close to having absolutely *no* wind in her sails as I've ever seen her, obeyed. She started the car. Before she buckled in, she turned around. "Adam, I give you permission to hate me for the rest of your life. But I did this for you. I had to try to make Frank do right by you. He needed to know what a wonderful man you are."

This did not go over as she hoped. Adam gave her the finger.

You can imagine the ride back to Framington. No conversation. Lots of throat clearing. All of us lost in our own thoughts. Barley frantically trying to keep Winnie focused on the road ahead. It was horrific. But we made it home.

Of course, as we drove up, we saw Dad pulling weeds in the front yard. He stood up and waved gaily. When we got out of the car, he came toward us with a grin. "Find any good bargains?"

Chapter Four

Sunday dinners at our house were usually pretty lively. Between Winnie's constant reminders to Adam to use his napkin, Dad's inquiries about how practice was going or, in my case, when on earth would I get around to helping him clean the garage as I promised, conversation usually flowed right along. This Sunday totally sucked. First of all, we had sandwiches, because Mom wasn't home to cook. Secondly, she couldn't look Dad in the eye full on. Thirdly, Adam wouldn't come downstairs. Finally, I was so nervous that I spilled iced tea all over the Formica.

Something had to give.

Dad asked what he thought was probably a pretty innocent question. "What's going on around here?" Then he added, "Where's Adam?"

That released the floodgates. Mom disintegrated. I know it isn't nice to say, but she blubbered into her hands and things got a little snotty around the edges. Her chest was heaving so much that when she tried to talk, all that came out was, "Whu, whu, whup, whup, whup."

Dad turned to me, of course.

"Mom? Do I tell him the truth?" As if, at this juncture, there was any other option.

She whupped her permission. So it was up to me. I had to think. How would I put this? What could I say to darling Roy Heath about his adulterous wife and nonson? My God in Heaven. So I started in.

"Dad, remember when I asked you how you met Mom? And you said something about how complicated it was between you, Frank Fletcher, Aunt Iris, and Mom?"

He nodded uneasily.

"It seems that things were even more complicated than you thought. See, oh, gosh, Dad, it seems that after Aunt Iris lost her baby, but before Fletch, I mean Frank, left town for good, he and Mom kind of hooked up. Once. Then Mom got pregnant. Totally by accident."

Dad nodded again, but painfully. "I know. Go on."

Wait. *What?* Then I remembered the part in Mom's dissertation in Dayton about how Roy Heath had supported her and married her. The part about the premature infant Adam. Oh, God! My dad was a *prince*. I regarded him with completely new eyes.

"Dad. How could you have done that? How could you have raised another man's son?"

By this time, Dad was openly agitated. "Mandy. We will go into that. But I have to know what happened *today*!"

I paused for breath. Maybe if Roy knew everything, this wouldn't be such a disaster. Maybe all we would have to do is salvage Adam. But no—Aunt Iris. Fuck.

"Anyway. Mom has apparently been worrying about how screwed-up this has been for so long. So Mom got me and Barley on Fletch's trail. Frank's trail. We weren't sure, but we found a couple of Frank Fletchers in Dayton. Mom dragged us all down there this afternoon to confront Frank." I stopped to give Dad time to digest so far.

He paraphrased: "Winnie convinced Barley, you, and *Adam* to go down there? Why did she do that?"

"I think she wanted me and Barley there for some sort of moral support. Plus, Barley was the only one with the Fletch addresses in her GPS. And Barley's good with maps, in case we got lost, which we almost did. Not to mention that Barley is a calming influence. And Dad, neither Barley or I have our licenses, so Adam had to drive."

"*She had Adam take himself to meet his biological father?*" Roy was incredulous. I didn't blame him. He looked over at Winnie, still whupping noisily. (At this point, I think she was forcing it a bit. Because she didn't want to have to jump in and finish the story.)

"Mom says she's given permission for Adam to hate her for the rest of his life. But she had to get down there to tell Frank off, and she told him about the divorce part. There was more. She told Frank she expects him to pay for Adam's college education. Because it's the least he can do."

Now, as you can surely imagine, we were sitting around the kitchen table behind plates of uneaten turkey sandwiches. There were still puddles of iced tea on the Formica. Napkins were crumpled. Roy shoved his plate into the center of the table and put his fists down rather forcefully. Mom and I jumped.

"WINIFRED HEATH. YOU COOKED UP AN IRRESPONSIBLE PLAN TO BRING ADAM AND FRANK TOGETHER JUST LIKE THAT? NO CONSULTING ME? NO WARNINGS? NO THOUGHT AS TO WHAT THIS MIGHT DO TO OUR SON? OR TO FRANK? GOOD GOD, WOMAN!"

I have to say that I was impressed. My dad, the former marshmallow man, had actually stood up to Winnie the whirlwind. Winnie the boss. Winnie the stout. It was amazing. But as soon as the man of iron had shown up, he disappeared. Roy Heath was suddenly wiped out. His face sagged, and the color drained out of his cheeks.

The flash and flush was gone. When he dropped into his chair, he was one defeated pharmacist, I can tell you.

He put his forehead on the table, his hands in his lap. For a minute, I thought he was taking a little nap. He snuffled, rolling his poor head back and forth against the surface of Mom's prize vintage 1950s dinette. Mom seemed to be quieting down. Instead of "whupping," it was more like "ish, ish, ishing."

"I had *ish* . . . *ish* . . . to do it, Roy. This has been eating away at me all these years. Iris is my sister . . . *ish*. If she wants to have a future with Don Horley or anybody else, she has to be free of Frank. I had to confess to my children what I have done. Whether they forgive me isn't important. But I had to tell the truth. *Ish*."

For a minute, I thought she was going to say she had to "come clean." That would have been more like a movie/soap opera script than even I could bear. But she didn't. Wait. There's more. After that last *ish*, Winnie dropped the final bombshell of the weekend:

"Roy, I don't know how you can be so judgmental. After all, you jilted my sister and broke her heart. I'm not the only one who's thrown a monkey wrench around in this family!"

Stunned silence that you could cut with a knife. This had gone from a shit show to what Adam aptly calls a "fuckfest."

Recap, because you are probably totally lost. Geez, me too, practically.

Way back when. Frank is a sexy redheaded musician. He meets Iris, and she kind of likes him. Then Roy Heath, the dashing pharmacy student, shows up and sweeps Iris off her feet. For some reason, he doesn't know he has done it or something, because he just thinks Iris is a nice girl. Iris has to get over it, because Roy isn't interested. Then one day Winnie enters from stage left, and Roy is smitten. What does Frank the Fletch do? He latches onto willowy Iris, and they get it on! Iris gets pregnant. The Fletch, who apparently is not all bad, agrees to marry Aunt Iris. Iris has to give up (my God, she TOLD ME THIS STORY) the love of her life—ROY—in order to marry her baby's father. She loses the baby. So awful. Fletch reverts back to the jazz man that he was formerly and disappears frequently for gigs.

I am pausing here for us to catch our breath.

Okay. Next, we find that Frank shows up one last time. Why hasn't been established. Knowing the players in this farce, there will be some really crappy reason for his return. Stick around for that outcome. Anyway, when he comes back, it is to give Iris some money, or play a gig in town, or tell her he has a girl in Toledo, or whatever. *But*, and this is the *big but* (OMG, pun on Winnie), he manages to get Winnie drunk the last night he's in town (or one of the nights, anyway), and just like in the movies, she gets pregnant with Adam. The Fletch disappears again. So Roy marries my mother, knowing that she is pregnant with another man's kid, and he loves them both.

You're welcome. Back to our shitball Sunday dinner.

"Now it's all out in the open. The whole tawdry story. I will take responsibility for what I did in the past. But what about you, Roy?" Winnie welled up again. Oh, God.

Roy surprised us all. He raised his head off the table, and he was smiling weakly through a few tears. There we sat. The rooster clock ticked. Cars vroomed by. A woodpecker tocked against a tree. You catch my drift: Time stood still. Dad wiped his face with the closest napkin and stood up.

"Winnie, you're right. We're all twisted up in this. I'm just as much to blame as Frank. I love you. I have always loved you. I never even had a *tiny* bit of romantic interest in your sister. How she felt about me was all in her own imagination, I guess. I love my son. He *is* my son. Frank is just DNA. Just Goddamn DNA."

Another perfect shot from a movie. Roy put his arms around Winnie's shoulders, pulled her out of her seat, and Jesus, they *both* started "whu, whu, whupping." It was way too private, and I was embarrassed, exhausted, angry at Winnie, Frank, and the world. I left them to it and went up to bed.

Adam had locked himself in his room. I could only imagine all that was getting his testosterone in a bunch. He must have been roiling around in there. But I couldn't think about him. I hadn't even had one second to figure out my own feelings about this unprecedented day in my life.

The first thing I did when I went into my room was slam the door. Some steam escaped. Then I laid (lay? I have no clue) down on my Winnie-coordinated bedding and cried. I cried for me, first of all, because, let's face it, teens are completely self-absorbed, right? Then my sorrow encompassed my dearly loved Aunt Iris, and I wondered how she would react to opening up all these old wounds. Finally, I cried for poor Adam, whose entire world had exploded over him like a volcano. Poor simile, but I was in the throes. I managed to squeeze out a few tears for Winnie even. Although I was furious with that man-killing fireplug. If only she hadn't wanted to get this off her chest. Yeah. Right off hers and onto ours.

This went on for what seemed like hours, but it was actually about ten o'clock when I began to come out of myself. I had personally both "whupped" and "ished" enough. I took a couple of jagged sighs, and dialed Barley on my cell. This was way too much for a text.

"Holy shit, Mand! I've been dying to talk to you, but I knew there was stuff coming down like crazy over there. How are you? What happened? Is Adam okay?"

"First off, I hate my mom. What kind of insane idea was this trip, anyway? And does she think that her proclamation that it's okay for Adam to hate her forever somehow absolves her of all of this crap?"

Oh, boy. Poor Barley. She got sucked right into the middle of this maelstrom that was my family. "Mand. You have to calm down. You have to try to put this in perspective."

"Perspective. Okay. Let's give *that* a try: The world is fucked up. Adults, who are supposed to be mature, go around having sex with the wrong people. Mothers suddenly announce that they have children from more than one father. Parents totally mess up their kids' minds. Oh, yeah, the perspective part—maybe we'll all get over this in about twenty years and get on with our lives?" I wanted to throw the phone up against my Better Homes and Gardens wall.

"Barley, you're my best friend, but this second? Perspective totally sucks. My family is falling apart right now. Any other suggestions?"

"Shit. Okay. Do you want me to come over? Or would you rather come over here?"

I considered leaving, but there was my brother down the hall, probably contemplating suicide or something. I had to talk to him. "Barley, I love you to the end. Really. But I need to stick around. There may be more crap coming down. I need to make sure Adam is all right. I'll call you tomorrow. Say a prayer for us over here! Bye."

First off, the fact that I asked for a prayer is totally weird, because the Heaths are not a religious bunch. Roy goes to church sometimes. The rest of us sleep in or watch cartoons. Well, Adam and I do that. Winnie is usually up before the crack, and she cleans stuff or makes pancakes. Praying? We've never even said *grace*, for Pete's sake. So it's really hardcore when I resort to asking for help from above.

I lay there for a while, considering what to do. I reached for my old Ted bear, who is the only stuffed animal I insisted on keeping during Winnie's last home scourge. Aunt Iris gave him to me on my sixth birthday, and as soon as I saw his little soft ears and button eyes, I melted. His fuzz has gotten me through a lot of crises. I clutched him to my neck. I inhaled him. He smelled like magic markers and dust. I buried my face in his softness and closed my eyes.

Have you ever tried to clear your brain of all thoughts? Like they do in meditation? It isn't possible. Those meditators are lying. Because I tried to wipe everything clean. I took deep, cleansing breaths. I pictured a peaceful, grainy white beach. I thought of the delicious smell of molasses cookies. I tried to relax my muscles.

Nothing.

All I could think about was the look on Adam's face when it sank in that he was this Fletch guy's spawn. Adam had turned green. You got it. That really happens. Not green like a pea or something—more like the white of his skin was replaced by a thin layer of puke. Horrible. I couldn't stop worrying about what he was doing in his room. He probably wouldn't let me in, but I had to check on him. So Ted and I padded down the hall. I knocked on the door. "Adam? It's me! Are you okay? Let me in—we need to figure things out!"

Silence.

"Adam! I need to talk to you! I hate Mom! Let me in!"

I heard a thud. He was heaving gym shoes at the wall. Another thud. Adam is a Neanderthal when it comes to sorting out his feelings.

"Adam, let me in this minute or I will ask Winnie to come up here and spill more of her guts!!"

That did it. I heard him shuffling to the door. The lock turned, and it opened a crack. I saw a bloodshot blue eye. We glared at each other for a sec and then I shoved my way in.

"Good God, Adam, it stinks in here! Open a window. Your flop sweat is nauseating!"

"Shut up, fuckface!" He sank onto his funky bed in despair.

"Wait here." I opened his door, looked both ways for parents. They weren't around. Probably downstairs, still hugging and forgiving. Ugh. I sneaked into the bathroom, and grabbed the Febreze. I hustled back into Adam's room with the stuff and locked the door.

After liberally spritzing all the decaying piles of clothes, shooting spray into the dozens of skanky shoes lying around and anointing the sheets, Adam, and the general atmosphere, I sat down beside him on the bed.

"Adam. Spill it."

He really looked lost. Kind of like he'd changed from a senior in high school right back to being five years old. His face was flushed, and all his freckles looked magnified. His hair was damped down and lanky. He looked deflated and small. And he smelled moldy. Some things don't change. But he was my brother. He had sustained a huge shock. So I took control of my gag reflex and reached out and gave him an awkward huggish kind of thing. He didn't even wrench himself away—that's how bad a state he was in.

"Shit, Mand. I don't know what to do." He rubbed his head and twisted a gingery hank of hair around his fingers. "I hate Mom right now. How could she be such a whore?" He banged his head against the Adam Dunn poster on the wall behind him. "HO BAG!"

Whoa. I looked at my brother. He was writhing around in obvious pain. Up to this point, I had never even given Adam credit for *having* any emotions other than lust. If that counts as an emotion. And suddenly, he was plunged right into the big five: Embarrassment, Rage, Resentment, Humiliation, and Betrayal. All in one afternoon.

I crossed my legs, Indian style. Might as well get comfortable. We weren't going anywhere. "Adam. You know that Mom is not a whore. She had sex as an adult woman. With one guy. You and I both know girls at school who've done much worse than that, and they're not only *not* hoes, they're the popular girls! The sexual revolution happened a zillion years ago, remember? So calm down about calling Mom names. It doesn't solve anything."

Okay. There I was, channeling Dr. Phil. Desperate times call for desperate measures.

"I hate Mom."

"I know. I hate her, too, right now. But Adam, she's our mom. She did this because in her own Winnie-ness, she thought it was the right thing. She was trying to *fix* what she did, and I'm sure she knew you would hate her. She said you could, right?"

That approach didn't help. Adam shrank down into himself even more. He looked like some sort of pathetic Muppet. He stared into space.

"Adam, we'll figure this out." I tried to sound optimistic. Adam shook his head. He sniffed and looked over at me.

"Get out."

I didn't have a choice. Plus, I really didn't know what else to do. So I took Ted and the bottle of Febreze and I left.

Life continued on like this, with our family suddenly behaving like we belonged to a weird Amish sect that allowed electricity and driving cars but still believed in shunning a member who violates a rule. Winnie walked around the house in slow motion, doing her best to continue being our mom. Neither Adam nor I felt much like talking to her. All right, I'll be honest: We left any room she had the balls to enter.

Dad was clearly suffering. I think he lost about five pounds the first week. He just couldn't snack with all the turmoil. Whereas we tended to make ourselves scarce whenever Winnie approached, Dad did just the opposite and trailed after her like a lost puppy, which, while it was intended to make her feel warm, loved, and forgiven, actually had the opposite effect, and Dad started to get on Mom's nerves.

She started snapping at Roy, her only advocate in the Heath clan. Oh, yeah. None of us had yet manifested the guts it would take to go over to tell Aunt Iris about all of this. That came later. Hold on.

You know how it is when you decide not to speak to someone? How the longer it goes on, the more impossible breaking the silence seems? Who will be the first to say something? And pride keeps the whole thing going way beyond what is sane?

I'd begun to have thoughts like: *Maybe I should casually say "Hi" the next time she comes in the room. No! That would be ridiculous, like I have amnesia or something and forgot what happened. Or: What if I cry? Will that bring her rushing to my side, and we can fall into each other's arms, sobbing and, incidentally, forgiving?* That seemed a bit of a stretch, even for me.

Meanwhile, Adam was staunch. Of course, he'd been the most traumatized by Winnie's "admit, repent, and pay for a college education" caper. I didn't expect him to soften much around Mom. But Dad visited our rooms on a nightly basis, trying his damndest to soften one of us up. I don't know what went on in Adam's den of stench, but here's the transcript of one of Dad's visits to my room:

Roy: *Mandy, your mother made a mistake. She has paid for it over and over. She has not lived one day since without regretting what she did. And she has such love for Iris. She wants to help her sister move on. Really, Mandy, she does.*

All of this delivered with a hangdog expression and sometimes with the addition of a little gift to sweeten the deal. He brought me a plate of molasses cookies and hot chocolate one night (they don't go together), and he also brought orange popsicles and packs of Nerds. Remember, the man has an entire inventory of Assorteds at his disposal.

Me: *Dad, I know. But Mom has humiliated Adam. Or ruined his life. Or both, probably.* (I usually took this moment to let my message sink in as I enjoyed the gustatory delight of the popsicle.) *Adam can't just forgive her with the snap of a finger. He's a seething mass of hormones, for one thing, and secondly, he's totally confused about everything. He doesn't know if he even wants to go to college at all. He wasn't keen on it anyway, and now he feels that the last thing he wants to do is take Fletch's money.*

Roy: *Mandy, what about you? Can you forgive your mother?*

Me: *I don't know.*

By this time, Barley was at her wits' end. She called frequently with requests to get together with me and Adam. But Adam was making himself scarce. He would leave the house in the morning, going out the front door so that he wouldn't see Mom in the kitchen, or he'd walk right past her, saying nothing on his way out. Winnie put up with this without as much as a whimper. I didn't feel like going to the pool and tanning. So poor Barley was left out completely.

In the meantime, Mom went over to spill her guts to Aunt Iris. I found this out when I went over there to keep Iris company and help her weed her garden. June was starting to bake, and Iris wanted to get her annual beds in order for the Fourth of July. This year she decided to have a red, white, and blue theme with white petunias, red geraniums, and electric blue lobelias from the garden center. But when she got there, the colors were just too glaring so she got white and pink petunias instead.

As we bent over the loamy soil (I got that from a book), sweat dripping down our noses, Aunt Iris said, "You had quite a trip to Dayton I hear." Understatement! She turned to look at me, her eyes glittering from under her straw gardening hat.

"How did you hear about it?" I asked. Knowing full well.

"Your mom told me. She said that she wanted to make things right. But she isn't sure she did anything but destroy her family. How do you feel, Mandy, about all of this?"

I, of course, had been thinking of little else since the trip. "I have a question for you. How do you feel about the fact that you lost a baby but your own sister had one? With your husband?"

"First of all, Mandy, this is all water under the bridge. At least that's what I thought. I was surprised Winnie decided to find Frank. But honey, she's been carrying that huge weight around with her for years. I guess she wanted to get it out so that we could all heal." Iris sat back on her haunches and scratched her forehead with her trowel, leaving a brown smudge above her eye.

"You haven't answered my question. What about your baby and Mom's? Well, Adam?"

There was a pause. A bee droned by, nearly scaring me to death. I hate bees. Birds rustled above us. Still, Iris sat, lost in thought. I could almost hear myself sweating.

"Mandy, honey, I'll be very honest. I never wanted to have a child. Really. I don't think I would have been cut out for that. To tell the truth, I never loved Frank. But he was so very attractive, and those red curls and muscles just blinded me to the truth. When I lost the baby, I was more guilty than sad. And the guilt just grew and grew."

I looked at my darling aunt. She twirled the trowel and stabbed it into the bed, lifting it and jabbing it back into the earth, over and over. I thought she might be crying, but it could have been sweat. Either way, she was obviously forlorn. She picked a white petunia with the non-trowel wielding hand and smelled it. They don't have a scent, by the way.

"What about Roy and Mom and stuff? Weren't you furious at Frank for being with my mom?"

Iris put the trowel down. She shifted toward me, dropped the petunia, and took both my hands. "Honey, I was in love with your father. I thought he was the kindest and most gallant man on earth." She smiled, probably remembering Roy when he was young and virile (ugh).

"Mandy, your father liked me, but he adored your mother. When she got mixed up with Frank, it didn't matter to your father one bit. What he did want was to protect your mom."

I hate all of this soap opera stuff right in my own life. It's pure shit. "But why did you all act like this? I thought adults knew better. This is so screwed up!"

"I agree." She let go of my hands and sat back with a sigh. "Are you furious? I don't blame you if you are. But Mandy, you should forgive your mom. If for no other reason than you need her. You're dealing with all of this, you're going into high school, which could be very difficult for you, and you need a mother now more than you ever have. Can you think about that?"

Iris went back to popping the petunias out of their plastic pots. The roots were gnarled up and she gently massaged them loose, then plopped them into the holes we had dug. She seemed to be concentrating very hard. I sat there, stunned.

The sun beat down on me. One fifteen-year-old girl, full of angst, and I wasn't even under any peer pressure yet. My brother was having a nervous breakdown, my father was beside himself, my friend Barley couldn't get through to me, and my aunt was loaded to the gills with guilt, forgiveness, and understanding.

"This is just fine and dandy for you, apparently," I said. "Forgiveness. I would like to know how to go about forgiving my mother for opening this huge can of worms. For destroying my brother. Oh, and by the way, I guess since she gave him *permission* to hate her for the rest of his life, that somehow gets her off the hook?"

"Time, Mandy. Time will heal. For now, try to understand. Everyone makes mistakes. Some of them are huge. Nobody is even close to being perfect. You will make mistakes, honey. You *will*. You can be sure of that. And you'll most likely have children. Think about all the mistakes you'll make before you are a mother. How will you want your kids to treat you if they find out about them?"

That night, when I lay in the dark, with the whoosh of the overhead fan and my pulse throbbing in my ears, I tried to imagine how Winnie might feel right now. I mean, people have sex. Some of my girlfriends do it already. There was a girl in the eighth grade last year who had a baby. We all sneered, "The condom broke!" I never even thought about the baby. That baby will grow up and learn about her mom. I don't know that girl from last year. I know she gave her baby up for adoption.

When she's old enough, that baby's mother will tell her about her "biological" mom. Will the child hate that girl who gave her up?

Sometimes, I despise life.

Chapter Five

Fourth of July. We usually have a big celebration. Iris comes over for a cookout, and Roy makes the most mouth-watering barbecued hamburgers and hot dogs. Winnie makes fried chicken and potato salad. And there's pie. We get hand-packed ice cream from Graeter's, and I usually get to pick out a bunch of candy bars from the store. Barley is there with sparklers and, of course, Adam shoots off the big stuff and we worry about the police stopping us. It's so much fun.

This year, not so much. Adam was still clenched all the time. Some progress, though. He talked to Mom, but only for necessary information, mostly with "yes" or "no." He still was gone a lot, but when he was around, at least he remained in the same room with Winnie for short stretches.

Here's the thing: Winnie just *took* it. My mom, the beast, was no longer a dynamo. Nope. She went through the motions around the house, dusting things without really looking at them, leaving crumbs on the countertops, and vacuuming the same spot on the living room rug over and over. She still made the beds every day, and she did the laundry. But the fire had gone out. Roy spent more time at the store. Winnie went in more, too. I guess it got her mind off the family. When I was home alone, it seemed kind of stale and empty. Every room had an echo.

Oh, Barley finally got through to me. We went to the pool, ate ice cream sandwiches that melted down our arms, and talked about things. Barley was focused on Adam. Of course, she has *been* focused on Adam ever since her hormones kicked in. But I have to say, she was really worried about him.

Adam stopped stuffing himself after the whole Fletch debacle. It had been two and a half weeks since Dayton, and he had probably lost fifteen pounds. He looked like something the cat dragged in. His cheeks were hollow, and the face that had been a sea of blue eyes and cute freckles had turned pale and gray. He almost never showed up for dinner, even when Mom made cheeseburgers and fries to entice him. He must have been existing on Twizzlers and Coke.

Barley declared that he needed a breakthrough. Yeah, right. What could break through to him was a mystery to me. I admit I wasn't happy with the Adam situation myself. I tried and tried to talk to him, but he just vegetated in his room, playing video games on his laptop or texting on his cell. Or sexting. Who knows.

So I worried about the coming holiday, Mom, school starting, Adam, and myself as a member of the Framington High School masses. Peer pressure, boys, pimples, and all that stuff. My plate was way too full in my opinion. If something didn't get solved around here pretty quick, I worried about getting an ulcer. It was obvious that I needed to consult Dad about medications for curing my jumpy gut syndrome.

I cornered Dad before he went to the store. I gave him a hug, which he most definitely deserved, and then I asked him if he had a minute for me. He smiled and said, "Surely, Mandy! Always."

We sat at the kitchen table, but only after I wiped it down with the dishrag. Good God, channeling Winnie! Symptoms of my own breakdown in the offing, surely.

I jumped up and got a glass of water (they always need water in emergencies, have you noticed? I armed myself in advance), and then settled down next to Roy.

"Dad, it's just awful around here. Mom is not herself," (I pointed to a dirty cup on the counter) "Adam looks like death warmed over, and I'm feeling like I need Prilosec or something. I wish we could turn the clock back! I'm so worried about everybody. What can we do? Can we do anything? Help, Daddy!"

Roy reared back in shock, because I'd stopped calling him "Daddy" when I was four. He knew this was a crisis for me. Obviously, he recognized the fact that we were all kind of crumbling to dust around here. His dear brown eyes were sad, but always the optimist, Roy replied, "Honey, don't be blue. I do have an idea, and since you brought this up, I can share it with you. But I have to tell you, it might upset you more, because it's kind of radical."

Remember, Roy Heath is the visionary. But in a kind of very conventional, your-local-minister sort of way. So my reaction was mild. "Okay, Dad, what?"

"We're going to go ahead with the cookout for the Fourth. The family. But I'm going to invite Marianne and Frank to come."

Shock and awe. He wasn't kidding. Good Lord. It took a few seconds to sink in, but when it did, my skittish stomach took a turn for the worse. I felt the acid rise into my throat, and up in my mouth a little. This was why you needed water in a crisis.

"But why do THAT? How will that HELP? God, Dad, just throw some fuel on the fire, why don't you?"

"Mandy, I've been thinking about it. We have to do something to address this with everybody present—you know, kind of like an intervention?" He clasped his hands as if in prayer.

First of all, how my father knew about interventions was startling, but then I reminded myself that he was a *pharmacist*, after all. They have to know all kinds of things about drugs and druggies. He went to a yearly convention in Chicago, and I bet they have guest speakers like Dr. Drew.

"Go on."

He looked at me, drinking water. (By the way, it did kind of help me calm down, and it diluted the stomach acid in my throat.) My hands weren't shaking quite as much, but I did dribble a few beads of water onto the Formica. I wiped them off with the palm of my hand. Winnie couldn't have cared less at this point.

"I think we need to get together—have all the players present—and talk things out."

I got it, but I'm not sure Dad did. "Do you know what happens in those interventions? I watch the show! Things blow up! People get violent. You have to have a trained professional present. You can't just put a bunch of people who hate each other in a circle and ask them to share! Somebody could go postal. And I mean Adam."

Dad nodded. "I know. It's risky. I've discussed this with Iris and she thinks that as long as Don Horley is here, we'll be okay. He's big, he's involved, of course—so it makes sense to have him come, and he can help if Adam gets unruly."

"Wait. Dad. Does Mom know about this?" I couldn't comprehend this all coming together. Holy Hell.

"Well, no. I don't think any advance warning would be advisable."

"But have you asked Frank and the Gypsy—I mean Marianne—yet? How do you know they'd even consider this idea? It sounds completely disastrous to me. Have you asked them?" I said this with my hand over my eyes, as if the world were coming to a quick and violent end right there in the vintage kitchen with all the rickrack.

Oddly, Roy smiled. I guess he felt really good about his idea of family feud right in our own home. "I've talked with Frank on the phone a couple of times since Dayton Sunday." (Oh, so now it has a name that will become a historic reference point.) "He's very contrite and says this whole thing haunts him. I think he needs closure as well as the rest of us."

My God. Closure. Dad was channeling psychotherapists, now. Really, did I want to get to know my parents this well? Did every family have as many skeletons rattling around in their closets as we did? So many that interventions were in order?

"Dad. Frank needs closure you think. But does his desire to let it all hang out mean that he wants to spill his guts and eat hot dogs at the same time? Will Marianne feel right at home waving sparklers around while hearing about how Fletch and Winnie *got it on*? How will you feel about your son having to confront *both* his dads? You talk about *fireworks* on the Fourth!"

Again with the movie and TV references, but this all was kind of like some surreal Wes Anderson film. I was expecting a bunch of Boy Scouts in uniforms to come marching into the kitchen any second.

Dad reached over and took my glass of water and had a sip. He pushed the glass back to me. "Unless you have something better and less risky in mind, I'm going ahead. Things have to be brought to a head so that Adam can come to grips with this. And Winnie is very sad." His eyes got a little blurry. "She's so sad. It has to get better. I'm inviting Frank and Marianne. I'm banking on them coming. Because they need closure too."

So our "family" at the cookout would include the elusive boyfriend with big muscles from wrestling around granite countertops, my best friend, as well as Fletch and the Gypsy from Dayton. With a big box of illegal fireworks. Naturally, all of it was a secret. *Shit, Dad, sounds like a plan.*

Dad got up and gave me an awkward—him standing, me sitting—hug. He finished the rest of the water in my glass, slammed it down on the table as if it were a tequila shot, patted my shoulder, and went into the garage. I heard his Camry roar to attention, the clatter of the garage door as it ground open, and off he went to count pills.

I put my head down on the cool Formica. I counted the little red and blue flecks. This table had been in the kitchen of probably some *Leave it to Beaver* family in the 1950s. I bet they said grace around it before they had baloney sandwiches and potato chips. Probably the worst crises they had were about the Beave getting a C on a spelling test. What was it with all these secrets all of a sudden? Our family had been plain and normal before this summer. Winnie hustled and bustled. Roy was peaceable and contented. Adam was the usual annoying, hormonal, and monosyllabic big brother. Then a bomb went off.

Right then, I knew this for sure: When I reached adulthood, I'd try very hard to think before getting sexy with somebody. For that matter, I might swear off sex altogether. Money, the root of all evil? No way. It goes right back to the Garden of Eden and the damn apple. I wondered if I would like being a nun.

I got up and refilled the water glass.

I haven't talked much about Don Horley. Mainly because that summer I hardly knew him at all. Here's what I knew from the few times I saw him, plus what Aunt Iris told me:

Don Horley was a big man. I'd say around six four. There were some awesome tattoos. One of a thunderbolt that started just underneath his hair at the nape of his neck and shot down the middle of his back. Not *at all* what I envisioned appealing to Aunt Iris. He was bald, but in that kind of sexy way. For all I know, he shaved his head. He had hazel "deep pool" eyes that looked brown sometimes and green sometimes (this from Iris—hell, I never got close enough to him to gaze into his eyes).

He'd gone to the community college to learn about construction work and then started his own business. I guess it just took off. So the countertop man was very successful. Anyway, back to the description. He reminded me of those big guys who look kindly and all, but if you cross them they can break your leg. He had massive biceps that strained the sleeves of his T-shirts, and legs like tree trunks.

Despite his looks, Don Horley was a sensitive guy. Why else would he fall for somebody like Aunt Iris? She told me that he asked her to play sonatas for him. Of course, he probably wouldn't know a sonata if it slapped him across the face, but she got the picture and they spent date nights at her house, Aunt Iris playing him Mozart and stuff. She said he perched on the edge of the sofa, kind of awkwardly (the bull in the china shop?) and listened with eyes closed and hands clasped as if in prayer, eyes kind of teary.

So here we had a He-Man with a soft side. I bet he never thought that having a willowy pianist for a girlfriend would get him sucked into this weird maelstrom of family shit. But according to Aunt Iris, Don loved to read poems, he was a great dad (oh, yeah, divorced ten years ago, and his daughter was in college at Ohio State), and he offered to dig a new flower bed for Iris, just in case she got a yen for more perennials.

Iris told me that on their first date, she and Don went out to dinner at Beth's Bistro, her favorite little restaurant. Beth, a gorgeous woman who used to be an interior designer, got sick of that and opened a little café where she specialized in Southern delicacies. In northern Ohio. Go figure. But I've been there, and the pecan pie is to die for. Beth serves the desserts herself, and she comes around to all the tables to "dish" with the customers. Iris said that Beth gave her the thumbs-up after she watched Don scarf down two pieces of the pecan.

Anyway, Don and Iris went there, and they talked about their lives and loves. She told him a little about Frank and her stormy marriage. How, ever since that, she'd been leery of serious entanglements. Don didn't mind. He told Iris he wasn't looking for a serious relationship either. He liked his life, and he admired the one that Iris had made for herself.

Iris told me that she and Don weren't really serious. I think she was lying, because she wouldn't want just any old guy to be included in our family business this way. I figured she had secret designs and desires that she wasn't admitting to anybody. Maybe she was waiting to decide if she wanted to marry him until after she saw what happened with Fletch on the Fourth?

Here's what I concluded about Don Horley and Iris: That they *should* get married. People needed families. I mean, their own families, in their own houses. Like the Marches in *Little Women*. *Little Women* was kind of like comfort food to me, but in book form. When times were tough, I liked to take it to bed with me and re-read it. I actually ate comfort food at the same time. So my copy of *Little Women* had mucho food stains on the pages. I'm a throwback, remember?

But back to the subject of families: the more mine was falling apart, the more I realized how much everybody needed their families. Families gave you strength.

The people you live with should always have your back. Like the time I got my period at school and didn't know it, and the kids humiliated me about the red stain on my jeans; Mom told me the story about the time she wore an old pair of underpants and the elastic snapped, and they fell down her legs—on the sidewalk in front of her high school. It made us both laugh, and I felt better. Winnie said, "If you don't have embarrassing moments like this, what will you have to tell your grandchildren?" That was such a great night. Mom knew I was feeling awful, and she stayed in my room with me until I went to sleep, gently stroking my hair.

It wasn't exactly Marmee and Jo, but it was close. I always wished for more days like that. Family days. Fires in the winter with crisp apples and cracking nuts. Mornings in our cozy kitchen, with Dad making pancakes, Winnie heating up syrup, and Adam grunting replies. Aprons with bunches of cherries and green rickrack. Smells of molasses cookies baking—spicy and raisiny. It was my security.

Up until this summer, our family was right up there with the all-time great families.

It made sense that Iris must miss that kind of family support. She had us, but what about the nights when she felt crummy, all alone in her cottage, with nothing but cold piano keys for company? It seemed obvious she would love having Don around, to hug her and do the "man" stuff like unclogging drains and killing spiders. I bet she wished for someone to watch old movies with late at night, or a man she could just hug anytime she wanted. I bet Aunt Iris was glad her sister dragged us to Dayton to create a big scene and push Fletch for freedom. This whole thing might not have been such a stupid move on Winnie's part after all.

Meanwhile, I'd been thinking more about Mom. With the fizz gone out of her, it was harder and harder for me to stay furious with her. I watched her trying to go through the motions, but every time Adam shunned a meal or refused to answer a question, she wilted a little more. Yeah, at first, I thought it was what she deserved. Then I missed my mom. The old Winnie: Winnie Heath, the invincible. I honestly never thought that there was anything in the world that could conquer her. So I couldn't help forgiving her a little bit more every day.

Meanwhile, Adam resembled a bomb waiting to go off. Barley and I talked ourselves sick about it. I had to tell her about Dad's plan for the Fourth, because *forewarned is forearmed*. Barley declared that one of two things would happen: either Adam would attempt to kill Frank, have to be physically subdued, and end up in therapy; or he'd be hit with the lightning bolt of forgiveness over a chicken leg, and he and Frank would bond for life. Guess which one I voted for.

I had to come up with a plan to break through to my gaunt, hounded-by-demons, Twizzler-eating brother before it was too late. First step—getting him to talk to me.

Here's what I did. I got three packages of Adam's most beloved Twizzlers from the store. And I snuck a couple of beers from the fridge in the basement. Dad hardly ever went down there for them, except when we had company over. The rest of the time, Roy wasn't a drinker. Except for at the pharmacy, where he got beer and Vernors right out of the cooler for free.

Armed with the loot, I waited until Roy and Winnie were sound asleep that night, and I padded down the hall to Adam's room. Stealth and contraband—I was counting on it. Of course, if I could have gotten a couple of joints it would have been better, but I was fifteen.

Right—that doesn't really mean anything. Okay. I was an innocent.

Tap, tap, tap. I whispered, "Adam, open up! I have gifts. We have to talk!"

Nothing. But I'd expected that this mission wouldn't be accomplished easily.

"Adam! I have alcohol! Let me in!"

I heard shuffling. Then fumbling. He unlatched the door and opened it a crack—I saw one bleary eyeball squinting out at me. I held up the beer. The door opened just wide enough for me to sidle in.

"Good God, Adam. This place is worse than usual. You can't just hole up in here. I think the atmosphere might be poisonous."

Adam's room was the color of cement, as I've mentioned. He had a double bed right in the middle of one wall. On the other wall were two big windows, with white mini blinds, installed by a hopeful Winnie during her, "If you decorate it, they will keep it clean" period. Dusty, *bent* mini blinds. He threw his basketball against them to spite Winnie.

Adam's walls were plastered, as I mentioned before, with a disgustingly tattered assortment of posters of sports and rock icons and naked girls. That night they were all half hanging down, so the tape marks on the walls made it look even more like some sort of slum dwelling. Added to it, the usual suspects: dirty socks, piles of clothes all over the floor, the gym shoes strewn around, and the atmosphere was funky to the ultimate. I breathed through my mouth.

He shut the door behind me and latched it. I surveyed the area for a safe place to land, and after handing off the Twizzlers and a beer to my brother, I used my elbow (I didn't want any direct contact) to nudge some odious-looking textiles off his desk chair. I sat down with my beer. We both took a swig. Then he stared at me.

"What do you want, snotnose?" (His fondness for me always apparent.)

We looked at each other. Me with my complete inability to solve this situation but hoping somehow that I could find magic words. Adam, looking lost and just about empty. It was the first time in my so-far-carefree life that I felt this heaviness. I wondered how many more shitballs I'd have to get hit with in the future. Suddenly, adulthood seemed like a long series of problems with no solutions and plenty of migraines.

But I tried. "Adam. This sucks. I don't even know how to *imagine* how you must be feeling right now. I see you going down the tubes in front of my very eyes. You have to snap out of this, somehow." (Bravo, me.)

He tipped up the beer and drained the whole thing. If I hadn't been in such a state, I would have given him a high five and congratulations. But I just watched him snork it down, wipe his lips with his forearm, and throw the bottle onto a stack of what looked like flammable rags. "No, you can't imagine, little girl."

He wiped his eyes with the heels of his hands. My God, he looked like he used to when he fell off his bike and tried not to cry. Adam, my big brother. The guy who used to point to his cheeks and say, "Now count the freckles—I am going to *punch you* for every one!" The boy who followed Winnie around the house singing the refrain from *Sesame Street*.

"Adam, this entire family is falling apart. Mom is having some sort of mental breakdown, as far as I can see. Dad is a mess. I'm worried that you're going to do something really stupid, dangerous, or both. So come on, we have to talk!"

He smiled at me. No, he kind of *leered*. "Mand, I hate Mom. She was a complete *slut*. And, wow—guess what?

I'm the product of her lust. So what? I'm supposed to be normal after this? Put it all behind me and figure out how I'm going to spend the money this Fletch guy is going to give me for school? Okay, gee whiz, maybe I will be a doctor, after all!" He belched. "Yeah, right. A doctor. I guess this whole thing has a real silver lining, Mand? I should be happy that Mom decided to take us to Dayton and spill her guts all over us? Good. Great! I will be happy about it. I will go down the hall right now and wake up Mom and Dad to tell them that I get it— Mom was doing me a *huge favor. A huge fucking favor*!" His eyes bulged, and a bright raspberry-colored flush crept up his neck to his cheeks. Oh, no. I thought he looked slightly vomitous.

"Adam. Calm down." I took another swig of the beer (how people drink tons of this stuff is a mystery—it is *so bitingly bitter*) and gave the rest to Adam. He rubbed the condensation from the cool bottle on his forehead. Then he slumped back against the wall. He closed his eyes and rolled his head back and forth against the wall the way he used to when he was a little napper who couldn't sleep.

"Do you know what I want to do?" he whispered.

"No, what?" I was really afraid of his answer.

"I want to leave here. I want to go somewhere where I can get away from all of this and make new friends. I wish I could go to a big city like New York and just disappear."

"Adam, you're eighteen. You just got out of high school. How would you get a job? It's expensive to live in New York. You can't just run away like that. You'd end up much worse than you are here! There are gangs, drugs, and stuff in big cities. You might get in some kind of crime ring and get killed!"

He opened his eyes and looked at me incredulously. "First of all, Mand, you are an idiot. Your entire viewpoint about what happens in big cities comes from all those stupid crime shows on TV. What, do you think I'd have to start selling my body in order to survive—yeah, like become a boy prostitute? Yeah, then I'd have to take heroin in order to get through the days. Shit, you're stupid! I'd use Fletch's money!"

"Oh, you're calling *me* an idiot. How are you going to finesse this big financial windfall, huh? Make up to Mom, smile a lot, and wait for the mail to come from Dayton with a huge check in it?" I reached out and pulled his big toe as hard as I could. Adam yelped and he swiped at me, but I was too fast for him and ducked. Adam spilled his beer. I shifted to avoid the puddle of brew as it flowed onto the spunky tangle of sheets on Adam's horrendously disgusting bed.

I continued, "Oh, and let's see—I don't recall any reaction on his part when Mom made her grand suggestion about Fletch owing you money. By the way, she said he owed you *an education*. Not a trip to the Big Apple. Did you hear him say 'Oh, yeah, Winnie! Great idea! Yes, indeed—I will go right to the bank ASAP and give this total stranger a fortune so he can go to either Harvard or taxidermy school!' Did you hear him say that, Adam?"

This wasn't going well. I had to regroup. I reached into the bag and pulled out a couple of Twizzlers and took a bite of one and threw the other one at Adam. He caught it, and we both munched for a while.

I started over. "Here's the thing. You know how they always say you have to make lemonade?"

"Huh?" He looked honestly confused, and the fact that he had a piece of Twizzler stuck on his upper lip didn't help.

"You know—when life gives you lemons, you make lemonade. This is definitely a totally lemony situation. We have to figure out how to" (I made a presto, presto abracadabra hand scramble) "mush things around and get a decent outcome out of all of this! Adam. It behooves us to look at this in a mature and emotionally balanced way."

Adam looked around. He surveyed his haven: a disgustingly messy, typical teenaged boy's room, located somewhere in middle America. Full of the trappings of middle class hormonal boy/man: the sports paraphernalia, shreddy wall posters of basketball players and naked women with ginormous nipples, battered mini blinds, dirty laundry all over the place, and remnants of snacks from long ago. In other words, a really safe, really great room. The kind of room every punk kid in the slums would die for.

"Shit." He was coming around, I could tell. "What are you suggesting, lemon girl?"

I took another Twizzler bite and chewed thoughtfully for a few seconds. They may be red, but they never taste much like cherries to me. I've always thought they should taste more fruity. "First, you know you can't run off anywhere, right? You and I are stuck right here with all of this. Correct?"

He winced, but nodded. "But I can't forgive Mom. Or Fletch. Or Dad, for that matter, for keeping *his* mouth shut about all of this and going along with Mom like some kind of puppy dog."

"Adam, I don't even know what forgiveness *is*. Let's not even think about that. But maybe we can try to remember that when all of this happened, Mom and Aunt Iris weren't that much older than we are now. They were kids. How many kids do you know who've made asshole decisions?"

I had him there.

"Okay. So this bunch of people made some shitty decisions. And now I end up with two fathers and surprise! I'm supposed to do *what* with all of this information?"

Well, I had him there for a *second*.

"Adam. Chill. We have to put this into perspective and cut them some slack. Frank had no idea Mom was pregnant. Yeah, he did have a one nighter with her, but come on, this is what men *do*. And Mom felt horrible about it for years. Enough so that she hatched a plan to make Fletch accountable to you, her adored son. Aunt Iris is kind of an innocent bystander, in my opinion. For God's sake, you can't fault Dad for being the stand-up guy that he is, loving Mom and you, and us, no matter what went on in the past. He's a *prince,* for heaven's sake!"

Adam softened. The pinched look kind of dissolved, and his eyes got a little brighter. His shoulders, which he'd been holding way up under his ears, dropped. He sighed. "Okay. I get you. All I can tell you is that I'll think about all of this. Right now, I'm beat. Mand, I just want to go to sleep."

I looked at him and smiled. Victory, at least a small one. I bent down and picked up a pair of sweatpants off the floor, shook the twigs, dust, and other detritus off them, and lovingly placed them over the wet beer spot on the mattress. Adam saluted me and settled down with a sigh.

I'd contemplated telling him about the surprise guests at the Fourth of July celebration but decided not to push things. Baby steps. I tiptoed out of his room, and gently closed the door. I snuck down the hall and crept into my room, shutting the door as quietly as I could. I threw myself face down on the bed, inhaling slowly—cleansing breaths. Dryer sheets. Aaah.

I tried to picture what my life would be like when all this shitty stuff was behind me. Summer over. High school. Maybe I'd be world-weary and jaded, due to my experiences as a member of a broken family—one that nearly shattered completely, but which I saved single-handedly. Mom and I would be chummy again. I could just about see it: Winnie, running for president of the PTO, with me as her campaign chairman. Me and Mom, taping up "Winnie Heath Won't Let You Down" posters all over the halls.

No. Wait. Winnie and me, at the mall, shopping for homecoming dresses. I would, of course, have a hot date, and so would Barley. The three of us—yeah, Barley and I trying on strapless bras and laughing at how stupid we look in the three-way mirrors. Winnie, egging us on, pointing out pink sparkly tops with long, tight skirts. Taking pastel dresses off the hangers and urging us to try them on. "You'll look beautiful in this!" Three-inch heels. Us tottering around, with Winnie coaching. "You have to stand up straight! Don't look down at your feet!"

No. Stupid. I took another deep breath. Underneath the dryer sheet perfume, my bed smelled faintly of potato chips with a smidge of sweat. I'd been neglecting changing the sheets since the drama began. Anyway. This: I was still furious at my mother, despite taking the high road with Adam. My mother had done what she had told me I should never do. She'd had sex without marriage. Girls who slept around were sluts then. Hell, they still are. Thus (deductive logic), my mother was a slut. Despite my speech to my brother.

I rolled over and stared at the ceiling. My mother was nearly an unwed one. "Kids having kids." So everything she'd ever told me about abstinence—bullshit. I felt like slugging her. Or shooting her. This whole thing? Just like in some flick.

Here is the scene from the movie:

> *Mandy rolls back and forth on her mattress, sweating. Her eyes are glassy. The hot breeze wafts in from the window, but it can't cool Mandy off. No, because Mandy can't stop the horrific mental image of her mother and Fletch rolling around in lust in the backseat*

of his Chevy. Her mother's hair, wild and springy, bouncing up and down with each thrust. Fletch, moaning in ecstasy, his hands clutching Winnie's shoulders, damp with passion, his pants down around his knees. "Don't stop, don't stop," she groans. He kisses her fervently on the top of her head as he comes.

Mandy's eyes fill with tears. "I hate you, Winnie!" she cries.

Mandy sits up on the bed, clutching the slightly dingy sheet, sobbing. The sounds of dogs barking are heard faintly in the distance. A car horn bleats. The house is silent, but Mandy knows that in each bedroom of the house, a similar scene plays out. Her brother lays writhing in anguish, his headphones blasting Mumford & Sons into his ears to drown out his fury. In their bedroom, Winnie, her floral cotton nightgown plastered to her sweaty thighs, paces, worrying that her children will never again love her. She is followed by her faithful Roy, who reaches out to her. But Winnie simply won't be consoled. The Heath family, all in hell, completely cut off from one another. End scene.

Shit. I embarrassed myself by imagining sex scenes sometimes (note to self: before becoming a screenwriter—have sex). But it was what it was. My life, the movie script. It just kept on rolling.

In the meantime, if I wanted to prevent murder and mayhem, I'd have to start cutting Winnie some slack.

Chapter Six

The Fourth was nearly upon us. At the Heath house, preparations were half-hearted, but we soldiered on. Dad prevailed upon Adam to mow the lawn in the morning. It had that grassy, fresh smell. The smell that apparently all dogs love to roll in. Winnie had the potato salad made by eight in the morning. Then she went to the store with a huge grocery list: chicken for frying, strawberries, whipping cream, lemons, cokes, tomatoes, and on and on (it wasn't a party unless it was a feast, in Mom's opinion). I heard her unloading stuff when she returned, and I wandered into the kitchen for some Cheerios.

As she bustled around, checking the cupboards to see what she needed, I tried to make good on last night's resolution to start forgiving her.

"Mom. You look nice in that pink blouse. Is it new?"

Winnie paused and looked down at her chest. The blouse was crisp cotton (Winnie frowns upon T-shirts) with white pearly buttons shaped like apples.

"Mandy, I've had this blouse for ten years. You told me last summer that you hated it."

So much for peacemaking. "I was wrong. It's nice. I like all your vintage stuff. You make a real statement." (Yeah, her clothing screams *old woman*, but I won't go there.)

Winnie wasn't buying it. She knows me too well. But she seemed happy that I was talking to her, at least. She gave me a half smile, smoothed her palms against her matching pink seersucker Capri pants (another oldie but goodie) and took some shopping bags out from under the sink. "Thanks for the compliment, honey. I appreciate it. I hope you understand how hard I'm trying to make tomorrow a nice celebration. I really am trying."

"I know, Mom. We're going to have a good time." I struggled for something else to add, to pump her up a little. God knows she would need it. "I bet we'll be surprised at the whole, you know," (searching for an old person term) "*shindig*!" (An understatement. Okay, inward groaning.)

Mom looked around our kitchen. The one she had so lovingly decorated. It was all Winnie: The café curtains above the sink, with their gingham checks. The white canisters with the ring of cherries on each one. The dishtowels with red rickrack and roosters. The red Formica table with the chrome edging and matching chairs upholstered in red pleather. The framed picture of the old red barn in the midst of Ohio cornfields that was a "steal" at the flea market. The rooster clock. She heaved a sigh, took one last look around and bustled into the hall for the vacuum (even when she's depressed, Winnie bustles). As she passed me, she put a hand on my shoulder for a sec. It warmed me up inside, just a tad.

I slurped my Cheerios. I love oaty things. In a continued effort to turn over a new leaf for Winnie, I actually got up, went over to the sink, and rinsed out the bowl. I dropped the spoon into the bowl and turned to go upstairs. A little buzzer went off in my brain: *Wait, you idiot! Put it in the dishwasher!*

This may be what maturing is like.

Barley called as I was changing my sheets. More maturity, I know.

"Hey, Mand. What's up? D'you want to go to the pool today?"

I considered it, briefly. "I can't. I have to clean my room and get ready for tomorrow's *big party*. But we need to talk. Can you come over? I promise I won't make you dust or anything."

"No prob! I'll be over in a few."

I was shoving a bunch of shoes into the back of my closet when Barley flapped in wearing apple-green shorts, a ribbed turquoise tank, and those Brazilian flip-flops that everyone but me knows the name of. They were pink, naturally.

She threw herself down on the newly organized and fresh bed, took a deep breath, and said, "Wow. The aroma of Clorox and lemon Swiffers. Marvelous, dahling!"

"Don't offer to help. I've nearly finished." I tried to look snarky but failed. I closed the closet door, switched on the overhead fan for some sorely needed cool (our AC doesn't do much upstairs), and flopped down beside her.

"We need to talk about tomorrow night. Or, more to the point, I need to *warn* you about tomorrow night."

Barley was examining her manicure. Bright pink polish. I noticed that she'd put white polka dots on her thumbs. "What do you mean?"

"Stop admiring your handiwork and I'll tell you. I need undivided attention here."

Barley put her hands down, shifted so she was lying on her side, and fixed her cat's eyes on my face. She looked worried. "Oh, no. What horrors await?"

Barley and I had gone from normal, boy and makeup obsessed teens to CIA operative level in a few short weeks. This summer was going to set the bar pretty high for the rest of our lives. I mean, really—what did we have to look forward to after this? Football games? Soccer tournaments? Going to work every day for the rest of our adult lives, noses to the grindstone? We may have peaked way too early. The rest of our lives could be a real yawner. But I digress, as always.

I sat up and took a deep breath. "Okay. Get this. Roy Heath, the peacemaker, has taken it upon himself to invite the famous Fletchers here for tomorrow night's festivities."

I knew there would be a reaction coming, and I waited. Barley didn't disappoint. It was as if somebody touched her bare skin with a hot curling iron. She leaped off the bed, her blonde streaks flying out in all directions. She clasped her head and spun around, shrieking. Then she dropped back onto the bed next to me, panting wildly.

"This will be a nightmare of epic proportions, Mand! Are they actually coming, though? Maybe they won't. I mean, *why* would they want to?"

I shrugged. "Roy told me they are. I guess they're just as screwed up over this as we are. Maybe they're looking for closure. Shit. I sound like Oprah or something."

Barley nodded. "Is there an action plan in place? You know, a SWAT team at the ready, in case Adam decides to kill someone, namely Fletch or Winnie?"

"That's the thing. I don't think Dad has thought about the potential for violence. I think he has a fantasy that if we get together with watermelon and bug spray, light a few sparklers and drink beer, all will kind of fall into place. Adam will hug Winnie, Fletch will hand over a wad of bills to finance Adam's education, and Marianne will pull out a guitar and sing peace songs. Dad just wants his old family back. Plus, he's been watching Dr. Phil in the break room."

Barley didn't even crack a smile. "God, Mand. Does anybody know about this? I mean other than us?"

"Yeah. Dad ran this past Aunt Iris. I guess she couldn't find a way to talk him out of it. Oh, and Dad invited Don Horley, too. For some added muscle, if we need it."

Barley looked up at the ceiling. She shut her eyes. "Adam knows nothing about this?"

"No. Should we tell him?"

Barley rolled over and got off the bed, flip-flopped over to the window and looked down into the backyard. "No. If we tell him, all hell will break loose. You don't want him to have any time to stew around about this and come up with some kind of plan. Worse, if he knows about this in advance, he might just disappear. That would be the icing on the cake as far as your mom is concerned. No. We have to consider all the possible outcomes and plan accordingly. Good God, your life is exhausting, Mand. Wait. Is Winnie also in the dark about this?"

I nodded. "The people who know about this are Dad, you, me, Aunt Iris, Don Horley, and the Fletches. That's it. The guest list is the four of us, Iris, Don, you, your parents, the Fletches, and on top of that Dad always invites everyone on the block. I have no idea how many of them are coming. But there will be small children involved. You know. This is why we always have the fireworks."

Barley slid down onto the floor, crossing her legs Indian style. She looked around my room. "Do you have a pad and pencil? We have to make an outline."

An hour later, we had compiled a list. Barley, her fingers covered in Cheeto dust (we had to have fortification for this, so I brought up Coke and snacks), licked each of her pink-clad fingers delicately, then picked up the list to summarize:

HEATH FAMILY FOURTH OF JULY DISASTER PLAN

1. Barley Crowder must arrive early. Her role: all-day cheerleader and buffer. She will ask her mother to bring over her famous sweet-and-sour pickles, which are a favorite of Adam's. This might help a little.

2. Mandy will hug Winnie and tell her she forgives her. Mandy will do this tonight before bed, so that Winnie will go to sleep a little happy. Mandy will be convincing and get over herself and her own anger, pronto. Too much is at stake to be selfishly annoyed at Winnie for one more minute. And Winnie needs to begin tomorrow with the knowledge that least one of her children still loves her.

3. Barley Crowder will stick to Adam Heath like glue all day. She will wear her most adorable outfit and will flirt with Adam as much as possible. Hormone Plan A. Let's face it: he is eighteen.

4. Mandy will confer with Aunt Iris tonight. Hopefully, she will have some ideas about how to keep her sister calm. Also, she will talk more about Don Horley with Iris. What does he know about this whole sexual debacle from the past? Mandy will find out just how Horley fits into the picture. Hopefully, Horley will be a designated asset at the party.

5. Mandy and Barley will help Roy set up the party. They will artfully pull as much intel as they can from him before the party: What did he tell the Fletches about the evening? Do the Fletches want to bury the hatchet, or are they just coming to pay their respects

for a few minutes, placate Winnie, and get the hell out? What are Roy's expectations of the evening? Why on earth did he decide to invite the Fletches, anyway?

6. Mandy will hide some beer in the bushes.

That was about all we could come up with. It was getting late. Barley had to go home and make sure that there were still some of her mom's pickles in the basement (everybody *loves* these pickles, and Mrs. Crowder can hardly make enough to meet the demand), and she wanted to prepare her parents for the whole thing. We felt that we needed the Crowders in reserve. After all, the more adults we alerted, the better. And who knows? Maybe Mrs. Crowder could shed some light on the whole thing—she has known my mom since forever.

After Barley left, I wandered around the house to see what was going on. Adam was nowhere. That must mean he was out doing something sweaty. Mom was in the kitchen putting potato salad together. I could hear her clattering around as I came down the stairs. I could smell hardboiled eggs and mustard. I adored my mom's potato salad. Actually, I adored pretty much everything Winnie cooked.

I'd classify her as an "all-American" cook. She knew how to make bread from scratch that smelled like yeasty heaven and tasted so homey. She made fried oysters for me at least once a month, even though nobody else in the family loved them. I drowned them in tartar sauce and just inhaled them. The molasses cookies I've already told you about. One more thing: Winnie would get up in the middle of the night and make you cocoa if you had a bad dream.

I sat down on the stairs for a second to ponder my mom. Okay. She did a "sinful" kind of thing way back then. But in this day and age, we know about sinful things that *everybody* has done. Presidents chase interns. Movie stars have affairs all the time. There are entire reality shows about baby daddies and bachelors choosing from a whole bunch of slutty-looking girls. Hell, kindergarteners use the F word. So who was I to judge Winnie Heath for something that happened nineteen years ago? The result was Adam, who, even though he was a jerk, was my only brother.

Okay. I decided to put the first part of the disaster plan into action right then. I calmly walked into the kitchen. Winnie had her back to me. She was chopping celery at the counter. She wore her apron with the apples and oranges on it, and it was tied in a snazzy bow at the back. Winnie always looked the part.

I cleared my throat. Mom turned, a paring knife in her hand. I smiled. "Mom, do you need any help? I could peel the eggs."

Shit. That was all it took. Winnie broke into a teary smile, rushed over to me (*watch the knife! watch the knife!*) and threw her arms around me. She hugged me so tight, I thought I might faint. After about a second, I put my arms right around her and hugged her back. Something let go in my chest. I put my head on Mom's shoulder. She smelled so good, like baby powder and fried onions. Mom smell. I had missed that.

She pulled away and smiled at me. I wanted to pet her face, but I held back.

"Okay, honey. You can finish peeling the eggs. Run them under warm water while you peel; it makes it much easier."

Scene from the movie:

> *The middle-American kitchen again. Rooster canisters. Black-and-white checkered linoleum tiles. Wood-grain countertops. Gingham*

café curtains—red checked, okay—yellow. Sun filters through the multi-paned window over the sink, illuminating the shiny dark brown hair of the teen girl and the wiry salt-and-pepper hair of the mother. They stand, chopping and peeling in companionable silence. Use filters to give the scene a grainy, old-fashioned feel (think old fifties movies).

Relieved and reunited, mother and daughter (I decided here that since it is actually going to be a movie, I will stop calling them Winnie and Mandy. Because who knows? Names have to be changed to protect the "innocent." Or in this case, my crazy family) stand in the kitchen side by side, the daughter peeling an egg and sneaking a bite here and there. The mother chopping celery like an expert, occasionally glancing fondly at her daughter. They make small talk, and the mother chuckles when the daughter pops yet one more bite of egg into her mouth.

Music swells over the scene. Maybe something country, like Garth Brooks singing "If Tomorrow Never Comes."

As the scene fades out, we see the mother and daughter each pick up a hardboiled egg and toast one another with them, cracking the eggs and laughing, then peeling them. Fade.

We had dinner in the *dining room* that night. I guess Winnie felt so happy to have me back on her side that she wanted to celebrate or something. Our dining room was nice, too, very tasteful; I have to hand it to Winnie there. Our dining room is a big rectangle. Two windows face the front yard and two face the side yard. Mom painted it light yellow about two summers before this, and with the white wood trim and chair railing, it looked pretty cheerful.

Two summers ago she was in her "window treatments phase," and she and Iris sewed the curtains, which hung from the tops of the windows and "puddled" (Winnie's word) onto the dark wood floor. They were silk or something, and they had gray-and-cream stripes. Pretty HGTV, if you catch my drift. On the floor was an old floral rug that Winnie had gotten at a garage sale somewhere—it had gray-and-blue flowers that matched the curtains.

Our dining room table was an antique, too. I've always loved that big rectangle of waxy, dark wood. It had been in our dining room for as long as I could remember. We also had Grandma's antique sideboard with the wavy glass doors, and it sat against the back wall with Mom's wedding china in it.

Mom set the table with light blue linen placemats and real cloth napkins. There was a Longaberger basket full of Golden Delicious apples in the center of the table. Apples, color-coordinated with the yellow walls. She had pulled out all the stops. Wow.

Roy sat at the head of the table, Mom was on one side, Adam and I on the other. Mom made Adam's second favorite dinner (we were having fried chicken, his first favorite, tomorrow at the party)—macaroni and cheese, salad with Thousand Island, sliced tomatoes, and real lemonade. This wasn't easy for her, because she'd spent the day making potato salad, Jell-O pretzel dessert, apple crisp, and deviled eggs for tomorrow. She was a kitchen slave for us, really.

I thought I'd try to get things rolling in the forgiveness department by saying to Adam, "Isn't this delicious? You know, Mom made this especially for you. Tomorrow she's making a huge amount of fried chicken for the party. Isn't that great?"

I may have sounded just a little forced. Adam gave me the stink eye. "Yeah, it's great." He said it unconvincingly and with his mouth full. It came out more like "Yea, iss gray." Then he continued to stuff his face, but he turned to his plate and kept his eyes down.

Mom jumped in. "I'm so worried it might rain tomorrow. It's been cloudy all day. Roy, have you looked at the weather maps?"

My dad considered himself almost a qualified meteorologist, albeit a very optimistic one. His favorite line was, "I think this is the closing shower." But he did have the Weather Channel app on his cell.

"Nothing on the radar. I think we're in the clear. Winnie, how many tables do you want me to set up in the backyard?"

Winnie looked momentarily like her old self. She gazed at the ceiling, squinting as she calculated: "Well, there'll be the four of us, the three Crowders, Iris and Don; and I'm expecting the Nelsons, the Hoffmans, the Phelans, the Flanagans, and probably the Garrisons." (All neighbors.) "I invited the Reeders, but I'm not sure." (They're old neighbors who moved away two years ago.) "But I'd say we need at least four long tables out there."

They nattered on, and I tuned them out and looked at Adam. He was staring fixedly at his plate and stuffing himself. Obviously he wanted to shovel it in as fast as he could and get the hell out of there.

I took one more stab at it: "Hey, Adam, are you going to help the little kids with the snakes and sparklers like you did last year? I think they like it better when you do it, because you use your scary voice and say stuff like,

'Oh, my God, it's a snake! It's going to bite you!' and then you tickle them. They love that. When I light their stuff, they just look at me and drool."

Adam took a long pull on his lemonade, draining the glass completely. Then he wiped his mouth with the back of his hand (Napkins? He doesn't use them) and burped. Dad shifted uncomfortably in his seat, and Mom shut her eyes for a second. Then he looked around at all of us and announced, "I don't know if I am going to be in attendance at the annual extravaganza."

Mom gasped, and Roy's eyes widened. I reached out to grab Adam, but before I could get a good grip on his greasy Queen T-shirt, he slipped out of my grasp and left the room. We heard the back door slam.

So much for the Mandy Heath forgiveness efforts.

I helped Mom clear the table. Dad gave her a hug and came around and kissed me on the cheek. "Don't worry, girls. Tomorrow will be great." Ever the silver-lining guy, Dad left to go down to the basement.

I had to talk to Aunt Iris.

Fourth of July. Sunny and clear. Too bad. I was hoping against hope that it would be a rainy day, and the whole shebang would have to be canceled. No luck. I lay in bed, watching the leaves in the maple tree outside my window. A robin was in there, tweeting away. I wanted to shoot him. Instead, I got up, threw on my robe, and schlepped down to the kitchen. I rummaged around in the cupboards, looking for something to eat, fast. I had a lot to do, what with helping Dad set up, trying to keep Adam around, and figuring out how to talk to Aunt Iris before it got too late. I needed to suss her out on what she knew about tonight. I found a package of strawberry

Pop-Tarts and stuck one in the toaster. As I poured a glass of orange juice, Winnie swooped in.

"Good morning, honey!"

She sounded a little forced. I thought it looked as if she hadn't slept much. She was a little rumpled around the edges. Of course, with all that was weighing her down, it was understandable.

"Mom, how are you holding up? Have you been able to talk to Adam at all?"

She frowned. "Not really. I'm hoping he'll soften up a little at the party tonight. He's always loved it before. Oh, Mandy. I am such a wreck." Her chubby chin wobbled a bit. "What do you think—will he ever forgive me?"

Oh, boy. If only she knew what was in the works. I was tempted to warn her. Should I? Visions of firecrackers, screaming family members, a violent Adam, people flinging food, screeching tires, or worse—murder—went through my mind. I made a split-second decision.

"Okay, Mom? I'm working on Adam. You know how hard Dad is trying to pull the family together after our Dayton trip. And you know how much he loves you, and us. So I just want to give you a little heads-up."

Winnie stiffened, her newest fruity apron rustling. She clasped her hands as if in prayer or something. "Mandy, tell me. What is it?"

It was too late to take it back, so I spilled it. "Dad has invited the Fletches to the party tonight. I guess he thinks we need to bury the hatchet or something. And they're coming. I wish we could invite Dr. Phil to come, too."

"What? My God—your father is out of his mind!" She turned to go, and I knew she was going to barrel right out in the yard to slap Roy or something worse, so I grabbed her arm.

"Mom! Stop! You can't let on that you know! This is a secret! Dad hasn't told Adam, either. We have to remember that it's *Adam* we have to worry about. Dad thinks that Adam needs to talk more with Fletch—I mean Frank. You know—to know him is to love him, or something like that. I don't know why, but Dad really thinks this will solve things. But I'm sworn to secrecy. So you can't let on that you know, Mom. The last thing we need is for *Dad* to be furious with you and me. Isn't having Adam on the verge of murder enough?"

Mom pulled out a chair and sat at the table. She motioned blindly toward the coffee pot. I poured us both a mug, even though I think coffee tastes like dirt. I pulled the half and half out of the fridge and served us. I sat down opposite her and we both sipped, thinking. I resisted the urge to run out the door, even though I wanted to. Iris would have to wait. Sometimes, you have to set your priorities. Winnie needed me to help her process this latest wrinkle in the family saga.

"How on earth did this happen? Your dad and Frank? They're talking? I don't get this!"

"I know. It's very confusing. Apparently Dad has called down there a few times. I guess he and the Gypsy woman—Marianne—cooked this whole thing up. I guess they both think we all need to spend more time together. You know, not exactly bonding, more like talk therapy. Dad says that the situation is not going to go away, so we have to face it. All of us. Adam. Mom, we have to focus on Adam."

"*Talk therapy*? Is there anybody in this group who is qualified to control what might happen tonight? *Talk therapy*, my foot! This will be a disaster!"

Mom was getting pumped up. Her face was beet red, and I could almost *see* her blood pressure going up.

"Mom, calm down. Aunt Iris knows about this, and Don Horley is coming tonight, too. Between him, Dad, and Fletch, if Adam gets crazy, they can control him. We have to think positively. Maybe tonight will be like Dad says: it will give us all a chance to discuss things and maybe forgive each other some. Maybe."

"Adam has no idea?"

I shook my head.

She drained her coffee, stood up, removed the new apron, and flung it into the sink. "Get dressed, Mandy. We're going over to Iris's house."

So much for the Pop-Tart and orange juice. I went upstairs to put on some clothes.

When we drove up to the cottage, we saw Iris bending over the geranium bed by the driveway. She looked so poetic in her floppy straw hat, wearing pink gardening gloves, old white Keds, and a sundress covered with orange poppies. She straightened up and turned, her hair escaping from the hat in romantic tendrils. I swear, the woman is right out of central casting.

"Hi, girls!" Iris wrestled out of her gloves and threw them in the grass. "Come on in for some iced tea!"

She knew we were coming, I bet.

We settled down at the kitchen table. Really, I have to give Don Horley props. The kitchen was so gorgeous. What a contrast from our 1950s all-American setup. If Jane Austen lived in Framington, her kitchen would probably look like this, with shiny surfaces, gleamy wood floors, soft floral curtains, and the square antique table. Aunt Iris kept a tray on the countertop with a "chintz" teapot, creamer, and sugar bowl. She told me that "chintz" was a kind of English china that was hard to find these days. Of course. Just right for serving Mr. Darcy. Or Don Horley, I guess. Anyway, Iris reached into her fridge for iced tea and lemon and poured us each a tumbler.

"Sit down, Iris. I want you to tell me what you think is going to happen tonight. What in heaven's name is Roy hoping for, anyway?" Mom took command, as usual.

Iris took a dainty sip of her tea. "Oh, dear. How do you know about this? I thought it was a secret!"

Mom reached over and uncharacteristically stroked my shoulder. "Mandy spilled it this morning. She thought it would be better if I knew in advance. She's right. I don't know what I might have done if I were to see Frank walk into my yard unannounced. A heart attack, maybe? Forewarned is forearmed, I always say." (Sidebar: I have *never* heard Winnie say this.)

Iris nodded. "I have to admit I'm relieved. Girls, I don't know what to expect. But I know that Marianne Gardner has been instrumental in all of this. Her heart is in the right place, and I think she and Roy both want this family to come together on this, rather than falling apart because of it."

So the Gypsy woman was good-hearted. Boy, Fletch had really lucked out in his life: first Iris, then Winnie, and now the Gypsy. Maybe there was more to Fletch than just supple lips and a saxophone.

Mom nodded in agreement. "The thing I worry about is Adam. He's so torn up over all of this. I wish I hadn't stirred things up! What will he do?" She seemed so forlorn.

Iris patted Mom's hand. What a contrast. Mom's stubby peasant fingers, her utilitarian fingernails next to Iris's ivory, smooth, graceful ones. "Winnie, I have faith in Roy. But more importantly, I have faith in Adam. You brought your children up to be kind. They're both smart" (*Adam?*) "and strong. I think we have to trust him. And you know, Winnie—Frank is not to blame. You are not to blame. People make mistakes."

I interrupted. "As long as we're on the subject, can I get a little clarification? What *is* it about this Fletch guy? How come *both* of you got mixed up with him? Is he some sort of swashbuckling hottie or something? I mean, really—tell me how this one sax player wormed his way into this family and fathered Adam? I don't get this—it's like a bad movie."

Mom and Iris exchanged looks. I waited. I drummed my fingernails on the tabletop for emphasis. Then I cleared my throat. "Somebody has to talk. Mom?"

Mom took a gulp of tea and set her glass down, emphatically, I thought. "Mandy, it's complicated." Her expression changed, and her eyes turned a brighter shade of blue. "Maybe it isn't so complicated. Yes. Actually, it's very simple: Iris and I were young. Our lives looked very long out in front of us. We didn't have any kind of crystal ball to show us the future. We didn't think about the impact of our actions. We just followed our impulses. Yes!"

She looked triumphant, sort of. "Mandy, we were young girls. Frank was a handsome and exciting man. He was talented. He had charisma. We both fell for it. Simple. And now? All of that has caught up with us."

So Mom was telling me that she was like I was right then. OMG. Barley and I. We were young, and we had a shitload of passion building up in us. Just like the rest of our generation. Just like all the generations of young people who came before us. Mom and Iris were no different then, than Barley, Adam, and I were *now*. Crap.

It *was* simple. People did stuff that they came to regret later. Yep. Humans were human. The light bulb went off.

"Mom. What you're saying is that you did what you did and you're paying for it now. So I should be careful for the rest of my life not to screw up?" I felt sweat dripping in the armpit area, once again staining my shirt.

Iris leaned forward, her slender hand still on Winnie's plump one. "No, honey. What your mom is saying is that you have to plunge right into your life. Don't be careful! Ever since Frank left me, I've been careful! Safe! What do I have to show for it? New countertops and nice flower beds? I would not trade that time of my life for anything! It was exciting and thrilling." She patted Mom's hand lovingly. "And your mom? She had the guts to have an adventure! She thinks it was a mistake, but her adventure resulted in Adam!"

Mom looked startled. I guess she hadn't thought of the Fletch thing as good luck. I guess she never considered how Adam got here as being fated or anything. Certainly not an *adventure*. I watched the wheels turning in her head. My God. Here the three of us were, sitting around drinking cold glasses of iced tea and having revelations.

For a few seconds, I envisioned this scene from the movie. I would cast some young unknown actress as Mandy, and I think Julianne Moore would be good as Aunt Iris, and maybe Camryn Manheim as Winnie:

> *Midday in northern Ohio. The two older women sit facing the young girl. The light filters through the curtains, casting a glimmer onto the antique table. The Mother, her hair all in place, her chubby frame encased in turquoise capri pants and a white sequined tunic top from Chico's, radiates anguished energy. The Aunt, her floral linen sundress stylishly wrinkled from her yard work, sips from the cut-glass tumbler of iced tea.*
>
> *As the discussion of youthful mistakes takes place, and The Girl realizes that her future is full of potential for both passion and error, we hear Carrie Underwood's "All-American Girl" swell in the background. The camera pans from Aunt to Mother, and finally to the Girl. As the scene ends (dialogue to be inserted later, when I have time to think*

about it), the final shot is of Aunt and Mother's hands, clasped in sisterhood, the pale one over the chapped, chubby one.

If I survived this summer, Barley and I would have to look into taking a film-making course at the community college in our spare time. I mean, really—when life hands you lemons, you might just have the makings of an independent movie. My destiny was beating me over the head.

Mom looked relieved, but she still wasn't totally calm. "So we just wing it tonight? I pray that Adam won't want to kill Frank. I have to trust my son? I don't think I can do that."

Iris got up to put the tumblers in the dishwasher. "Let's keep our fingers crossed and see what happens. If you can't trust, then fake it."

Mom shook her head. Then she took hold of herself. She smacked the top of the table for emphasis, her wedding ring making a sharp TING. "We have a lot of work to do. Let's go, honey. Iris, thanks for the pep talk. I guess I have to put my trust in the universe." (Mom? Really?)

I was relieved to see my mom back to her usual. Winnie was a piece of work, no doubt about *that*. We got up, and the three of us filed outside like soldiers. Iris kissed me and hugged Mom. As we backed down the driveway, Mom rolled down the window and called out to Iris, "See you tonight! Gird your loins; it may be a hell of a party!"

It was the first time I had heard Winnie swear.

When we got home, Dad was wrangling tables in the backyard. Adam was nowhere to be seen. Winnie and I, apparently not only reconciled but joined at the hip, simultaneously chimed, "Where's Adam?" To which Dad looked at us funny and replied, "I sent him out for more charcoal."

Still in sync, Mom and I both winced and said, "Oh, no!"

Dad was incredulous, but he continued, "What's the matter with that?"

Mom gave him a poke in the chest. "Roy, Adam doesn't want to be here tonight. He's said so. Giving him the car keys was not the best decision."

"I didn't give him the car keys. He hoofed it over to the Sunoco station. He said he needed some exercise. That boy has way too much energy, if you ask me."

Mom poked Dad *again*. He staggered backwards. "For God's sakes, Roy, how could you invite the Fletches" (OMG, she was saying it now herself) "and not tell me?"

This whole thing was going to become a broken record. I stepped up to the plate (okay, too many metaphors, I know).

"Guys! Let's not hash all of this out. There isn't time. We have a party to organize, Adam to locate and, hopefully, a complete reconciliation and happy ending to formulate. So let's return to our obligations. Mom—kitchen. Dad—what do you want me to do?"

Mom shrugged and toddled off to fry chicken. Dad turned to me and said, "How did she find out?" As if he didn't know.

"I told her. I felt that if she was going to get hit right between the eyes or get caught flatfooted," (it must be metaphor day) "she needed some warning. Don't worry. She's glad she knows. Now let's sort out this smorgasbord of illegal ordnance, shall we?"

So Roy and I commiserated while separating the cherry bombs from the rockets. Dad always goes across state lines to get huge "value packs" of assorted fireworks, and we always start with the little stuff like snakes and sparklers and work our way up to the big bangers. Adam is our keeper of the matches, and he's the one (let's face it; he's young and virile) who insists on setting off the big ones. Since he was gone, I asked Roy how he felt about doing the entire show by himself if Adam stayed AWOL.

"I feel confident Adam will show up at some point before dark. After all, he doesn't know about Frank and Marianne coming. Or does the whole world know by now?"

Ah, Dad was mad at me. Damn. "In my defense, Pop, I had to tell Mom. Really. I think she might have had a stroke or something if Frank just wandered up the driveway, you know?"

Roy looked at me funny. I've never called him Pop, for one thing. And second, I think maybe he hadn't actually thought about just how much of a shock the "surprise" might have been for Winnie.

"Dad, you really love Mom, don't you? How did you wrap your mind around the fact that you weren't really Adam's bio-Dad? Was it horrible for you?"

Roy chewed thoughtfully on a firecracker for a sec, then tasted the gun powder and spit it out. "Quick, Mandy—bring me a beer!" I brought two. I untwisted the caps, and handed one to Roy. I took a swig of the other one, and he didn't even blink. *Score!*

Anyway. Roy took a mouthful of beer and gargled it around a little and then spit it in the grass. My God, we were like two cowboys out on the town after a roundup—swigging and spitting.

"What was your question, again?"

"Dad, let's sit down on the grass for a break. How did you feel about Adam not being your bio-son? Were you totally bummed? Or what?"

"Oh, that. Honey, here's the thing: I was in love with your mother. You have no idea what a completely exciting woman she was back then." (And I don't want to, now, BTW.)

I held up my hand to ward off any further details. "Dad, I am your daughter. Just edit yourself accordingly."

He grinned. Dad has very cute teeth. Kind of ridgey, and the front two have just enough of a gap to make him look a little bit like a hick. A lovable one, though.

"Okay, honey. What I mean is this: your mother is so full of energy and sizzle—whoops, I mean electricity. Being with Winnie was fun. She always had something sassy to say and all kinds of ideas. She was so vital. Iris was pretty and a truly kind person, but she didn't have much spunk. Winnie drew people to her like flies to a flame."

I groaned.

"Honey, I'm being as G-rated as I can! But I'm not really talking about sexy stuff, anyway. It's so hard to describe. Okay. Let's talk about dogs. If I went to the pet store to get a dog, I'd pass right over the Afghan hounds and go straight to the beagles. Beagles love to run, and once they catch a scent, *off they go*. Afghans look good strolling along leisurely on the leash. But when you let go of a beagle, she's off to sniff out an adventure. I guess I just like beagles."

I tried not to picture my mom as a beagle in an apron, running after a squirrel. Or a beagle digging holes in the yard and dropping geraniums in them, one by one.

"Dad, I kind of always pictured Mom as a pug, to be honest."

He hugged me hard and chortled. Well, chuckled, but I like chortle. I put that one in my mental lexicon for use in future screenplays.

"Mandy, you may be right. She looks more like a pug. They're damned cute. Dogs aside, the bottom line is that I loved your mother then, and I love her now. She isn't perfect, but nobody is. I married her knowing that I'd love the baby. And who could have resisted Adam? He was seven pounds of red and wrinkles when I first saw him, and I *was* his father. Period. No regrets, no turning back. Then when your Mom got pregnant with you, my prayers for a family were answered. One boy, one girl, both mine. I'm a simple man, Mandy. I don't look for complications."

Once again, "simple." How weird. Both Mom and Dad. Simple. This whole thing was getting kind of cosmic, if you know what I mean. We continued sorting the firecrackers from the cherry bombs. I'd already put all the sparklers in a plastic tub. Tonight would be epic, and we'd probably set the entire neighborhood on fire.

"Dad. One more question. A big one. Why Fletch and Marianne?"

"Honey. I'm not really sure why I called them. Marianne answered. We had a nice talk, and I think it helped her understand us all a little better. I reassured her that neither Winnie nor Iris is holding any kind of torch for Frank. I told her Winnie has been punishing herself for her indiscretion with Frank ever since it happened. I told her that Adam was a wonderful boy," (wow—suddenly Adam is golden) "and that both she and Frank would like him if they got to know him. Then I guess it hit me . . . the only way for them to get to know Adam and the rest of us was up to me. So the invitation kind of happened."

"But why keep it a secret? Because you felt that the whole thing might be a disaster? Or what?"

Roy put down his package of Terrible Roarings (those Chinese can really come up with good names, right?) on the grass, and he scratched the stubble on his chin. It affected me like nails on a blackboard, and I flinched. But I said, "Go on."

"I kept it a secret so that Adam wouldn't work up a head of steam in advance. That boy can be volatile." (Speaking of Terrible Roarings.) "I knew that if Winnie knew, she'd obsess about it until she broke out in hives. Secret was the only option."

"Wait. Mom gets *hives*?"

"An expression, Mandy. An expression."

What peer group he ran with that used "getting hives" to mean flipping out was a mystery to me. Maybe the guys at pharmaceutical conventions? Maybe they think in terms of stuff like eczema and hives? Kind of their lingo? Who knows.

"I get it. Well, Dad, I'm keeping my fingers crossed. Barley and I will be here to help if things get hot. Barley is wearing a particularly sexy outfit tonight, in hopes that Adam will get all hormonal and forget to be furious about anything. And of course, Don Horley and the neighbors will be around. But, Dad? I'm telling you this as a respectful and upright fifteen-year-old: we have beer in the bushes. I think you'll agree that for tonight, there should be no such thing as underage drinking. We may all need to get drunk as skunks."

I just love Roy Heath. Because he grinned from ear to ear, gave me a high five, and handed me a six pack.

Chapter Seven

Oh, boy. I tell you, if this summer was any indication, my life was going to be eventful. I may have been looking my destiny right in the face: I guess that people who come up with the ideas for movies and TV shows must get their ammunition from real life. Maybe those intricate plots don't just come from their imaginations. And *soap operas*? I used to think all of that intertwining of the cast members' lives was crap, but now I knew better. (So this is why I'm writing all this stuff down. I may need to remember the details later on, when I'm a member of the screenwriters' union, and contemplating my Academy Award-winning storyline. Yeah.)

So. The party. Where to start . . .

I spent the rest of the afternoon in my room, sorting through my makeup, arguing with myself whether or not to put some of it on. I hated all this stuff, but Barley said that we would need to wear it in high school *every day*. I disagreed, but Barley knew best. It pays to have a gloriously beautiful best friend. I knew she'd come in handy—so I sat there, reading the labels on the mascara tubes, trying to get in the right mindset to follow her advice.

I put on some eye shadow: "Evening Smoke." Barley said that dark-eyed people should stick with natural tones and stay away from blues and greens and stuff. Too garish. Then I put on the mascara: "Evening Velvet." I was entirely thankful that I got this stuff free at the store. There were real benefits to having your dad as a pharmacist—I was saving my own cash for college.

I applied some blusher: "Peach Perfection." *Ugly.* I looked like a Barbie doll. So I rubbed that off. The eyes were enough to start. A little lip gloss? Okay. Fine. Then I put on my denim shorts (a wardrobe classic, according to Barley—they wouldn't ever go out of style—thank God. A person must stick with classics, because following fashion trends? Way too exhausting) and a white T-shirt. Plain. Another classic. That tiny little chocolate stain on the front probably wouldn't be noticeable . . . it would be dark out there.

Flip-flops, blue. Okay, then. I surveyed myself in the mirror. Gazing back at me was a tallish, moderately cute teen girl, with dark brown hair touching her shoulders. A little too bushy, but hell, it was very humid out there. I did have to admit to myself that I needed to contemplate getting some sort of hairstyle before too long. Welp. So much for saving a lot of cash.

My posture wasn't great. I straightened up and looked a little better. My boobs (what there were of them) stuck out a little more, and I had to admit that good posture does make your stomach look flatter. I guessed I passed muster. At least to myself. Of course, my standards were pretty low. Barley might think I would need to change shirts or something, but I decided I looked totally fine. Done.

I went downstairs at around five to get a snack to tide me over. Mom was in the kitchen, organizing the condiments. She had artfully arranged mustard, ketchup, mayo, pickles, and chow chow (nobody likes it but her, but she keeps putting it out, year after year) on a wicker tray. She was rummaging in the cupboards for additional sides—she thinks some people need stuff like steak sauce and barbeque sauce on their burgers.

Mom looked nice. I could tell she'd put a lot of thought into her ensemble for tonight. She was wearing brand new pink linen slacks from the old lady store. We call it that because they do a land-office business in caftans and tunics—you know, the kind of store that specializes in garments to hide the hips. On top, she had on a breezy, orange-and-pink flowered tunic top with a hem that was lower over the rear. You get the picture: She was stylin'.

To top it off, when she turned to smile at me, a bottle of Worcestershire in one hand, and a Stubbs Original Bar-B-Q Sauce in the other, I saw that she was wearing hot pink lipstick that made her lips look like Pepto-Bismol and some green eye shadow. Probably "Emerald Sparkle." It had a little glisten to it. She looked cute, in her determined way. I had to give her a hug.

"Be careful! You don't want to get anything on your shirt!" Mom said, backing away. "Oh, too late. There's a spot of Worcestershire on it."

I guess it wasn't as minuscule as I thought. "No, it's okay. It was already there. I don't think anyone will notice, really. They'll all be looking at Barley." I hoped.

"Oh, honey, don't worry. You're right. This will be an eventful night. No one will be thinking about you." She paused. "That sounds terrible. But you know what I mean, don't you?"

I nodded vigorously. "Mom. I know exactly. Are you nervous?"

What a stupid question. Of course she was nervous. Her life was hanging in the balance.

"I'm terrified. You know, I'm glad this is out in the open. I just want to get this behind me—us—and move forward with our lives. But Mandy, I'm kind of shaky!" She put the bottles down on the counter and extended her hands in front of her (OMG, she had on a charm bracelet) so that I could see them tremble.

"Mom, I bet things won't be disastrous. It will go better than you think. Remember, you have all of us on your side."

She smiled, a bit ruefully, I thought.

"And Mom? You look really pretty. I love your eye shadow. Barley says that blue-eyed people can really pull off colored shadow. The green really sets off the blue of your eyes." I thought a compliment was in order.

Winnie touched her eyes and looked grateful. We basked for a moment in the love, then she started whirling around again, adding the sauces to the tray. "Take this out for me, will you, honey?"

So here's the menu. In case you want to throw a Fourth party: Cold fried chicken (Winnie makes it early and puts it in the fridge—we like it cold better than hot). Hamburgers, which Roy insists on calling "hamburgs," hot dogs, and a few brats for the sake of variety, all barbecued. Potato salad, sliced tomatoes, sweet-and-sour pickles from the Crowders, and coleslaw. Neighbors were bringing desserts (Mrs. Reeder's were the best; she makes cakes from scratch) and stuff like baked beans and Jell-O salads. It was always a feast. Whether anybody would have an appetite after the Fletch debacle remained to be seen.

I took the tray out back, where Roy was setting up the lawn chairs and stuff. We only had about ten, but the neighbors brought chairs, too. I noted that Dad had arranged the paper plates, cups, and napkins on one table. So I put the condiment tray with them. We had three other long tables set up at the edge of the yard near the driveway, awaiting the food. Dad, of course, had brought red, white, and blue tablecloths from the store, and matching Tiki torches were stuck around the edges of the yard. Only Roy would think of that: He ordered all of this cool patriotic stuff from a special catalog. We sold out of it fast at the store. Roy was a visionary, like I said before.

It wasn't too bad, for a July evening. Luckily, a breeze was wafting through the trees so the humidity wasn't that oppressive. By the time people started coming, it would probably be a little cooler, around eighty-two degrees. Thank God for that—tempers would probably be hot enough!

My dear dad was all decked out himself. Roy was a devotee of theme parties. He was wearing dark blue Bermudas. Sandals—he liked to wear them with socks, but we broke him of that habit. So, okay, fine. On top, he had on his "Independence Day" shirt—white, with stars on the collar, and stripes running vertically down the front. More stars on the back. My dad, the true geek. On vacation, he was a total tourist, with shirts like this, and lots of maps sticking out of his pocket, cameras around his neck. So I wasn't surprised.

"Hi, honey. Nervous?" As if he had to ask. I nodded.

"How's Mom?" He looked pained.

"Dad, what do you expect? She's reeling around the kitchen like a crazy woman, rooting around in the cupboards for additional goodies to bring out. And probably wiping down the counters for the hundredth time. She's a mess. You know, her usual maniacal behavior, amped up."

He shook his head. I bet he regretted this whole thing. But what could any of us do now but hope for the best?

"Where's Adam? Have you seen him? When is Barley coming over? Do you think it will be too hot out here tonight? Where's the charcoal? Have you seen Adam?" He wandered off into the garage, looking forlorn, still babbling. Oh, man.

Just then, Barley arrived. Early, thank God. She looked like a vision in turquoise short shorts, which looked fantastic with her tan legs. White tank top, with turquoise piping (where does she *get* this stuff?), and a little thin necklace with a pink crystal heart. White sandals with sparkly turquoise sequins. Her hair was slightly curled around her head, like an aura, and it looked freshly highlighted. Her green eyes were encased in thick black mascara, which made them look huge and very deep. In short, she was her usual gorgeous self. I waved at her, wanly. I didn't even get up. Drama has always fatigued me.

"Hey, Mand!" She wafted over in a cloud of citrusy perfume. "Hey, you have some schmutz on your front."

Okay. Tiresome. "You're about the hundredth person to notice. Should I change?"

Barley closed in, looked at the spot, and then laughed. "Well, no one ever expects *you* to be perfect. Ha ha! Don't worry—no one will be focused on you tonight."

I winced. The consensus. She was right. Tonight would live in infamy, but not because of my chocolate stain.

"My parents are coming over in an hour. Where's Adam?"

Good God. Where was he? I hadn't seen him since the morning.

"Shit. I don't know. We better look." I hated to get up. But we had to patrol for the missing bro.

Adam wasn't in his room or anywhere around the house. He wasn't in the yard. Or in the garage. The fireworks were in there, all in order, but no Adam. We didn't want to alarm Roy, who was starting up the grills. So we scouted around the neighborhood. We walked around the block, peering down driveways. Nothing. We circled back to our house and sat on the front steps.

"I think he might have run away." After all, he'd said he would.

Barley nodded. "But Mand, your cars are all here. He can't have gone far."

I thought of his bike. Shit! I grabbed Barley, and we ran down the front walk, around to the driveway and into the garage. His bike was gone. "He left on his bike. That fucktard!"

Barley brightened. "This might be a good thing. If Adam doesn't show up tonight, this whole thing might be a non-event. As a matter of fact, let's keep our fingers crossed that he *doesn't* show up, you know what I mean?"

It *was* a revelation. My God, it might be the best thing ever if Adam spent the evening at a friend's, or, I don't know, riding around town. I didn't care where he was. I just hoped he would stay there.

People started arriving around seven. It was getting cooler. The smell of charcoal and grilling was in the air. I inhaled the deliciousness of sizzling steaks—someone behind us was T-boning. I usually adored summer evenings like this, when you smell the summery cooking, hear children squealing, and the splash of swimming pools. We had four pools in our block alone. I always wished we had one. But not tonight. I was wired.

Barley and I hung around the edges of the yard at first, just surveying the scene. There were the Garrisons, wearing tennis whites, carrying what looked like brownies. The Garrisons were known for their brownies. They put pieces of Hershey's dark chocolate in them. Gooeylicious. And the Smiths from across the street strolled in. Gretchen and Charles. They were old folks with snowy white hair, and they were *always* together. Gretchen wore tan slacks, so did Charles. Of course, they both had on red golf shirts. She had on white Keds with little ankle socks. He had on wingtips. Wingtips with black socks. Ha! Kind of cute. They always brought homemade chocolate chip cookies, with *huge* pecans in them. Yum. But I wasn't very hungry.

The crowd got bigger, and Roy started cooking the burgers and dogs. Mom began setting out the stuff from the kitchen. The platters of chicken looked delectable in their crispy brownness. Mom surveyed the crowd and went back into the house for more food.

"Hey, we need to see if your mom needs help." We hustled into the kitchen, where Winnie was taking the potato salad out of the fridge. She looked a bit pinched around the edges.

"Here, girls. Take this out there and put it somewhere in the center of the table with the entrees. Wait—here's a serving spoon." Mom looked like she was getting a headache.

"Chin up, Mom! Adam's nowhere to be found. Maybe he won't show up and then the evening will be regular! Don't look so stony!"

"Yes, Mrs. Heath. It will probably be a fun party!" Barley gave her most encouraging grin. Mom relaxed a little. Then she got all tightened up again.

"But what if he's really *gone*?"

I put the bowl of potato salad on the table for a sec. "He took his bike. He isn't in Cleveland or Chicago or anything. He's around here someplace. Don't worry. Hey, Mom, do you want a beer or something? You need to relax."

Now, the idea of Winnie Heath relaxing is ridiculous right off the bat. But using alcohol to do it? Unheard of. It was worth a try.

What do you know? Wonders never cease: *Mom nodded.* "Yes, a beer sounds good. I have to go out there sooner or later. Mandy, take the salad. Barley, here's the bowl of coleslaw. Now let's just go out there, have some beer, and *mingle*, by God."

As it got darker, we saw flashes of lightning bugs stabbing through the yard. I loved them. I never put them in jars when I was little the way everybody else did. It seemed too cruel. One time, Adam killed some and smeared the fluorescence all over his face and ran around screaming. Oh, yeah, him. I wondered where he was.

Barley and I loaded our plates with chicken and slaw. I added beans, a few sweet and sours, and a dollop of potato salad. I didn't want to eat too much at first because I loved to load up on desserts. We got some beers and sat down in the grass to eat. It was so companionable. A good crowd. I looked around at the scene.

And action:

> *A typical Midwestern backyard party. A large white foursquare home, viewed from the rear. Surrounded by a white picket fence, the yard is decorated for the Fourth, with bunting draped over fence and garage, Tiki torches blazing. Tables groan with picnic fare. There is a crowd: old men in khaki trousers, wearing L.L. Bean broadcloth sport shirts and bow ties, their wives in garish sundresses and white sandals. Young corporate-looking couples, the men in Ralph Lauren polos, their wives bedecked in madras and Pandora bracelets. Children scream and beg for sparklers, their parents try to ignore them, concentrating on their wine coolers and gossip.*
>
> *Two teenaged girls sit at the edge of the lawn, excited to be drinking beer with their food, feeling the beginnings of a nice buzz. Suddenly, a rather Bohemian-looking couple*

stroll down the driveway. He is tall, lean, and excitingly red-haired. He wears tight, faded jeans and a white T-shirt. His left earlobe is pierced with a single hoop earring. Strategic tattoos. He is lavishly but alluringly freckled, a leather and silver braided bracelet around one muscular arm. She is beautiful with her wavy dark hair, piercing black eyes, and dark skin. She wears a flowing, fiery skirt that grazes her ankles, gladiator sandals, and a tight, red tank top. No bra—you can see her nipples pointing out. Her huge silver hoop earrings swing and catch glints from the torches. Colored bangle bracelets chime on her wrists.

Cut.

Yeah, here they came down the driveway. Fletch and Marianne. They were carrying a giant glass bowl of fruit salad. They looked a little bit out of their element: hipsters at a Star Trek convention.

Roy looked up from the grill and dropped his tongs when he saw them coming. He elbowed his way past Mrs. Garrison, almost knocking her down in his haste to get to the Fletches. He edged his way through the other neighbors, goosed Mrs. Crowder by accident, and blew over to Mom, grabbing her by the elbow before she could protest, and sort of dragged her out into the driveway to greet Frank and Marianne. OMG.

Mom was nervous, and the way she snatched the bowl of fruit out of Marianne's grasp was telltale. I couldn't hear what Mom said, but it was probably something garbled like, "Oh, hi! How are you both . . . let me take that from you . . . come on in . . . nice night . . . we have food . . . where's Adam . . . have a beer or light a sparkler . . ."

Barley and I tensed. I set my plate down in the grass. I grabbed Barley's hand and squeezed. "Finish your beer. We're going to need to be drunk for this."

I have to give Fletch and Marianne credit. I'm sure they were shitting themselves inwardly, but they smiled and nodded at Mom and Dad. With Mom on one side and Dad on the other, they faced the crowd.

Mom peeled off with the fruit salad and made a big show of placing it prominently on the dessert table. Roy began escorting the Fletchers around, introducing them, and as they got a little closer, I overheard:

"This is Frank Fletcher and his . . . partner, Marianne Gardner. They are friends of ours from Dayton." (*Ha!*)

Just then, Iris came out of the house where she must have been powdering her nose or something. Right on cue, Don Horley, muscles blaring, materialized out of the sea of chattering neighbors. Gluing himself to her side, they walked up to meet Fletch and Marianne. Iris, ever cool and otherworldly, reached out to give Fletch a semi-hug. You know, like they do on all the talk shows. Don stuck out his arm for a handshake, and I could swear that Fletch flinched just a little.

"Mand, come *on*. Are you in this family or not?" Barley scrambled up, pulling me by the hand. "We have to go over there! Solidarity!"

I tried to brush the grass clippings off my knees as Barley pulled me forward. Awkward. Thank heavens for the beer. It took the edge off, and I was able to force what was probably a clownish grin. Marianne smiled back at me, but of course, with her white teeth and flashing eyes, she looked bewitching. Iris looked bemused, and I thought I heard Don Horley hiss. Maybe not.

"What a gorgeous night! I understand there will be fireworks!" Marianne beamed our way.

Double entendre, if I ever heard one. But Marianne reached out and patted me on shoulder, very disarmingly. I was kind of in a "deer in headlights" trance, then Barley elbowed me. I giggled. Maniacally, probably.

"Yes, we have a bunch. Adam is supposed to set them off later." (OMG, another double entendre—when will it all end?) "But he's currently unavailable." With this, I hoped to be swallowed into the bowels of the earth. No luck. Marianne continued smiling, but with a bit less wattage.

Barley jumped into the breach. "Would you both like to have some food? We have tons, and it's all good! If you'd like a burger, Mr. Heath will be glad to make you one. Or a hot dog. We also have Mrs. Heath's famous fried chicken and all kinds of sides."

This was the ice breaker that we needed. Fletch seemed relieved to have some sort of suggestion for an activity. "That sounds great. We're starving."

"Mandy and Barley, get the Fletchers—I mean Marianne and Frank, some drinks," Dad said. (He was mortified, I'm sure; he knows Fletch is still married to *Iris*). "Marianne? Beer? Wine? Frank?" (A hearty chuckle.)

We all stumbled, in a clot of nerves and forced merriment, over to the food table. Marianne and Fletch took plates, and although I'm sure neither of them felt one bit like noshing, they each took some chicken. Marianne put a pickle on her plate, and served Fletch some of Winnie's potato salad. She grabbed a few napkins and two forks and swung around to look for a place to sit.

Winnie, all manners and hostessy, rushed over and announced, "I've cleared the picnic table over there for us. Guests of honor, you know!"

I groaned almost audibly. Here we were, the Heaths and Fletchers, settling around the picnic table, one big, jittery, unhappy, and freakish family. The table seats six, so Mom and Dad mashed themselves on one side next to Iris. Don planted himself next to Fletch. Marianne sat on the end, her thigh touching Frank's. Barley and I stood, stiffly, next to Marianne. No room for us at the table. Everyone stared as Marianne picked at her food, bracelets clinking, and Frank swilled the beer that Barley brought over from the cooler. No words were spoken. Marianne stopped eating.

More silence. Then, as it always happens when no one knows what to do or say, we all started talking at once. So it sounded like:

"Ohgoshdeliciouschicken lovelynight Ihearfireworks lookafirefly OHMYGODTHERE'SADAM!"

He emerged from the kitchen, holding a beer and glowering at the masses.

Under the glow of the light over the back steps, Adam looked even more tightly wound than usual. Even his curls looked tight. He looked like Frank's evil doppelganger. OMG. I suddenly realized that everyone in the backyard was probably thinking the same thing and doing math in their heads, adding up the twos to equal four. Shit.

He hadn't seen us yet, and as he peered around, Dad got up to intercept him. Dear old Roy Heath, the prince among men. Dad clapped his arm around Adam's shoulders and steered him over to our table, all the while speaking into Adam's ear. By the time they reached us, Adam knew the score, and he was literally vibrating under Dad's arm. Don Horley stood up and closed in on Adam's unprotected flank. Mom looked artificially bright. Marianne was frozen, her bracelets silent. Fletch looked like a man about to be executed.

"Adam, I invited Frank and Marianne tonight. It seemed the right thing to do. I think we should all get to know each other better."

Luckily, our neighbors were decent people. None of them moved in to eavesdrop. The Crowders, forewarned, picked up the pace of their chatter, and Mrs. Crowder laughed loudly, as a decoy maneuver. Mr. Crowder pretended to choke on his drink, spluttering and coughing. The Crowders were true friends. The neighbors, busily trying to save Mr. Crowder's life, momentarily forgot the drama unfolding at our picnic table.

Mom stood up, motioning for Adam to take her place at the table, but Adam didn't budge. Instead, he looked wildly around him, taking in the assorted friends and neighbors. He turned on Mom.

"What the FUCK do you think you're doing here? Isn't it enough to screw up my life? Now you need to spread it all over town that this guy is my father? You need all the neighbors to see how much we look alike? Shit, Mom! What's next? Are you going to ask Aunt Iris to divorce him so that YOU can marry him? So I won't be a BASTARD son? Huh? I HATE you!" At this point, he was shrieking.

This was shit scary. Adam by this time was frothing at the mouth, and some of his spit struck Mom on the cheek. She began to sob, sinking back down at the table, head in hands. Iris instinctively wrapped her arms around Winnie. Marianne jumped up, her flaming skirt nearly tripping her up, and she rushed around the table and hunkered over Mom, crooning "Sssh, sssh."

Then everybody began churning—Adam wrenching away from Don and Dad, the neighbors who weren't saving Mr. Crowder moving in to cluster around us, Barley and I swirling in confusion. Then *boom*! Adam flung Dad's arm away and punched Don Horley in the gut. So much for *that* tough guy! Horley just crumpled to the ground. People froze. Stunned, I watched Adam run past the Crowders, shoving his way past poor Mrs. Reeder, who dropped her wine. Then he pushed some little kid with a popsicle against the fence and pounded his way out to the driveway and into the night.

What a scene.

The camera zooms in:

> *The backyard, which moments before looked like a typical summer gathering, has morphed into chaos. Paper plates and napkins are strewn across the grass. Camera zooms in on a cheeseburger abandoned by the fence, ketchup oozing from the bun onto the grass. A few children begin to cry. The guests are confused, and normal movement stops. For a moment, the scene resembles a still photograph taken by a bystander after a crime has been committed: frozen stances, faces blurred and white, mouths open.*
>
> *Then, as the realization sinks in that this is a private and turbulent family crisis, the guests begin to drift toward the driveway and down the block, carrying lawn chairs and half-empty platters of food. A few people say goodnight, but within a few minutes, the Heath's yard is empty, except for the sobbing Mother, wreathed in the arms of the Daytonian Gypsy and the Aunt. Everyone looks shocked, winded.*
>
> *The two Teen Girls are agitated and clearly at a loss. The party is over. But all over the neighborhood, there won't be much sleeping tonight—bedrooms will be buzzing with conjecture. "What happened? Did you see how much that man and the Heath boy resembled one another? I bet there's a story there!*

Who was that woman who looked like a folk singer? Why was the Mother in tears? My God, I didn't even get to have dessert!"

Cut.

The Crowders were the last to leave. They circled around the yard, cleaning up. Barley's mom carried platters of food into the kitchen, motioning for me and Barley to help. I was glad to follow orders, and so was Barley. As we lugged the remains of the evening into the kitchen, covering stuff in cling wrap and filling up trash bags, Mrs. Crowder said a brilliant thing:

"Mandy, things will probably get worse before they get better, but honey, they *will* get better. Life has a way of going on."

We did a pretty good job of putting stuff away. Barley filled the dishwasher. Dad and Don, once he got his wind back, busied themselves folding up the chairs and carrying empty tables back into the garage. Fletch and Mr. Crowder gathered up the beer cans and bottles and put them in the recycling bin beside the fence. The men covered the grill and stashed the used sparklers in our trashcans. They put out the Tiki torches. Then Don, Dad, Fletch, and Mr. Crowder carried in the three coolers, still loaded with beer and wine. There we were, all of us, standing around in Winnie's kitchen like a bunch of zombies. There wasn't a spark of life left in any of us.

Because during the entire clean-up operation, Mom sat at the picnic table, weeping in Marianne and Iris's arms.

After the Crowders left, taking Barley reluctantly with them, Don, Dad, Fletch, and I sat around the kitchen table, drinking beer. We weren't nearly drunk enough.

"How long do you think they'll be out there?" Frank asked. He looked exhausted. I knew he wanted to leave, but he was marooned in the kitchen as long as Winnie was sobbing in the backyard.

"As long as they want to. If she wants to cry all night, let her! We'll stay here all night if we have to. This whole thing is my fault." Dad looked teary. "What was I thinking, inviting you and Marianne?"

I wanted to ask that same thing. I kept quiet, but really, what kind of optimist was Dad, anyway? Did he think Adam and Fletch would bond? Did he want to prove what an open-minded pharmacist he was, embracing all of this soap-opera crapola? Did he want to show Mom how much heloved her by forgiving all of her shenanigans with Fletch? Why did this evening have to happen, anyway? Where would we go from here?

Fletch looked like a burned-out rock star, his too-long gingery hair flecked with gray, purple circles under his hollow eyes. He reminded me of Mick Jagger. You know, old, haggard, used up, but nonetheless kind of cool. "I don't know what you were thinking. I don't know why I came. I don't know shit right now."

We nodded in solidarity. It got pretty quiet. All you could hear was the hum of the dishwasher and the occasional sigh from one or the other of us. It was tragic, all right. I felt extremely tired. I just wanted to go to bed, but that would put me in the "kid" category, and I wasn't about to admit that I wasn't one of the guys. Not on a night like this.

All of a sudden, the screen door opened, and Mom, looking calmer and less blotchy, came in, followed by her loyal henchmen, Iris and Marianne. Roy jumped up and reached for her, but Mom wrenched away. "I'm exhausted and through for the night. Leave me alone. I'm going to bed." She lurched away from the crowd and disappeared. Her faint footfalls on the stairs were followed by a decided *slam* of the bedroom door.

"Okay, folks. The show is over. Let's get out of here and let these people recover."

I'd never heard this much out of Don Horley's mouth before. Masterful. He grabbed Iris by the hand, saluted Dad, and led Iris, who looked concerned but helpless, out the door. Another couple gone.

Fletch was still looking haggard, his eyes deep and gouged out, kind of like black holes in a night sky. (I got that from Stephen King or somebody.) Marianne looked around at us, probably thinking we were a bunch of hapless losers. Then she poked Frank between his shoulder blades. He jerked to attention. "I wish we could stay and help you, but we have a long drive back to Dayton. Roy, thank you for inviting us. I wish things would have ended more successfully." As she spoke, she urged Fletch out of his seat, turned him toward the back door, and with her arm around his sagging shoulders, maneuvered him out, gently latching the screen door behind them.

So it was just me and Dad. He smiled at me in his dear and ever cheerful way, his eyes crinkling around the edges. I loved him so much.

"Honey, it's been a hell of a day, hasn't it? Don't worry about Adam. He'll be okay. I'll leave the door open for him, and I bet he'll be back before long. You look totaled! Me, too. I bet we'll have humdinger headaches in the morning! Let's go to bed."

I slid out of my chair, and Dad and I pushed the coolers against the wall so that Adam wouldn't trip over them when he got "back before long." (Wishful thinking.) Then I gave Roy the absolutely biggest bear hug I could muster in my inebriated state, and I sobbed a tiny bit. Dad rubbed my back, and we rocked back and forth, just the way we used to when I sat in his lap after a bedtime story.

It was time to give it up. Dad turned out the lights, leaving the one over the sink on for Adam, and we went upstairs—me to my solitary bed, and Dad to face Winnie. The next thing I knew, Dad was knocking on my door. It opened a crack, and Dad whispered, "Mom has locked herself in. I am going downstairs to sleep on the sofa. Don't worry, Mandy. She just needs to be alone."

I blew him a kiss. "See you in the morning, Dad. I love you."

I heard him tiptoe downstairs. I was too exhausted and tipsy to react to one more thing. I let my head hit the pillow and I was out. Like the proverbial light.

Chapter Eight

I was only fifteen, but I felt like a centenarian. Because this summer was so full of life events, I felt forced into premature adulthood and beyond. Holy crap. I kind of wished I *were* like that Proust guy, with a life full of tiny details brought on by some sort of butter cookie. Apparently, he wrote that entire book based on taking one cookie bite. The woman at the library said that it bored *her* to death, and she gets *paid* to read everything. Right then, I'd have paid good money for a boring life. At the rate things were going, my autobiography would make a good *horror* movie—or maybe a country-and-western hit song, if nothing else.

Here's the next installment:

I woke up on the fifth of July at around noon. My lips were all dry and chappy, and I felt like hell. My bladder was screaming. My head throbbed like a bitch. My tongue felt like a damp, mildewed towel. As I teetered into the hall toward the bathroom, nearly wetting myself, it registered in my swollen brain that Mom and Dad's bedroom door was open, the bed was empty, and it was made.

This seemed like a good sign, and I fantasized about tea, French toast, and aspirin downstairs, with a soothing hug from Winnie thrown in. Maybe she'd make bacon.

After I peed, I leaned over the sink to wash my face in cold water. It was a shock to my hungover teenaged system. I raised my head to look at what hell had wrought, and my God! The girl in the mirror looked like some sort of grayish, wrung-out zombie. This drinking stuff was completely for the birds, really. If college meant doing this every weekend, I decided right that moment that I would matriculate without liquor, for shit's sake.

Anyway, I made my achy way back to my room and removed my beer-soaked and smoky clothes from the "celebration" and put on the loosest elastic-waisted sweats I owned, and tried not to wince too much as I pulled a clean T-shirt over my throbbing head. As I shuffled downstairs, I was sad not to smell bacon.

Sitting at the kitchen table was dear old Adam, shoveling the breakfast of champions into his pie hole. He glanced up at me. "You look like shit."

"So do you. Every single day. When did you come crawling home? Where is everybody? Do you know if we have any industrial strength aspirin?"

He sneered. "For your information, beer breath, I came home around two a.m. I just got up, and I haven't seen Mom. Dad is still passed out on the sofa. Look in the medicine cabinet for pills, you idiot."

OMG. Dad was still passed out? Mom was gone? I hurried into the living room, where sure enough, Dad was curled up on the sofa in a sort of fetal position, with the crocheted pink afghan we've tried to give to Goodwill a hundred times covering his legs. It was his favorite thing, that afghan. I think his mother made it or something. Winnie hated it; however, every time she put it in the Goodwill bag, Roy fished it out and said something defensive like, "You don't understand the term 'sentimental value,' do you?" Anyway, he looked pitiful and vulnerable. Not the way you want your father to look, I can tell you.

It got worse.
Here is the scene from the movie:

> The Teenage Girl, completely wilted and forlorn, her eyes ringed with dark circles and last night's mascara detritus, enters the living room. The blinds are drawn. It is a typical middle class, Midwestern, situation-comedy living room: beige wall-to-wall carpeting, a fireplace with the obligatory landscape by a "good" local artist hanging over it. A chintz sofa with matching drapes: the local interior designer's take on that famous decorator—is his name Marco Buatti or something? Two puffy upholstered chairs opposite the sofa (which contains the recumbent and snoring father), in a forest-green velvety material. An oblong coffee table, with a box of monogrammed coasters (the Mother likes her initials), a dish of ancient, dusty potpourri, and an art book (the Mother has it out there for "atmosphere") between the chairs and sofa. Walls painted a tasteful greige (again, that designer who thinks it's "classic").
>
> The Father groans and turns in his sleep. His Daughter approaches, hoping he will wake. Only then does she notice through her hungover daze that he clutches an envelope in his fist. It says "Roy" (well, you know, I'm going to change the names, but this consistency is getting kind of difficult) on it, and it is, naturally, in the Mother's handwriting.

Fade.

I kid you not. There was Roy, looking like something the cat dragged in, hanging on for dear life to what was obviously a note from Mom. This did not bode well, and I knew it. At this point, I felt that I might as well go for broke. There wasn't going to be any bacon this morning. Maybe forever. Shit. I leaned over and jostled Roy's shoulder, whispering (okay, shouting) "DAD, WAKE UP! WHAT THE HELL IS THIS NOTE?"

He struggled to regain consciousness. His eyelids fluttered a few times, and he hacked a few times, sounding just like those sickening old men in nursing homes. I wasn't in the mood for coddling just then. "*Dad.* Sit up! Give me the note!"

I snatched it from him as he tortured himself into a sitting position. As soon as he was upright, I plunked myself down beside him on the sofa. I did the respectful thing: I asked, "Can I read this?" as I tore the note out of the envelope.

Shitballs and turds. *Winnie had left us.*

"ADAM, GET YOUR ASS IN HERE!" I hadn't realized how much screaming hurts your head when you've had a hundred cans of beer the night before. I guess Dad didn't either, because as soon as I yelled at Adam, both Roy and I fell back against the sofa cushions, holding our heads and moaning.

It took Adam about ten seconds to join us. During which Roy and I continued groaning, and I felt like hurling into the potpourri. But the moment passed. Adam looked grim as soon as he saw me holding up the envelope. He sank into the chair across from Dad. "Oh, no. What is it? Did Mom commit suicide?"

I told you Adam is an idiot. Anybody who knows Winnie Heath knows that she would never kill herself when she could kill the rest of us instead. I held up my hands for silence and opened the note. I read it aloud.

The sad sack family is assembled in the living room. The Father, looking wan and grayish, parked next to his rumpled and alarmed Daughter, who holds the letter. The errant Son, wearing a cereal-stained Eminem T-shirt and soccer shorts, leans forward in the faded velvet chair, his green eyes burning.
The Girl sighs and begins to read.

This was not what I expected. Winnie was turning the tables!

> Dear Family,
>
> They say the road to hell is paved with good intentions. I certainly know that now. I had nothing but good intentions when I made the decision to tell Adam about Frank and vice versa. I wanted to be honest and to try to have something good come out of the mess I made in the past. I wanted Adam to know his true identity. I wanted Iris to be able to get a divorce and remarry, if that is what she wants. I wanted Frank to get to know his biological son, and perhaps do him the favor of contributing to his education. And I wanted Roy to know that no matter what I have done, I love him and know that he has been the best REAL father any family could have. And Mandy, I wanted you to understand that everyone makes mistakes, even your mother.
>
> But instead of receiving understanding and support, I got a neighborhood scandal, judgment, and a furious son. I was humiliated by the appearance of Frank

and Marianne. Roy, I know you meant it to turn out well, but it didn't.

I am leaving for a while. I need time to think. As you read this, Iris, Marianne, and I are on our way to Marianne's summer cottage in Michigan. The three of us need time to regroup. If you need to reach me, don't. Do NOT call me on my cell phone. Do NOT email me. And forget trying to text me, either. I don't know when I will be back. You three are perfectly capable of taking care of yourselves.

Just make sure you keep the kitchen clean, run the dishwasher, and take out the garbage. If you don't, there will be cockroaches.

Mom

It took a minute for the gravity of the situation to sink in. On me. Of course, Adam and Roy were a little taken aback, but they were not processing this note the way I was. Because I knew immediately that my screwed-up summer at that moment had morphed from shitty to completely fucked up. Because not only was my brother angry and not completely my biological sibling, my father suddenly alone and vulnerable, my mother holed up someplace up north in a cabin with her "sisterhood," probably giving one another pedicures—but now *I was the woman of the house.* And I had no idea, for instance, why there was a "delicate" cycle on the washing machine.

"How long do you think they will be gone?" Roy asked, sitting up warily.

Adam snorked. You know, that thing boys do that sounds like they're going to spit a huge wad of something disgusting onto the floor. Thank God nothing emerged. "She's being a drama queen! Let her stay there forever for all I care! We don't need her!"

"Oh, yeah. Like we don't need clean clothes, food, and a cockroach-free environment! Dad, Adam—who do you think makes this house run like a well-oiled machine? *Mom*. And who do you expect to take her place? *Me*. I'm warning you: this isn't going to be pretty. You two think I'll just step right up, don't you? No sweat, we have Mandy!"

Nearly in tears, I turned and ran up to my room, which still smelled like Pledge and Febreze. But not for much longer. Then I sobbed.

You're probably thinking feminist thoughts right now. Like, "Oh, this will be a great opportunity for Adam to learn how to separate the whites and the colors and for Roy to learn to make Hamburger Helper. But I was a realist. I knew that Roy worked very hard at the pharmacy, and the likelihood that he had the energy to learn to cook after bringing the bacon home was nil. And Adam? Are you kidding? Would you trust a guy who likes to spit on the sidewalk to do your laundry? Of course not.

So it was going to be up to me. My imagination kicked in.

The scene from the movie:

> *The produce aisle of a neighborhood grocery somewhere in the Heartland. Amidst rutabagas (??) and heads of romaine, the Teenage Girl wanders, studying the carrots and potatoes. How many of these should she buy? Would she be able to fit a whole chicken, carrots, potatoes, an envelope of*

Crock Pot Chicken Fricassee Seasoning, a quart of milk, and a box of Cheerios in her backpack? She grabs three organic carrots and two potatoes. As she trudges listlessly toward the checkout counter, she pulls two expired coupons out of her pocket. Realizing that she will now have to pay full price for the Cheerios and milk, her heart lurches. Will she have enough to cover it?

Camera pans to a single tear trickling down her cheek as she gazes out the plate glass window of the store and swivels to a close-up of her Schwinn, chained to a cart corral. The audience realizes how desolate she feels as we hear "Seven Nation Army" by the White Stripes swell.

We watch as she hands the plump, smiley Winnie-ish checkout woman the crumpled bills from her pocket. She gets back a nickel and three pennies. She smiles ironically as she loads her backpack. She scuffs out of the store, and we watch from inside as she unchains her bike, plunks onto the seat, and pedals off dejectedly. Music and scene fades.

    I was working up a good feeling-sorry-for-myself wave of emotion. Choking on my sobs for effect. There was a knock on my door. Dad.
    "Honey, can I come in?"
    "Sure." I sat up and wiped my eyes.
    "Mandy." He looked like he was trying to hold back from puking, but in an optimistic, Roy Heath way. He smiled. Or his lips did. The rest of his face was a little

chalky. "Honey. Don't take this all on your shoulders. We're in this together."

This little speech failed miserably because defeat was written all over Roy's hangdog smile.

"Dad. This situation sucks, and you know it. Mom left us. Yeah. While she is *finding herself*, or whatever she's doing up there with Aunt Iris and the Gypsy, we're here alone. You, me, and the seething hormonal asshole that is Adam. Don't try to put a good spin on this. Let's not look for the silver lining. Because there isn't one."

He sagged a little more. Honestly, it made me want to find Winnie and shoot her or something. I just couldn't wrap my head around all of this. What started out as kind of a wacky adventure went completely sour, and now our whole family was a fractured ruin.

"Dad, why did she do this? Why did she want to confess about Adam and everything? Didn't she realize what would happen? I'm so mad at her right now! I thought I understood, and I thought I forgave her. But I'm furious all over again. And I'm not sure if Adam will ever recover."

Roy leaned back on my headboard and took a deep breath. He banged his head lightly against the antiqued blue boards a couple of times. I watched him try to collect his thoughts; I could see the tired wheels turning inside his head.

"Mandy, I don't know the answer. I'm not a very deep man. I've tried my best to love and support your mother, but I've never claimed to know what makes her tick. I've spent a lot of time thinking about this, but I just don't know. But I do know that your mother has never gotten over the fact that she got pregnant as a single woman. It wasn't something she ever intended to do. She's been full of guilt over this our whole married life. I think maybe she needed to get it off her chest. I think she wanted the family to know. She hated secrecy."

"You mean she wanted to tell Adam about Fletch so that Adam would hate her for it? Mom has a guilt complex? She needs to punish herself?"

He nodded wanly. I sat there for a minute. I did a quick review of my summer so far. An absent mom who was apparently into martyrdom. A brother who was into victimhood. My aunt, who was sucked into this maelstrom of drama. Poor Don Horley who never signed up for bodyguard duty. Fletch, the bio-dad, and his partner, the Gypsy. Everybody was caught up in their own version of this disaster. So, me? I guess I was the least affected.

I could see that not only was I going to have to learn how to make meatloaf and sanitize the countertops—it was more than *that* pain in my ass. I was also going to have to whip the remains of this family into some kind of shape. I could deal with Winnie later. At the moment, action was needed. Our sorry lives here in Framington would have to turn around while Mom was on sabbatical, vacation, or whatever she was doing up north. It was me or nobody.

"Dad. This has to stop. I mean, it will make a great movie, which I plan to write, but in the meantime, we have to get a grip."

Everything was okay for about two days, or as long as the Cheerios and lunch meat lasted. Then things got a little dicey. The weekend was coming up, which meant that both Dad and Adam would be around the house more. This meant food. So I called a meeting. Or literally, I dragged Dad and Adam into the kitchen on Thursday. I opened the fridge.

"Tell me what you see," I said, gesturing into the abyss.

Adam and Dad looked blank.

"Exactly! *Nothing but condiments and about an inch of milk.* This is serious. We have to work together. Apparently, I'm in charge of nutrition. In case you don't recall, I can't *drive*. We need to go to the grocery store and we might as well go together, as the two of you seem to be free at the moment."

Adam rolled his eyes. But he pulled car keys out of his pocket. Dad got up.

"Wait, you guys! We have to make a list! We have to talk about how this whole thing is going to work—the groceries, the cooking, the laundry, the cleaning. We have to do this right, because if there's one bug in this house when Mom comes back, we will be toast."

Dad sat back down.

I thought it might be a good time to spill my guts completely. "Dad, how long do you think this Mom thing will last? Has she left for good? I mean, is there anything you need to tell us?"

Adam clenched up. We both watched what little color was left in Roy's face drain out completely. All of a sudden, he didn't seem able to keep up his optimistic façade. He sighed. "I don't know. I really don't know."

Not that any of this was Adam's fault, but he was sitting right there.

"*Adam, you suck.* If you hadn't been such a dickhead, Mom might still be here!"

Adam whirled on me. "Shove it, wormface!"

Dad clearly wanted us to shut up. He shook his head. "Look, you two. Acting like spoiled brats won't help the situation and using foul language won't, either. Let's make the list and divide up the rest of the household tasks." He sighed again, this time more heavily and with great resignation.

So we put hamburger, bread, milk, Cheerios, eggs, boxed mac and cheese, lunch meat, soup, and hot dogs on the list. Toilet paper. That covered the basics. It was all we could muster at that moment. We moved on to the roster of chores, with me on cooking (?), Adam on laundry, Dad on vacuuming and kitchen cleanup, and each of us on the honor system for bed making and stuff. In other words, nothing else would get done.

In the car on the way to the store, we tried to be chipper. Dad turned on the radio. Adam changed the channel to the ESPN sports report. So we chugged along, listening to talk about the coming football season and training camp. Boring, but normal, at least. We filed into the store, and I grabbed a cart. Dad had the list, and Adam slunk along, trying not to act as if he was one of us. Typical. The other shoppers must have wondered who this pitiful little group was, since none of us knew where anything *was* in the place, and we kept repeatedly circling around the aisles, looking.

> The three sad sacks enter the store: the Father, in plaid Bermudas, black ankle socks, dingy gym shoes, BAYER ASPIRIN emblazoned on his T-shirt; the Son, in red soccer shorts, flip-flops, and a weary-looking tank top; the Daughter, her brown hair pulled back in a messy ponytail, worn pink sweatpants with stains, Birkenstocks that have seen better days, and a yellow hoodie with cutoff sleeves. They pass the cereal without even seeing it and have to double back for Cheerios. At the butcher aisle, they ask the man behind the counter what ground chuck is. They wander as if lost.

It was a kind of bonding experience. Adam had no idea there were so many laundry products. We decided maybe we should get some of that all-fabric bleach because our clothes would need all the help they could get. I threw some spaghetti in the cart, along with a big jar of sauce, figuring that would be an easy dinner. Dad was incredulous at the price of NyQuil—we have it at the pharmacy for seventy cents less. All in all, it was pleasant.

On the way home, Dad hummed. It made my heart swell.

When we got back, Adam decided to do a load of wash. He passed through the kitchen and said, "Hey, where's that bleach stuff?" I fished it out of the grocery sack and stuck it on top of the pile of laundry he was clutching.

As he went down into the basement, Dad called after him, "Remember to separate the whites and colors! And read the directions on the soap—don't put too much in!"

We heard a grunt in response. We continued unpacking. Dad was filling the cupboard above the stove, shoving stuff out of the way to make room for the cereal. I didn't have the heart to tell him that Mom put the cereal in a different cupboard. He had his back to me, and I decided that it might be a good time to ask him a burning question—when I couldn't look into his eyes:

"Dad, are you going to call Mom? I know she said not to, but I wondered. Maybe if you called her, she'd explain why she left and stuff." I winced a little.

"Mandy, let's take a break. Sit down." He looked very sincere. Just what I dreaded. I pulled out a chair and plunked down, trying not to seem as worried as I felt. Dad sat carefully across from me, his hands flat on the Formica.

"Mandy, I know this is all very hard on you. And it's a crisis for Adam. Your mom probably didn't think that this whole thing would kind of blow up the way it has. I know I didn't. It's tough, just tough." He reached over and rubbed my shoulder in a quasi-comforting way. Then he shook his head and paused.

"I don't really know how to handle this. Do you think that if I called your mom, it would make things worse? I was thinking that I should wait at least a few days. Maybe she'll call us?"

Now, having your father ask you for guidance is just *wrong*. Suddenly, the roles were switched, and Dad was the kid and I was the adult. Damn. I had to wing it. "Well, I think we should give her a few days, right. To sort things out in her own mind. And stuff. Yeah." (So far, so good, right? Not.)

Roy smiled, wanly. Wan. We three were wan these days. Adam was slightly more aggressive in his wanness, but we were definitely on the wan side. I sighed this time. Dad nodded in agreement. I decided to push this whole adult advice thing.

"We need to work on Adam."

"Honey, nobody can *work on* Adam. He had a shock. He feels the way he feels. You're not going to be able to talk him out of anything. The best thing to do is leave him alone."

So Roy morphed right back into being the all-wise elder, thank God. Boy, seeing him weak and needy was way too unsettling. I was so relieved he'd bounced back to himself in a matter of a couple minutes. Just to be sure, I wanted to reinforce. "Dad, of course, you're right. You're always right. I love you." It worked. Roy beamed. For a split second. Then a tiny bit of doubt crept in behind his smile.

My cell twinkled the theme from *The Simpsons*. It was Barley. She wanted to know how things were going. "Is everybody in one piece over there? Have you heard from your mom?"

"No. But I had a talk with Roy just now while we put groceries away. He seems shaken, then okay, then wobbly again. To top it off, I have to make dinner from now on. So I'm screwed. And with Adam doing the laundry, probably all of our whites will be pink. Life is hell over here."

Barley is the best. First, she asked me what I was going to attempt to make for dinner. I mentioned ground chuck, which I'd become an expert on just hours ago.

"What will you do with this chuck? Make burgers?"

I didn't buy buns at the store. "Shit. I don't have buns or anything. What else can I make?"

Barley is so helpful in a pinch. Blue ribbon. "Mom makes great meatloaf. You need an egg and some onions and stuff. Do you want me to bring the recipe over? I can stay for dinner."

"I would be forever thankful. And not that you need any wardrobe advice but be sure to look good. Adam needs all the positive stimulation that he can get right now."

Cut to a couple hours later. Barley, in splendiferous white short shorts, a Juicy Couture striped orange and pink tee, and glistening manicure. Me, in the same old, same old. And seated at the Formica, gazing at Barley's ass, Adam.

"The recipe says to put the meat in a mixing bowl." Barley looked around.

I got a big Pyrex one out of the cupboard. "Check."

"Okay. Now put in the meat."

I unwrapped the chuck and plopped it in the bowl. It was cold and red. How Mom did this was starting to impress me.

"We have to chop an onion. Do you have one?" Barley turned and pointed to my sullen sibling. "Adam! If you're going to sit there, be helpful! Get an onion!"

"Shit if I know if we have onions. I'm only supposed to be in charge of laundry."

I pointed at the fridge. "Look in the drawer that says 'produce.' While you're in there, the recipe says we need an egg and ketchup."

Adam rummaged around in the fridge, mumbling. He seemed to stay in there for a long time. He straightened up, shut the door, and put eggs, mustard, an onion, and some oatmeal on the counter. "I couldn't find the ketchup. Mustard is just as good. I think Mom puts oats in meatloaf."

The fact that Adam even speculated on Mom's meatloaf ingredients was astounding.

Barley was apparently equally taken aback. "What, do you *help* her make meatloaf?"

Adam smirked. "No. But I pass through the kitchen occasionally. I live here, you know. And Mom always puts oats in the meatloaf."

I saw this as a Dr. Phil moment. "Don't you wish Mom were here right now? Making dinner and doing the laundry correctly? Making our lives worth living, instead of the hell we find ourselves in right this moment?"

"Whoa, turdhead. It isn't my fault that Mom unloaded a mountain of crap on this family—on me. That isn't my fault! It's hers."

Barley whirled on Adam. "You are a self-centered asshole! Your Mom didn't *do this to you*. It's something that just happened! Do you think for one second that you will *never* make one mistake in your life that you'll be sorry for later? Huh? Do you feel so perfect that you can place judgment on your mother for a mistake she made when she was *just about at the age you are now*? Think about it, Adam. Have you ever wanted to screw a girl? Or have you screwed a few already?"

Adam's face blazed. It matched his hair. "Shut up, Barley!"

"No, I won't!" Barley lurched toward Adam, put her hands on his shoulders and shoved him into a seat at the table. "Sit down! You too, Mand!"

Geez. I sat.

Barley looked at us, her face reflecting the dim opinion she held of the both of us at that moment. "Okay. This family is so fucked up right now. I'm going to have my say, and I'm only going to say it once. Winnie Heath is a good woman. She is a good mom. Roy Heath is a smart and fine man. They have *two*, yes *two*, good kids. The fact that there was some drama that went on when they were young and foolish is completely beside the point!"

She punctuated this by smacking Adam on the shoulder.

"So here we are. Adam, you have two fathers. Lots of adopted kids do, too. Lucky for you, both of yours are just fine, okay? You didn't discover that your bio-dad is a junkie or a pimp, for God's sake! And when your mom decided that she wanted to tell the truth, she was trying to come clean for your sake, for your aunt's sake, for Fletch's sake, and for her own sake. Apparently, Jack Nicholson was right—*'you can't handle the truth.'*"

She sat back in her chair, triumphant. I felt she deserved a round of applause, so I clapped. Adam apparently thought she was full of shit, because he got up and slammed out the back door.

Dinner time. The meatloaf was awful. Not only does mustard give it a tang that is not delightful, but I learned that potato chips are not the best accompaniment. Roy was even hard pressed to come up with a compliment: "Honey, this might be better with some sort of green vegetable. Is there any barbecue sauce in the cupboard?"

It was nothing like the usual meal with Mom around. First of all, I didn't set the table. She always did. With place mats and a centerpiece, even if it was only one little flower or a seashell or something. I just threw some forks on the table and put a roll of paper towels in the middle for napkins. It was pitiful before I even took the greasy (note to self: ask the butcher why the hell ground chuck is so damn fatty), grayish lump out of the oven. And each white plate with a slice of the stuff and a pile of potato chips? Forlorn.

"At this rate, we'll all die of either clogged arteries or malnutrition," Adam offered. So I slapped him. This put a damper on conversation. Dad got up three times to look in the refrigerator.

"Okay. I promise to start watching one hour of The Food Network a day. Next time we go to the store, we need to spend more time in the frozen prepared dinner section." I sighed.

Adam brightened. "Yeah. DiGiorno pizza. We can find out if it's as good as delivery. It has vegetables on it, so it has the food groups covered. If you get the deluxe. And buffalo wings. Let's get some of those."

Dad kept on eating his gray stuff. I love Roy Heath. With each bite, he stifled a shudder, but he seemed determined to finish his dinner. I have to admit that the barbecue sauce helped.

"Dad, really. Are you going to call Mom? Am I allowed to? Because I could ask her for some recipes and instructions and stuff."

Adam jolted upright. "*No!* Leave her out of this! She deserted us. Let her have her little vacation, or whatever it is! We don't need her here."

Dad shook his head. Really, it was such a surreal situation, with the three of us sitting around eating what might as well have been prison food.

"Adam, your mother left because this whole thing blew up in her face. Whether or not I call her is none of your business. I suggest you start thinking about ways to bring the family back together, not keep it apart. We can't live like this, without her, and you know it." (He indicated the "meatloaf" with a nod.) He took a sip of tepid water. That was the beverage of the evening.

Adam, not one to have the lightning retort, spluttered a little. "Dad! How am I supposed to feel? Can't anybody understand this? What she unloaded on me? How fucked up it is?"

Once again, the matching face and hair.

"Adam, what do you want us to do? Do you want me to divorce your mother? Would that help? Do you want me to have her killed? *What*? *What* do you want?"

Sheesh. Escalating emotions from the friendly pharmacist. I felt I had to step in to restore some calm.

"Look, guys. We can't go back and have a do-over. Adam, you know this, don't you?"

The face got redder, if that's possible. "Why is everybody expecting *me* to change? I got a mountain of crap piled on me, and you all expect me to smile and hug Mom about it? Why is this whole thing up to *me*?"

I knew what was next. The bolt out the door. "Adam, don't even *think* of running out of here! You can't keep running away from this. In my humble opinion, you just love being a drama queen..."

Nobody would have predicted what happened next. Nobody. Adam put his hands over his face. His shoulders began to shake. First I thought he was laughing. Then both Roy and I realized that Adam was sobbing. The big, angry boy just dissolved.

I guess both Dad and I somehow knew that Adam needed to break down. He couldn't carry all of his anger and hurt around anymore by himself. It was paralyzing. He sounded all hoarse and jaggedy. It made the hairs stand up on my arms. Dad bowed his head. It was a few moments that seemed like a week.

So we three, in Mom's cheery red fifties kitchen, sat together in sadness and confusion. I don't even want to contemplate *that* scene from the movie.

Finally, Adam wiped the snot from his nose on his arm (whew, back to normal) and looked at us. "What am I supposed to do? I don't know what to do." He sniffed.

I waited to see what Roy would say. In the meantime, I tore off a fresh paper towel and slid it to Adam. He looked blank. "Oh, for God's sake, Adam—blow your nose!"

Dad didn't look inspired. I don't know why we always expect dads to be crammed with wisdom, but I guess it comes with the dad territory. He took a beat to look around the kitchen and take another sip of water. Stalling. But who wouldn't, in this miserable situation?

"I don't know, Adam. All I can think of is to give things the 'tincture of time.'" (Oh, boy—that old saw. It must be in the Pharmacist's Compilation of Platitudes.)

Dad took a paper towel for himself and wiped his brow. "Nobody has the perfect life, you know. This is just a problem. It isn't the end of things for us. It's a challenge, that's all. Adam, you don't have to figure this out right this minute. None of us do. I think that's why Mom had to get away with her sister and Marianne. She needed time to figure things out."

Adam shook his head. Still teary, but now not so fiery red. "Dad, I don't know how to figure this out. I'm stuck."

I had a brainstorm all of a sudden. If Mom needed time with "the girls" to figure out all this stuff, then turn about would be fair play! "I know what we should do, guys. Mom is communing with Aunt Iris and Marianne Gardner up there in that cabin. To figure things out. As a group. We can do the same thing here!"

They both looked at me like I was an alien.

"You know! We can have a group, too! Let's invite Don Horley and Fletch over this weekend."

I might as well have suggested that we get naked and run around the block. Dad's eyes opened wider than I had ever seen them. Adam blanched. Went from red to white in one nanosecond. They both went slack-jawed. It wasn't a pretty sight, I can tell you. You could have cut the surprise in the air with a knife.

So I had to continue. "Let's face it. Fletch is now a huge part of this family, whether we like it or not. That fact won't disappear. And Don is, unfortunately for him, tied up with Aunt Iris, so he's a big part of this stinky equation. You guys, we can't figure this out alone. There are a bunch of players in this game. We have to get them together."

Yeah, I know. Probably too much metaphor; I need to work on that.

"What do you think?"

All three of us were ready to try anything at that point. The shit had already hit the fan. What more could happen?

Adam was too weak to fight anymore. Dad was always hopeful. It was the right combination, I guess. They both nodded in agreement. Oh, my God. I was going to host a Heath/Fletch/Horley bonding session. "Okay. I'll call and invite them over on Saturday for pizza. Not the DiGiornio stuff. We'll order from Fazio's. We need the good stuff."

Adam stared into space, his blues looking pretty watered down. Dad slapped the table decisively. "Okay, honey. Good idea. We'll have pizza and beer. I'll call Frank and Don. What time should I say? Six?"

So with one swift move on my part, we had a plan. Sort of.

Chapter Nine

Saturday morning was bright and clear. Of course, I was the only person to notice, because Dad went to the store and Adam usually sleeps until noon. Anyway, the sun was beating down by nine and there weren't any clouds floating around in the sky, so it would be a hot one. No eating in the backyard. I cranked the AC up high, and then sat on my bed with a grocery pad. I needed a list. Shit, I was the hostess!

First on the list was straightening up. Newspapers were all over the couch in the living room. Last time I counted, there were six pairs of gym shoes in the front hall. You could write your name on the dining room table, for God's sake. I was beginning to regard Winnie as some sort of household wizard. How did she *do* all this stuff?

Two. Make the downstairs bathroom less disgusting. Frank and Don might have to pee. Use the spray bubble stuff all over everything, and pour Clorox in the toilet.

Three. Make sure we have paper plates and napkins. Tell Dad to bring some beer home.

Four. Be sure to tell Adam that attendance is mandatory or Dad will murder him. Check.

As I was pondering, my cell sounded *The Simpsons*. Barley. "Hi. Hey, do you want to help me clean the house today for the big manly bonding session tonight?"

She coughed at her end. "Not really. I might be able to come over for a while later. I have to go school shopping with Mom this morning. That reminds me. If your mom doesn't come home soon, you'll have to talk your dad into giving you some cash so that you can get some clothes. You can't start school with the rags you're wearing now."

I replied with as much machismo as possible, "Look. My clothes are perfectly fine. Well, not really. But Mom will be home before school starts. Right now, Vera Bradley backpacks are the furthest thing from my mind. I have to focus on the powwow tonight."

Barley is very understanding and supportive. "Mand, I know you have a lot on your mind. It sucks. Okay. Yeah, I'll be over later. Don't forget to spray some room freshener around. Things are getting funky over there."

I hung up, feeling a little better. I put on a pair of boxers and a tank and went downstairs to assess the condition of things. On the way down the stairs, I noticed a slight grittiness underfoot. Shit. Add vacuuming to the list. At this rate, I'd still be cleaning house at midnight.

There was mail on the floor. A couple of bills were still stuck in the slot. I bent to gather everything up and saw that Winnie had sent each of us a postcard. She must have mailed them the second she left. Oh, right. This was my mother. I put the other mail on the hall table and sat on the stairs with the three cards.

Mine had a picture of a sunset over the water, with the outline of a loon or something flying through the pinkness. I turned it over.

> Dear Mandy,
>
> I hope you are holding up! I am feeling better and figuring things out. Take

care of things as best you can. I love you!
(Keep the kitchen clean!!)

Mom

Not much info there. I wished she'd said something like, "On the way home now. Things will go right back to the way they were in the spring." Of course, that wasn't possible, but still. I looked at the one addressed to Dad. It had a picture of the shoreline, with a black Labrador running in the distance. Classic gift shop postcard—could have been from Bermuda or Florida. Generic.

Roy honey,

I hope you are holding up! I am ok. Be sure you are eating a balanced diet. I am not answering my phone, so don't keep calling. I need more time. Give the kids hugs from me. I will call you soon, I hope.

X Winnie

So Dad *was* trying to talk to her, with no success. Wow. I wondered if Iris was answering *her* phone. Somebody up there had to be communicating. Good thing the guys were coming over, actually. If Iris was talking to Don, or Marianne to Fletch, we might be able to suss out when they were coming home. Or what in God's name they were planning up north.

I looked at the front of Adam's card. It was totally different. She couldn't have gotten this one at the same gift shop. It was much thicker, and it had ragged edges, like the fancy stationery you see at the Hallmark store. It was light blue with little gray flecks all over it. And there wasn't a picture on the front, but instead, in a fancy font, it just said:

Love Conquers All

Dear Adam,

I think about you every minute.

Love,
Mom

Okay, then. I felt a hundred years old.

I folded mine in half, and then in half again. It was a little oblong of Mom. I put it in the breast pocket of my tank top. It gave me a tiny bit of courage. I set Dad's and Adam's back on the hall table with the other mail. A sigh, and then I had to go to work on the house.

It took me from noon until four to do the cleaning. Yikes! I guess the living room looked okay after I was done. I threw away the newspapers. I used a Swiffer cloth on the tops of all the tables, and let it go at that. But the bathroom was awful. Why men can't pee without getting it on the floor around the toilet is totally ridiculous. The scrubby bubble stuff turned *yellow* when I sprayed it around the base of the toilet. I actually gagged. It took almost a whole roll of paper towels to get that place in order. By the time I was finished sterilizing, I needed to rest.

I had a Coke and laid (again, this verb is completely ridiculous, laid? lay? Shit!) on the sofa for fifteen minutes. I took cleansing breaths and tried to think of some good platitudes to get me through the kitchen cleaning. The only ones I could think of were: "Don't throw the baby out with the bath water," and "A stitch in time saves nine." So I hummed the entire score of *Lion King*. That was somewhat refreshing. Onward.

In the kitchen, I almost lost heart. Adam had apparently made nachos last night. It smelled like a bad Mexican restaurant. There was an empty bag of Fritos on the counter, along with a bottle of taco sauce, an empty package of shredded cheese, and an opened can of sliced olives on its side, olives and juice splayed out all over the Formica. Little black eyeballs. Crumbs everywhere. Dabs of sauce on the floor. And of course, a plate in the sink with encrusted cheese that would need to be chiseled off. Darling Adam. I wanted to get the leaf blower and blast everything out of there and start fresh. I was really starting to think of Winnie as some sort of epic Wonder Woman. This whole housekeeping thing? Overwhelming. No wonder Martha Stewart was almost a goddess.

I got out a garbage bag and threw in all the nacho remnants. Dirty napkins and an empty Cheerios box were on the table. In they went. I opened the fridge and removed the empty milk carton, three despicable-looking cartons of moldy leftovers, and a green thing. I think it used to be an apple. They all went in the trash bag. I had to make room for all the beers and leftover pizza. I hoped we'd have leftovers. One less meal for Mandy to make.

I dragged the bulging bag across the kitchen and hefted it onto the back steps. I'd ask Dad to put it in the trash later. I had to focus on washing down the countertops. (I went and got the scrubby bubble stuff from the bathroom for this; I figured that what's good for bathrooms can't be bad for kitchens, right?)

I swept the crap on the floor into a little pile and pushed it under the rug by the sink, wiped the table with a sponge, and loaded the nacho-cruddy plate and milky Cheerio bowls into the dishwasher. It was already full of dirty dishes. Most of them looked pretty disgusting, with smears of ketchup and little dried piles of muck. Thank God for the dishwasher cleaner that says "no need to pre-rinse." I put in one of those little miracle pods, slammed the dishwasher door, and pushed the Steri-Clean button. I thought that would be in the best interests of all of us. I hoped the cheese would come off Adam's plate without clogging the innards of the dishwasher.

By this time, I was exhausted. I needed a nap. That's when Barley wandered in. As usual, she was a vision in pastels. In her hand was a bag from Bath & Body Works, tied with a pink satin ribbon. "Mom and I felt sorry for you. Our treat. It's peach scented shower gel and lotion. We thought it might give you a lift."

This girl was a true friend. I took out the bottles, unscrewed the lotion and sniffed. Peachy heaven. As we trudged upstairs, Barley gave me a thumbs-up. "Good job on the cleaning," she said. "Well, maybe this?" She pointed to a discarded orange rind on the newel post. "Men don't really notice stuff like this, but garbage on the banister is a little gross."

In my room, I took the peachy bottles and put them on my dresser. As I folded the bag and put it beside them, it occurred to me to ask Barley if she wanted to be at the pizza event. I needed moral support. "Hey, can you come over for the pizza party tonight? I'll be the only girl. You're a lot faster on your feet than I am. I need you. Can you? Will you?"

Barley arranged herself on my bed. Really, the girl looks like a GUESS advertisement without even trying. "Mand. You don't need me here. This is a family thing."

"Oh, yeah. Like Don Horley and Fletch are *family* now."

"Oh, Mand. You know what I mean. This is all about your family. Whether you like it or not, Don may become part of it, and Fletch *is* part of it. More or less."

My stomach lurched. It felt like I might hurl. So I laid (I wondered if Proust knew the participles of this cursed verb?) down beside Barley on the bed and put her hand on my forehead. "Feel me. Do you think I have a fever?"

"Why, are you sick?"

"If I say I'm mortally ill, will you come over?" I gagged a little, for effect.

Barley rolled her eyes. "You feel fine to me. But I'm not a nurse or anything. Since you're staging your own death, fine. I'll come over. I happen to be dateless tonight. Well, I am most nights this summer. I think your family drama has negatively affected my social life."

Barley actually did have a social life. Boys drifted over to her house all the time. Even some of the older ones who could drive passed by her house and honked. There hadn't been an actual one-on-one, long-term boyfriend yet, but she had all the opportunities. Barley was picky. Neither of us really wanted to have sex yet. Or at least, Barley was humoring me in that department. Like she said to me one night on the phone: "Look, if sex is all it's cracked up to be, I'm certainly going to wait to have it until the guy I'm with has outgrown pimples." That made me feel better about myself. But for all I knew, Barley was going to orgies in her spare time.

Barley was wise beyond her years. As far as I was concerned, sex had a way of completely ruining your life. Example: my mom. So I didn't want to go anywhere near boys until I actually had to. Let's face it, sex scared me. As you know by now, I was short on experience and long on sexual anxiety.

"Do you have some kind of plan?" Barley asked as she pulled a few stray strands of her shiny hair behind her ears. "Like are we going to play poker or something?"

I took her hand off my forehead and rolled over to face her. "Are you kidding? You want three men who are already on thin ice and Adam the walking time bomb to start *betting on cards*?" I thumped my forehead. "Really. There will be a murder in this house before long. *No.* We're going to have pizza and beer and Coke, sitting in the kitchen like civilized beings, and I pray that the worst thing that will happen is that Adam will fart."

Barley looked thoughtful. "Do you think you should call your mom or something? Or Iris? Just to let them know what's going on here at home?"

I'd thought of that. "Yeah. I wish. But Dad says we can't. She doesn't want us to, obviously. So I haven't. I think maybe he's talking to her on the sly, but he isn't saying anything."

Barley started to giggle. "Okay. No poker. No talking to Winnie. So what, we should play charades? Or hokey pokey? No! SIMON SAYS. That'll break the ice! 'Adam! Simon says pull down your pants and show your ass!'" She fell back on the bed, dying of laughter.

"Barley, you just want to see Adam naked. This is not the time or the place. I hope there will *never* be a time and a place for that. Shit."

Barley sat up with a saucy gleam (take that, Mr. Proust) in her eye. "But Mand. If I marry Adam, we'll be sisters and friends forever. That's my plan. We can have a double wedding."

I pulled a pillow over my face. This was sickening for real. "Oh, my God, Barley! This is not the time or place for your fantasies. Wait." I removed the pillow and stared at her. "You've *planned* this?"

She smiled wickedly. "Of course. I've planned to marry Adam since we were in fifth grade. That's when he started getting hot. Well, that, and he kissed me under the mistletoe last year, and that really decided it. He has a lot of potential, you know, sexually."

Oh My God. Could my life get any more complicated and sickening? I couldn't deal. I rolled over onto my stomach and groaned. I considered writhing, even.

Barley started to laugh. Then she laughed more, and pounded me on the back. "Sisters!" She spluttered. "No—more like Siamese twins! Wait. Awkward during sex with Adam."

"EEEEEEEEW! This is not something I can unsee now!" I put both my hands over my eyes and gagged.

She fell back on the bed and we both nearly died laughing.

Barley went home to change (totally needless, but she's like that), and I laid down on my bed to rest. I pulled my old, nearly fuzzless Ted bear to my face and took a deep breath of my childhood. It smelled like a combination of sour milk and dust. Took me back to the days when Winnie was here, I was small, and we had a clean house, balanced meals, and happiness.

I shut my eyes and took another whiff. Adam used to have a Ted bear, too. Except his was constantly involved in nearly fatal accidents in which that poor little Ted (named Body, by the way—Adam was weird even then) lost limbs, and Winnie had to sew his legs and arms back on. Finally, he resembled a faded brown war veteran with prostheses (Winnie had to rebuild his legs with old towels, and we don't have brown ones, so Body had one dirty yellow terry leg and a filthy gray one).

Adam loved that bear, though, and he used to tag around the house after Mom clutching Body, offering to vacuum. He wanted to give Body a "ride." Mom, being wise, always said no, and then Adam cried. He'd get the vacuum out when Mom wasn't home, and vroom around the house with it, Body attached to it with

Adam's Sunday school necktie. He was such a pushy, resolute little kid.

Adam had always challenged Winnie, come to think of it. He tried to get her to buy him inappropriate stuff for his age a lot. Like the time he wanted a moped when he was in fourth grade. Mom said he'd kill himself on it. He wanted a bow and real arrows with sharp points on them in sixth grade, and Mom told him she wasn't going to be responsible for Adam murdering one of his fellow Boy Scouts. He wanted to learn how to shoot a gun last year, and even though he put up a good argument in favor of conceal-and-carry and saving people in the mall when crazy shooters showed up, Winnie was totally staunch.

It occurred to me that Adam *was* a lot like Mom. He had that dogged determination and complete self-confidence that Winnie had. They didn't look much alike, what with Mom being short and kind of stocky, and Adam having that long lean body. But they both had those blaster blue eyes. When they fixed you with a stare, it was hard to keep from disintegrating under it, if you catch my drift.

Do they say that people who have the same disposition butt heads? I figured this was partially why Winnie and Adam were on the outs. She thought she knew exactly how her "summer revelation" would play out. Every single family member would fall into line as she figured they should. She didn't factor in her almost identical-in-temperament son. Who was as stubborn as she was. Dad and I learned early on that "going with the flow" was a handy way to survive Winnie's dominance. But Adam took her on every time.

I turned over on my stomach and rested my head on Ted's smooshy back. In my mind's eye, I pictured Adam and Mom, the day Mom would finally come home.

A hot, steamy, and bright afternoon in early August. Framington, Ohio. The street is nearly deserted and the heat pumping off the sidewalks creates wavy lines. Yards are starting to brown in the usual late summer drought. The Ohio foursquare sits in the middle of the block, its front porch shaded by the maple trees that wilt listlessly in the heat. But even the shade on the porch is halfhearted.

A burgundy SUV revs down the parched street. As it passes, a dog barks in the next block. Driving the SUV is a small, fierce, and determined woman with springy brown hair and bright blue eyes. She drives the car as if it is her own personal chariot. When she reaches the foursquare, she pulls into the driveway by stomping on the gas pedal and wrenching the car to the left, screeching tires and raising a small dust cloud.

She shoves the gearshift into park and flings the door of the car open. The heat hits her like a slap in the face. She exits the cool interior of the car, hoisting her short legs over the driver's seat and onto the running board. Before she heaves herself forward, she stops to look at the house. Her house. The one she has lived in her entire married life. She glances up at the second-story windows, half expecting to see a face looking out at her. She pictures the dear face of her husband, with his soft eyes and kind smile. Or the animated face of her teenaged daughter, with huge, surprised eyes and an excited grin. Or perhaps the freckled and handsome face of her nearly adult son, with his hooded eyes and rusty curls.

But there is no one. She sighs and exits the car. As she trudges down the driveway toward the back door, the gate creaks open and out rushes her son, Adam, wearing basketball clothes and carrying a ball. She can't help but smile at his mismatched socks, high-top black sneakers and torn shirt: her dear and slovenly kid!

He looks up in mid-dribble and he sees his mother. They both stop short, face-to-face: the gangly boy with the ball, and the little firebrand who is his mother.

Seconds pass. Adam (I have totally given up on the Boy, the Mother, et. al., too hard; will work on this later) is frozen, his face devoid of emotion, almost trancelike. His mother's smile fades. She brings her hands to her cheeks and tries to cover her eyes, but it is not soon enough for her to hide the tears that well up. She drops her head to her chest and sobs, "I am sorry, Adam. I am so sorry." They remain rooted—the tense boy and the sorrowful, sturdy little woman. She knows it is futile. She attempts to brush past her son. She just wants to escape the heat, to get into the cool house and lie down on the sofa. She desires the security of home, no matter how broken up it is.

As she moves past her son, their shoulders touch. She can feel his whole frame shake. Suddenly, he drops the basketball, strangles a sob, and wraps his arms around her. They both shudder and cry, but amidst the sobs the boy can be heard saying, "Mom. Mom." In the background is some sappy old-school music, like the instrumental version of "The Way We Were" or something.

Fade.

I opened my eyes. Yeah. As if *that* was gonna happen. I blinked a few times to deconstruct the scene and then tried to decide what to wear for the pizza party. That sounded way too innocuous, like something normal people have. Not people like us, who have broken-up families and biological mayhem going on. I chose to go casual chic. I took a fast shower, and after slathering on Barley's peach lotion liberally, I put on a pair of fairly clean jeans, an actually clean Coldplay T-shirt, and flip-flops. I blow-dried my hair. I figured that I needed to look as presentable as possible. I studied my face in the bathroom mirror. Normal. No pimples. Hmm. Mascara or other embellishments? I decided against them. No one would be looking at me tonight, anyway, and even if they did, eyes would skim over me and move directly to Barley, as always. *Gross.* If Don Horley or Fletch looked at me or Barley and noticed stuff like mascara? I got a little sick at the thought. So I shook myself out and left to go downstairs.

Dad was pacing around nervously in the living room, plumping pillows and dusting the coffee table with his sleeve. I felt for him. This was disaster in the making.

"Dad. Roy. Let me just say right now that I totally have your back. I think this evening will be a good thing. So you really shouldn't look so bleak." I said this while stopping him from taking a used Kleenex from his pocket to wipe down the mirror next to the fireplace.

I pushed him down onto the sofa and sat beside him. He'd nicked himself shaving this morning, and there were two scabs on his face: one just under his left earlobe and one on his chin. The little red spots made him look even more vulnerable than usual. So I patted his leg.

Dad put his hand over mine, comfortingly. "Honey, with your mom and the girls gone, I want to do something constructive at my end. You know, get the guys together and have some conversation."

He looked at me with an expression that spoke volumes. He knew this was so *lame*. But I also sensed desperation in the tilt of his half smile. Here was kind, dear Roy Heath, trying his best to make it all better. Just like he does at work, when the pills he dispenses actually do help to make stuff better. I bet he wished there were pills for this situation.

"Oh, Dad. This is going to work. You know, the conversation and pizza and all." I patted him again, and then we just sat in awkward silence, Roy with his scabs and hope in his heart, and me with Coldplay across my shirt: *When you try your best, but you don't succeed . . .*

Barley showed up at the back door a few minutes later, resplendent in torn jeans, a tightly fitted, black-and-white horizontal striped, off-one-shoulder top (it would never even occur to me to try on something like that), black sequined flip-flops, and gleaming hair. She smelled like some sort of exotic flower. Of course. At least the men would have something to feast their eyes on. During clashes.

"Where's Adam?" she inquired, after giving a thumbs-up on the clean state of the kitchen. "He'll be here, right? I mean, I didn't spend an hour getting ready for nothing, did I?"

"Dad told Don and Fletch to show up here around six thirty." I pulled my cell out of my pocket and checked. "It's five thirty now, so let's hope Adam will come home in time. Dad made it clear he wanted Adam's sorry ass here this evening."

"You mean he isn't here now?" She grimaced. On her, it looked adorable. "Mand, you know as well as I do that the chances of him coming home for this are slim to zilch, right?"

She followed me up the stairs, nodding her approval at the banister (I'd thrown away the orange rind), and into my room, where we both fell onto my *almost* nicely made bed. I mean, I do my best, but Winnie I am not. Hospital corners are her thing, not mine.

"Barley, what do you really think is going to happen? I mean, what if Mom and Dad get divorced or something? I'm so scared about this. For one thing, I need her. She's totally annoying, but she always has my back. And shit, if she doesn't come home soon, this housemother stuff will kill me. I have a whole new appreciation for home-cooked meals and clean laundry."

Barley ran her hot pink fingernails through her highlights.

"Oh, Mand. Of course she'll come home. For one thing, I bet that cabin up there in the wilds of Michigan or wherever isn't even heated in the winter. Plus, Iris can't give her piano students the complete shaft. Who knows if Marianne has a job? Those women are not going to become *roommates,* Mand! They are grown-ups. They have *lives.* They'll be back. For God's sake, it isn't *Roy* she's trying to escape. It's the whole Fletch/Adam thing. Something will have to break in that situation. Adam may be eighteen, but he has no real skills. I don't expect him to run out of here to make his fortune anytime soon. He's just trying to figure all of this out.

Trust me, deep down inside that curly red head is a guy who misses his mom, too."

I rolled my head back and forth on the pillow. It's soothing. I look a little mental doing it, but I have always used the head-roll method to relax me when I'm stressed out. I considered Barley's words. I needed to be hopeful. So I decided to believe her. "Barley, how is it that you are so wise and also so *hot*?"

She rolled her eyes and laughed. Then she looked me over. "This is what you are wearing tonight?"

"Hey, this isn't a cocktail party, and I'm way too exhausted from sanitizing the house to worry about how I look. This is fine. Or as fine as it's going to get."

We heard the back door slam, and the thuds of Adam's gym shoes as he came upstairs. Thuds of doom, as far as I was concerned. I sat bolt upright. So did Barley. It was tense, all right. We saw the flash of red hair go past. Then the footsteps halted. Adam wheeled around and stuck his head in my room.

"Don't even start on me, girls. I am running on empty."

"Adam, are you ok? What's going on?" Barley patted the spot on the bed next to her. "Sit. You need to cool off before you get in the shower."

Adam looked wary, but he nodded. Barley smiled, and that did it. He came in and sat beside her. "I can't deal with this. I can't deal with Mom being gone. I am totally pissed off at her, but I feel shitty about making her leave."

Adam surprised me with this. "You made her leave? What do you mean? You told her to go away? When?"

He rolled his eyes at me. "Mand, you idiot. NO. I didn't tell her to go, but why do you think she left? For a little break? A vacation? She left because I hate her!"

I sighed. "Adam, you didn't make Mom leave. In case you have forgotten, there are a lot of players in this little tragedy. You can't take all the credit. Remember that Mom started this whole ball rolling. I bet she blames herself for everything—you hating her included."

"Yes, right." Barley reached out to pat Adam on the back, but changed her mind at the sweatiness, and put her hand back in her lap. "Adam, just try to chill. Take a shower and put on some clean clothes."

"Yeah. Right. I will go take a shower and try to turn myself into a good boy. Fuckin' impossible." With that, he turned his sweaty old self around, stomped into his room, and shoved the door closed. We heard a ball hitting the wall.

"Everyone at this end is present and accounted for," Barley said. "What is that classic movie line—put on your seat belts because there might be turbulence?" Close enough. Close enough.

At about six, Dad yelled upstairs. "Girls, come down and call in the pizza order! Adam! For God's sake, get in the shower!"

Don Horley arrived first. Barley heard a car pull up and hopped over to the window. "Oh, my God, Don Horley has a *car*?"

Just then, Adam was schlumping down the stairs, and he sidled over to the window behind Barley (a ploy to get next to her ass) and looked over her shoulder. "Not *just* a car! It's a 1967 Mustang! Sweet!"

So, of course, Adam ran into the hall, threw open the front door, and raced down to see the shiny red thing up close. He left the door open, naturally—so all the heat from the outside wafted in. Dad, as saintly as he is, was irritated and said, "That damn boy" under his breath as he went to shut the door. We heard him exclaim "*Wow*," and he left, thoughtfully shutting the door after himself.

"What is all the commotion about some car?" I asked, but went over to the window to look myself. Okay. I got it. The thing was vintage, all right. Its shiny cherry redness would have looked good parked in Winnie's kitchen. I don't know anything about cars, but this one was obviously old and obviously retooled within an inch. It was a convertible. Don and the men were milling around it, marveling over the black leather interior, general chrome-iness, and fancy wheel things. Hubcaps? Whatever they call them, they were pretty cool.

Apparently, Iris had hooked up with a totally hip guy who had a shiny bald head, muscles, a Harley, and this Mustang. Hmm. My Aunt Iris, whom I had always thought was kind of lackluster in a luminous way, was maybe more exciting than I thought. The men in her life? A saxophone-playing, redheaded rock star-type husband, and a biker bearing sparkly black countertops and a vintage Mustang? I wondered what she and Don *really* did over at her house when alone. All of this stuff about listening to the piano with tears in his eyes? Pmff. I bet Don was all hot and bothered, gazing at Iris's gleaming ivory arms or something like that. Leading to God knows what kind of rolling around and kinky sex. OMG.

After totally circling the car like vultures for an eternity, they trooped into the house, laughing and slapping each other's shoulders like good old boys. At least Don shut the door after them. Dad led them into the living room. Awkward. We all stood there, clearing our throats and shifting our weight from one leg to another. Finally, Adam slumped into a chair, throwing one of his legs over the armrest, which Winnie forbids.

This kind of broke the ice, and Dad said, "Sit down, girls, Don. I have beer and Cokes. Does anybody want anything?"

Adam looked up hopefully. "Yeah, Dad. I'll take a beer."

I smirked inwardly. As *if*. But you could have knocked me over with a feather when Roy answered, "Sure. Don? Beer? Girls? Cokes for you two?"

Barley and I nodded, stunned. Don smiled and offered to help carry in the drinks. As soon as their backs disappeared into the hall, I hissed, "Shit, this is serious business when Dad thinks it's fine to let Adam drink himself into oblivion right here in the house!"

Adam narrowed his eyes at us and hissed back, "Shit to you, Mand! I could use something a lot stronger than *beer* tonight..."

"What do you think is going to happen?" Barley whispered. "Adam, are you going to maintain control? Or am I going to have to get out my brass knuckles?"

Adam snorted and rolled his eyes. "As if. Shut up, both of you." He shook his finger at us. "You don't even have a clue what it's like to be me right now!"

"Oh Adam, cut the drama. And don't point, it's rude. Shh. Here they come!" Barley cocked her head in the direction of the kitchen.

They trundled in, Dad carrying two cans of Coke, and Don juggling three bottles of beer. He handed one to Adam and gave Dad his. Adam immediately started throwing back his beer, drinking as if his life depended on it. Dad motioned for me and Barley to get off the sofa so that he and Don could sit down. I scrambled off the sofa and sat on the floor, crossing my legs, juggling my Coke. Barley was just lowering herself and her can of Coke into the chair next to Adam when the doorbell rang. *Fletch.*

My stomach lurched. I nearly spilled Coke in my lap. Barley stood up very straight, shook her gleamy hair (probably to clear her head), set her Coke down on the coffee table (*coasters, coasters, we needed coasters*), and went to answer the door. Thank God. The rest of us were carved in stone. There was the usual helloing and small talk in the hall. Barley sounded gracious and self-possessed. I wanted to be her. No news there. Dad and I stood. Dad's knees cracked. I nearly fainted.

So. First in was Barley, a gracious smile lighting up her face, her cheeks a little paralyzed-looking. Towering over her, a similar frozen smile on his face, was the Fletch. Tight jeans with a knee hole and hanging threads, vintage Frye boots, and his muscles nicely arrayed in a tight Rolling Stones T-shirt. This man looked as out of place in our G-rated living room as a hookah pipe in a kindergarten classroom. I know. I need to work on my comparisons.

He was carrying an old, cracked leather case. Ah, the saxophone! So there would be music. I was kind of relieved. We needed some kind of diversion, since playing poker wasn't an option. Maybe some jazz would be just what the doctor ordered.

Barley, still beaming artificially, looked around and announced, "Here we all are."

This was going nowhere. Frank stood in the doorway, clutching his instrument case with whitened knuckles. I felt trickles of sweat running down my armpits into my bra. Adam belched. Roy, bless his soul, took charge. "Frank, I see you brought your sax? Great! We'll have music later! Sit down. Adam, go get Frank a beer."

Adam, who was shooting the proverbial daggers with his eyes, remained seated. He looked about fourteen, ragged sweatpants and basketball shoes, his leg still hanging over the armrest of Winnie's pristine armchair. I could see a few whiskers that he'd missed this morning, making his face look slightly dirty on the left side. Pitiful. All at once, Adam leaped up (the boy is a panther) and hurtled out of the room.

Fletch tried to disguise the fact that Adam nearly made him jump out of his skin by dropping his case on the floor, where it clunked and landed on its side. Dad chuckled heartily. Frank ignored the sax, entered warily, and sat down on the sofa, followed by Barley and Dad. So there we were. Dad, Don, and Fletch in a row on the sofa, all looking at me.

It crossed my mind that now would be a great time to run out of the house and away for good, but I squelched it. "Frank, have you heard from Marianne?" I figured I might as well cut to the chase. "We haven't heard much."

Frank ran a hand through his hair. Adam's hair. "I talked to Marianne this morning."

Pause for effect. Yeah. It was electric in there.

"They're all fine. The weather is cool but not rainy. They take a long walk every day. Marianne says it's excellent sleeping weather."

Was the man trying to *torture* us? Would he tell us what kind of *birds* they were seeing in the woods? What they had for dinner every night?

Dad, thank God, said, "Is Marianne sharing with you any idea of when they plan to come home?"

Adam burst in, slammed a beer in front of Frank on the coffee table, and threw himself back in his seat. Frank looked scared for a second, then continued, "Not really. She said that they're all three having long talks."

Adam threw his head back against the chair. Barley looked as if she might bolt at any second. You could cut the tension with a knife. I wanted to go get one and kill myself. Or Adam. A nice bloodbath to end this summer of weirdness. Suddenly, my brother blurted, "It's my fault that Mom and them left."

I think Adam surprised *himself* with this sudden admission. His face kind of collapsed, and I think I heard a "glunch" in his throat. And he went for broke: "Mom isn't a ho or anything. She just made a mistake; I get it.

I kind of hate her for it, but I don't *want* to hate her. But cut me a break; I never asked to have two fathers." He closed his eyes. "But I guess I don't want to ruin your life, or Marianne's, either."

Oh, the eloquence. But I have to say it did the trick. Frank smiled. Barley finally *stopped* smiling. Dad heaved a relieved sigh. The creases I thought were chiseled between his eyes disappeared as if by a poof of magic. And I nearly crapped myself at Adam's feeble but sincere words. I never would have predicted them. Never in a million years.

The doorbell rang. Pizza had never come at a better time.

We sat around the Formica table and demolished one large pepperoni and one large double cheese with sausage. After a few beers, the men relaxed even further and we actually made conversation. Frank asked me what I wanted to be when I got older, and I told him that our lives were all movie scripts. He didn't laugh. He even asked me about my future writing career.

When all that was left were crusts and crumpled napkins, Fletch said, "How about some music? It might settle our stomachs."

Barley clapped. "Oh, yes! We'd love that, *wouldn't we, Adam?*"

Adam actually smiled.

Then we got a big surprise. Don Horley, the man of the sparkly countertops, got up and left. "Just a minute. I'll be right back."

We were momentarily stumped. I took that opportunity to reach for two beers: Barley and I deserved them after this cathartic evening, I thought. And my God, Roy nodded. This evening had loosened him up, all right.

Don walked back into the kitchen just as Fletch did. Don carried his own leather suitcase.

What the hell?

"This is an accordion. I play it. Have been since I was eight. I'm not at Frank's level with the sax, I'm sure, but I thought he might bring his instrument, so I thought I might as well bring this."

Wait a minute. The picture in my head of what Iris and Don got up to in the evenings abruptly shifted.

> The gloaming. A living room in a small cottage. Candles are lit on an upright piano. A breeze comes through the open window and rustles the muslin curtains. A willowy woman sits at the piano, her graceful fingers at the keys. On the striped sofa, a large, bald, and heavily muscled man sits. He holds a white, marbleized accordion with silver rococo trim. They eye each other, and the woman gives a downbeat with a nod. And they begin to play boogie-woogie. He keeps time with his heel on the carpet. She laughs, tilting her head back, her long, taffy-colored hair in whorls around her shoulders. (Music by some old black musician; research needed here before scene is written.)

Fade.

I get ahead of myself.

Roy jumped up from the table. "Let's go into the living room! More space and comfortable chairs. Don, do you do polkas? I love the Beer Barrel . . ." and he kept muttering about polkas and Spanish ladies as we moseyed into the living room, leaving the dinner mess behind. Winnie would have died.

Frank and Don sat in the two armchairs. They carefully placed their cases on the floor at their feet. The unveiling! I've seen saxophones before, but none up close. And none this gleaming. Frank's looked like he polished it daily. "Frank, do you polish this thing?" I asked.

"Daily." Called it.

We craned our necks to see what was under the red velvet cover in Don's case. He smiled at the group, his fingers stroking the coverlet. "This is the instrument that Lawrence Welk made famous. Or infamous."

Barley looked as confused as I was. "Who?"

"You're way too young. Frank, I bet you know who Welk is."

Frank laughed as he fingered the keys on the sax. "My grandma loved him. Made me watch the reruns with her. His accordion virtuoso was Myron Floren. You take after him? Mandy and Adam—you and Barley might have liked Lawrence Welk." He chuckled. "Very PG. Lots of bubbles and dancing. There was an Irish tenor, the champagne lady, and polka, polka, polka."

Barley rolled her eyes. Adam said, "Not! Sounds like a show for old people."

"It was," Don said. "It was a guilty pleasure for a lot of young people. I watched it with my grandparents, too. I kind of grooved on the music; they had top-notch musicians."

"Guess what?" Frank interrupted. "The sax has always been cool, but the accordion is *coming back*. Lady Gaga plays it. Madonna has used them in her act. I see it in movies all the time. In Europe, they're on practically every street corner."

"Wow." Barley stood up. "Let's see it, Don!"

Reverently, Don lifted the red coverlet. My God. Splendiferous is all I can say. It was made out of what looked like aged white marble. Creamy and swirly. Plastic, Don told us. There was a whole bunch of silvery trimming all over it. Ivory and black keys on one side, lots of black buttons on the other. The bellows were red, with a beautiful black diamond design. It looked supple and

I was dying to push a key. Over the top of the keyboard was the word BELTUNA in beautiful script.

Barley, ever the interviewer, leaned over Don's shoulder. "How does it work, exactly?"

"Frank's sax has a single reed. He presses one of his buttons and it closes a hole and changes the length of the airflow in the horn and makes a sound. Each hole—a different tone. On the accordion, there are many, many reeds. Each individual note has a reed. When you press that key and the air is flowing, you hear the tone. Frequently, there are several different reeds on each note so you can change the tone of that very note."

Adam couldn't help himself. He leaned over Don as well. "What are these buttons for on the other side?"

Don answered by playing a chord, pushing the piano keys first. Then he repeated, pushing a couple of buttons and the keys together. "They change the register, change the key, and provide the background accompaniment to whatever you're playing on the piano—like keys operated by your right hand. Hear it?"

Wow. Then Frank joined in with a couple of chords. "Okay. Let's warm up a little."

They tootled around for a few minutes, all of us fascinated. Especially Adam, which I would have never predicted. He burst out, "Come on, guys—play something!"

Frank looked at Don. "Folk? Do you know 'Ramblin Boy?' It's a good one."

Don smiled. "Of course!" They began and Don sang, "*Fare you well, my ramblin' boy . . .*"

We were hushed. It was beautiful. Like we were all connected somehow, with the music dissolving our anxieties. It seemed to massage our frantic heads somehow. Roy was entranced. Barley gyrated with the beat. Adam was transported. I was about to burst with relief; I thought the night was going to be disastrous, not a hootenanny, for God's sake.

"Don, how about some polkas? Frank, can you play polkas? I love polkas."

Frank said, "Don, I can play anything you can. You start, I'll follow."

Don adjusted his accordion on his lap. The thing looked like it weighed forty pounds. Forty pounds of gorgeous sound. "Sure. This one is called the 'Too Fat Polka.' Not politically correct, but you kids will like it, I bet."

> *Oh I don't want her, you can have her, she's too fat for me*
> *She's too fat for me*
> *She's too fat for me . . .*

We all joined in on the second chorus, Barley strutting around like a pregnant woman holding her belly. Adam actually *laughed* at her. Don followed this one with "Roll out the Barrel" and "Pennsylvania Polka." By the end of those, Roy and I had polka-ed around the living room and we were sweating.

"We need a break. Mand, go get some more beers." I was not about to argue with Dad on this one.

We went from polkas to the Weavers, and on, naturally, to Pete Seeger. I think that Roy always kind of wished that he had a little more of the vagabond in him: we'd had *The Weavers' Song Book* lying around since I was small. Then of course, they launched into the Guthrie father and son, and finally, on to Bob Dylan. At last, an artist Adam, Barley, and I could faintly relate to.

Before the evening was over, Adam had brought his grotty old guitar down from his room. He strummed along, although I think Adam had had exactly one lesson in his life and could play two chords. But it was starting to be kind of fun—a *dysfunctional* hootenanny, all right. By eleven thirty, Barley and I went into the kitchen for a break.

"Fletch isn't all bad," Barley noted, sitting at the red Formica, smoothing out her hair. "He seems to be interested in getting to know all of us. He isn't pushing himself on Adam or anything."

"I know. I guess if you have to have two fathers, Fletch is good for a spare one. Maybe we all need extra parents."

I reached into the cupboard for some Cheez-Its. I'd been religious about keeping the cheezy snacks around for her—still in her cheese phase. I sat down, passed her the box, and we munched companionably. There was a break in the music in the living room, and we heard Adam's unmistakable shuffle coming toward the kitchen.

He appeared, his curls sweaty, his eyes shooting out glints of either nervousness or energy, or both. "Hey, girls. What's up? Hand me some Cheez-Its."

"Have a seat, bro. You want a Coke or a beer or something?"

Adam lurched into a chair and grabbed a fistful of crackers, and, of course, stuffed them into his mouth. "Ithjwoew a beer."

Barley rolled her eyes. I decided that we were too young to become alcoholics, on top of everything else, so I got three Cokes out of the fridge and passed them around. We cracked them open and glugged. Adam, having swallowed half the box of Cheez-Its, took a breath. The fingertips on his right hand, I noticed, were red and sore-looking from all that strumming. He rubbed them against his palm. He'd probably get blisters. "When do you think Mom and them will come back?"

I shrugged.

Barley, who is, of course, wise as well as beautiful, said, "Adam, don't you think it might be sort of up to you?"

He looked surprised. "What do you mean?" He put his right index finger into his mouth. It must have really been sore.

"You just *told* us that your outburst on the Fourth kind of sent her packing."

I have to admit I'd been thinking along these same lines, but since I was the one trying to keep the home fires burning and the toilets clean, I'd been afraid to say anything like this. I mean, really. I watched Adam for a reaction. The last thing we needed was for another family member to defect. Shit. I was tempted to kick Barley under the table.

Adam looked at me.

I didn't say anything. I just took a big drag on my Coke. Tension.

"What? D'you think I should go and get her or something?" Adam said, examining his wet finger. "Like, steal Dad's car and go up there?"

I have to admit, I hadn't thought of this.

"It has merit," Barley pronounced.

"Wait. First of all, we can't steal a car. If we asked Dad for his, he'd insist on coming with us. And he can't, because he has to work at the store, for God's sake. We can't *all* just go up to Michigan on a wild-goose chase for Mom. We don't even know where they are!"

Barley leaned forward, raking us both with an intense stare. Those blue eyes were relentless when she aimed them at you. "Fletch knows where they are. It's Marianne's house. He's probably been there a million times. If we asked Don, he'd drive us up there. I know he would, because I actually already suggested this to him. He says it's a slow time for his countertops at the moment. Remember, he has the Mustang."

"*What?*" Adam shot out of his chair. He almost knocked it over, but I caught it just in time. He glared at Barley. "Goddamn it, Barley, this is none of your business!"

Barley crossed her arms calmly. "It is too. I'm practically in this family, and I'm the only one thinking clearly about all of it. Well, not counting your dad. Or Fletch. Or Don. Nobody seems willing to *do* anything to fix the situation. Because, honestly, they don't have a clue. Because really, Adam, this is between you and your mom. Why do you think Winnie confessed all of this? To piss you off? To make you hate her? To break up this family? Noooo. She did it to finally tell you the truth and let both you and Fletch realize who you are to each other. She just wanted to be honest. I'm sure she didn't think she'd lose her whole family over this."

I could imagine Adam's chest was about to explode. Everything bulged. His eyes, his biceps, the little veins in his temples, his cheek muscles. Pressurized.

"Isn't that *tough* for poor ol' Winnie, then?"

A weak rejoinder. Even Adam realized that. He blew an explosive gust of air out of his cheeks. Everything else kind of deflated along with it. His whole body shrank down. He sagged and leaned against the sink.

"Come on, Adam," Barley said. "How long are you willing to punish your mom?"

Adam stood there, leaning against the sink, his face white, his fingertips red, and his fierceness extinguished. A broken boy.

I stood up. "Did Don ask Frank how long the drive is up to the lake?"

Chapter Ten

That night, everything buzzed around in my brain. First, I relived the entire musical soiree. Fletch was actually a genuinely nice man. Anybody who would react kindly to the discovery of a nearly grown son *not* from his undivorced wife? A guy who'd come over for dinner twice, never knowing whether or not he would be shot and killed? A keeper. I was actually looking forward to having our family expanded with music, culture, and geniality. Plus a gypsy. And Dayton is a nice town, so going there would be fun.

My dad. The prince among men. Roy, who discovered that the love of his life was pregnant, not with his child, and *married* her anyway! Roy, who was the best dad in the world, always happy and optimistic, always supportive. My dad, who always smelled just perfect: a combination of Head & Shoulders freshness and a dash of Listerine, layered with Bounce. In other words, as perfect as Winnie could make a man smell. Roy Heath, the visionary pharmacist who kept his heart staunch and true, despite the challenges. A man who smelled like a dad but was actually a knight. I rededicated myself to Dad that evening. I would never let him down.

Don Horley. Wow. Another prize in disguise. Who knew that the countertop king would drive a Harley *and* play the accordion? Oh, yeah, and possess such a hot ride? My Aunt Iris was evidently not a colorless recluse after all. She had a wild side. All those nights I pictured her playing solitaire or plinking out sonatas? Not the case. She had a lover and accordion music.

Mom. Phew. I really admired Winnie. A great mom. The pinnacle of housewifely skill. A helpmate. And all the while, she carried this secret around about her son. I wondered how horribly guilty she felt about Roy's devotion—if she really deserved it. I tried to put myself into Winnie's head all these years. See, I thought that Mom was just a happy camper, wielding the vacuum cleaner, sterilizing sinks, and making mac and cheese.

To me, her helping Roy out at the store proved she was kind of a feminist. Other than that, I never gave my mom any kind of thought. I never wondered what went through her mind. I never even pictured her as somebody who was once my age. I didn't give her any credit for being an actual three-dimensional being. To me, she was just a *mom*. I guess I had assumed that the only person in my world with any depth at all was me.

Which brought me to my brother. If somebody had asked me before this summer to describe Adam in one word, I'd have said, "Sweaty." Again with the one dimension! In my own selfish way, I had pegged Adam as just a bundle of burgeoning testosterone, monosyllabic and irritating. Adam, who looked like a cross between Shaun White and a rocker. I thought about all the things I never gave Adam credit for: keeping his mouth shut when Dad made awful jokes. Mowing the lawn in hundred-degree weather—no complaints. Riding his bike around after he got his license, mortifying for most guys. Not my brother. Adam, who never beat on me the way some big brothers do to their sisters.

I thought about all the time Adam spent alone in his room. I had supposed he was masturbating or doing other disgusting things, when he must have been actually *thinking*. Really. And now he was somehow having to come to grips with the fact of Fletch and Roy, Winnie and Fletch, and Winnie and Roy. I was having a lot of trouble figuring out how I felt about all of this, and I was not the one who suddenly had two dads. It certainly wasn't sitcom material for any of us. I had to give Adam all kinds of props for trying to unwind himself and for being willing to reach out to Mom.

Now we were going to go on a road trip, orchestrated by Barley Crowder. The girl wonder. Miss Popularity, who picked me, the awkward one, to be her best friend. Barley, who for all I know wasn't actually still a virgin (I didn't want to know, in case Adam was involved), who stuck with me despite the fact that I was most certainly a virgin and scared to death of the actual sex act. Barley, who remained a bestie in spite of my bad haircuts and embarrassing moments in the cafeteria. I thought about how we were probably sisters from another life. And the fact that Barley, deep down inside, loved Adam. And maybe he loved her, just not consciously.

I shut my eyes for the seventieth time, trying to go to sleep. But all I could see was this:

> *A hot Monday morning in August. Speeding down the highway, passing brown medians and scorched trees, is a shiny red Mustang, vintage. Top down. Radio blaring. Inside, their faces windblown but looking hot in spite of it: the bald driver—his Ray-Bans glinting in the glare. Beside him in the shotgun seat, a sullen man-child, wearing a green bandana over his orange curls, wraparound sunglasses, and a frown. In the back, gyrating to the tunes on the radio, two girls. One is blonde and glorious, her tanned skin set off by gold hoop earrings, white*

> sunglasses, and a sequined tank top in a blazing shade of melon. Beside her is a dark haired, worried-looking plonk of a girl, her brown eyes shielded by green drugstore sunglasses, her dance moves forced. They whiz down the highway toward the unknown.

This wasn't going to be any fun at all. And Mom didn't know we were coming. Barley said the element of surprise was going to be our winning strategy to dissolve Winnie's anger and bring her home. I slept maybe one wink that night.

Don had told us that we could make it from Framington to Aldrich, Michigan, where the cabin was, in one day. About five to sixish hours of driving. None of us had any idea whether or not we'd be spending a night and coming home the next day with Winnie tucked between me and Barley in the backseat, or turning right back around and coming home with our tails between our legs. Dad advised us to pack one set of clothes, pj's, and our toothbrushes. Of course, in Barley's case, a makeup case, hair dryer, and three changes of clothing.

Dad, I could tell, was so hopeful. On Monday before we left, he brought out a cooler filled with all sorts of goodies from the store: Cokes, some Snickers bars, sandwiches from the vending machine (turkey and cheese, the best), a couple of those Lunchables for good measure, and Diet Pepsi. He handed over a bag filled with packs of peanuts, trail mix, gum, and snack bags of chips. As if we were going on a trek into the frontier or something. His heart . . . always in the right place.

Don showed up just as I was finishing my cereal. As he walked into the kitchen, his muscles flashing in a tight black T-shirt (*boy, have I been underestimating Aunt Iris*), Adam came down, wearing a tattered gray gym shirt, ancient blue nylon soccer shorts, and flip-flops. He had a backpack, though. So he was ready.

"Hey, Adam." Don smiled.

"Hey." Adam, in his usual non-effusiveness. He pitched his backpack onto the back steps and turned to root around in the fridge. "Do we have any cottage cheese or anything? I have a stomach ache." My God, we were starting out right.

Roy entered, as if on cue, his white lab coat crisp, and his smile just a little forced. "Adam, wait a minute. I have some Zantac and Rolaids. I'll go and get them. You can take some now and put the rest in your suitcase."

"Dad. Nobody has suitcases anymore." Adam paused. "But thanks."

Roy, glad for something to do, bustled out. We heard him hurry up the stairs, followed by rummaging noises from the bathroom.

"Don, do you want toast or anything? Or instant coffee? We have to wait for Barley to get here. She texted a little while ago and said she was up and going to be over here . . ." (I looked at my cell phone) "well, fifteen minutes ago. But it won't be long."

Don sat down at the table and nodded. "Yeah, Mandy, some instant coffee would be great."

We were sitting there, sipping coffee, munching on snacks, or sucking on Rolaids, when Barley knocked on the kitchen door. Dad motioned for her to come in. She entered in all her splendor. Barley is so glam, I just can't stand it. Here I was, in my usual old jean shorts, rumpled white Gap tee, and battered old blue Nikes. In walked Cameron Diazy Barley, clad in a misty pastel green Ralph Lauren Polo and gladiator sandals. She had on green barrettes, eye makeup, and everything. We all kind of basked in her glory for a sec, then she dispelled the atmosphere with her usual aplomb by yelling, "YEE HAW! ROAD TRIP!"

"Have you had breakfast?" Roy asked. He went to the fridge, opened it, and peered in. "It seems that Mandy has been to the store for provisions. We have eggs and bacon. Would you like some? Adam?"

Adam clenched his midriff and shook his head. Barley beamed at Dad and said, "Thanks, Mr. Heath, but I had breakfast at home. We need to get going before it's too hot."

With that, Dad was all pharmacist. "Does everyone have sunscreen on? If you're going to be driving all the way with the top down, you need sunscreen. Wait—I'll get some SPF 50." He bustled back upstairs. We looked resigned.

After he forced us to slather ourselves, Dad zipped the sunscreen into my backpack and we went out to the Mustang, which Don loaded carefully. We stood around for a few minutes, awkwardly hugging each other goodbye, and then we got in. Don backed down the driveway, and as we waved gaily (well, Barley and I) to Dad, Adam slumped down with his earbuds tightly screwed in, and the odyssey began. Top down, sun shining on the houses and lawns as we passed.

I bet Roy felt lonely. But I know him. I bet he went into our kitchen and cheerfully did the dishes and swabbed the counters (anti-bacterial soap), with pleasing Winnie in mind. Because, of course, Dad was an optimist. Roy Heath, ever loving, ever hopeful.

We drove toward the highway interchange to go north. I thought about a phrase my English teacher said about something. I hadn't been paying attention much that day, but this one thing she said stuck in my mind: "It's not the destination but the journey to reach it that's interesting." So far this summer, eight short weeks, had been a hell of a journey. And now we were going on a *real* one. I pledged to tell my English teacher about this when school started. Because I just bet that *this* destination would be a humdinger. Our journey was only the beginning. I was willing to bet actual money that something monumental awaited us there in Michigan.

If you think that riding in a convertible with the top down is fun, breezy, and adventurous, you're mostly wrong. Riding on the highway in an old Mustang, going sixty-some miles an hour in the second week of August is *hot*. Windy, gritty, and hot. Not to mention noisy. After the first hour, I wanted to put the top up.

"Hey, can we put the top up?" I said, or actually kind of yelled. I was in the backseat with Barley, who, naturally, looked brilliant with her hair blowing all around her flawless face, her sunglasses setting off the look. She could have been on a fashion shoot.

"Mandy, this is a vintage car. It doesn't have air conditioning. We can put the top up, but we'll still have to have the windows open," Don yelled back, as he turned his head to face me (*scary, Don—eyes on the road*).

Adam, earbuds firmly in place, didn't move. Barley smiled, held one marvelous tanned and freckled arm above her head and waved at the man in the shiny red Beemer who was passing on the left. He, of course, was thrilled and nearly swerved off the pavement. I was overruled.

"Okay, then, can we stop at the next rest area so I can go to the bathroom and splash my face with cold water? And enjoy the still air for one minute?"

"Good God, Mandy. I had no idea you were so fussy." Barley smiled, though. "Yes, Don! I could use a rest stop, too."

Adam pulled the plugs out and turned around. He looked a little dazed still. But maybe a little bit of courage, or optimism, or something other than anger, was building. His jaw wasn't as tight. And his shoulders weren't up around his ears any more. "Hey, Mand. When we get back on the road, you can ride shotgun."

How generous of him. I wondered if he was considering my comfort or getting closer in proximity to Barley the glorious. It didn't matter. "Yes! Because I think I'm also getting a little nauseous back here. Riding up front will be much better. And I want to get some of Dad's Rolaids out of the trunk."

Highways in northern Ohio are kind of boring. No spectacular mountains, huge stands of pine forest, or shimmering lakes around here. No. Flatness and farms. Corn. Soybean fields. Lots and lots of Bob Evans and Cracker Barrel billboards. On the median strips, there's an occasional stunted-looking bush or small strip with the sign: "Do Not Mow—Wildflower Prairie," which in mid-August looked like tiny hayfields.

It was not panning out to be any sort of wild and scenic adventure thus far, I can tell you. With the sun beating on our heads and particularly searing on our noses, I was thankful for Roy's insistence on the sunscreen.

About fifteen miles later, Don signaled right and pulled off at the Highland Hills Rest Area. I wondered if the Ohio Department of Highways people were ironic. Anyway, Don parked near the limestone-and-glass visitor information area. How nice. There was a stand of vending machines, and a sign on the glass entry doors to the main building said "Free coffee inside." We filed in and Don headed over for some coffee. Barley and I peeled off into the ladies' room.

Public rest rooms could be the subject of an entire documentary, I think. Some of them are just gorgeous—these are the ones in fancy restaurants. I went in one with Mom once; I think it was their anniversary or something, and so we drove to Columbus for a special dinner. The restaurant was called Shimmer. The ladies' room really did. It had gold leaf on the walls, a fresh flower arrangement on the counter between the sinks, and each stall had a gray-and-white marble floor and louvered doors. The spigots were little bitty waterfalls. Compare and contrast: the rest stop had gritty beige subway tiles, dirt buildup (let's hope it was dirt—it was *brown*) in the corners, that female farty smell that we all recognize from sordid rest rooms, wet paper towel litter everywhere, and one stall without a door. I just wanted to wash my hands and get out of there but, as I turned to go, Barley grabbed my arm.

"Wait. We need to talk a second."

"Can't we talk out in the lobby where it isn't so stinky?"

Barley wrinkled her nose but shook her head. "No. It's about the trip. Adam hasn't said a word. Don't you think we need to *talk* about this thing before we just show up? I mean, get a *plan* together or something? Don't you want to know what Adam is going to do and say to the women? I mean, we know he can be a loose cannon. Come on."

I tried not to breathe too hard while answering. "Well, yeah. But what should I say? What about you? You always seem to have the entire world under control. What if you start the ball rolling? No loose cannon pun intended."

Barley stifled a cough. We had to get out of there. "Okay, let me think. When I start the conversation, *you have to join in*. We need to get a meaningful dialogue going in that car before we just show up at the cottage!"

"Okay. Now let's go before we die of inhalation poisoning."

We exited the main building to see that Don had set up Roy's cooler on one of the stained and pitted concrete picnic tables out in the "grassy" area. At least it was in the shade of some sort of gnarled, big scabby tree. Spread out on paper towels (thank God Don was trying to keep us from picking up picnic table plague) were Dad's sandwiches and snacks, along with the drinks. It looked very inviting, actually. Don smiled at us as we approached. Adam sat beside Don at the table, luckily without the earplugs.

"Sit down, girls. I thought we should have a bite of lunch before we got back on the road." Don picked up a sandwich and held it out to me. I was famished. I took it, sat down, and unwrapped it. One bite. The salty smoked turkey, the mustard, and the soft bread were a symphony of packaged-sandwich perfection. One bite was all I got before Barley, who plunked herself down gracefully and put her elbows on the (shudder) bare table, started in with the dialogue.

"Okay. We'll be there in a few hours. Have any of you thought about how this whole thing will pan out?" (Significant glance at Adam.) "Do we know what we're going to do? The women aren't expecting us. We assume they'll all three be there, with welcoming arms. But come on, how likely is that to happen? Adam, what are you going to say to your mom?"

I nearly gagged on the Muenster in my sandwich. Nothing like the direct approach. But Barley knew what a Neanderthal Adam was most of the time. I guess she figured she had to slam him with this right between the eyes. Adam, who was ignoring his sandwich in favor of drinking down an entire can of Coke without taking one single breath, nearly choked. But he swallowed down the last of his Coke without spitting it out, put the can down on the table, and burped a few times. With his hand over his mouth; I have to give him that.

"I dunno."

Adam, the mellifluous.

Barley sniffed. "This is my point."

Don, who had finished one sandwich and was loosening the cling wrap on another, added, "That is a good question, Barley. First, the women might not even be home. We need to consider that. If they are, they might not be all that happy to see us show up."

I put down my sandwich, making sure it didn't touch what looked like the scum of an old dollop of chocolate ice cream, probably left on the table from some snotty-nosed kid a hundred years ago. "Yeah. What if they yell at us and tell us to turn around and go home? Mom made it pretty clear she didn't want us to call her on her cell, and she isn't even opening any emails. If Dad's talked to her, he hasn't told us. So. What if they slam the door in our faces?"

Adam looked pretty miserable. "Yeah."

Don swallowed a bite and took a sip of Coke. "I don't think they'll slam the door. Iris isn't that mad at anybody. She's just there to support Winnie. I have no idea why Marianne offered her house to them. My guess is that Winnie isn't mad at *us*. I think her beef is with Frank."

Barley cut in. "Wait, Don. You've been talking with Iris?"

Don looked uncomfortable. "We've had a few conversations. Iris told me to keep them to myself. She doesn't want to get more caught in the middle than she is already. If that's possible."

The sun was getting pretty beastly. But we didn't budge from the table. At least there was a little breeze, and the leaves in the dry tree above us jangled. Don filled Styrofoam cups with ice cubes and passed them around. I applied mine to my forehead. Adam just held his. Barley put a couple of cubes down her bra and shuddered with delight. That woke Adam up a little.

"What has Aunt Iris told you?" Adam asked. "I mean, what about Mom? What's Mom doing up there? Is she mad or sad or what?"

Don considered for a few seconds. "Iris hasn't really given much information about what's going on up there. At least, not what's going on in their heads. She mostly says it's very pretty and that they're swimming in the lake and having healthy meals. There isn't a piano up there; she did say that."

"What the . . . ?" Adam spluttered. "Come on, Don! She must be saying *something*. You have to tell me. Us."

Don crumpled his cling wrap into a tight little ball and set it carefully on the table. He looked around at us as if we were freaks of some kind. "You kids." He snorted ruefully. "Your self-absorption knows no bounds. Has it occurred to you that this is bigger than just you?" He waited for a response. There wasn't any. We were struck dumb.

"Every single one of us is affected, you know. Geez, Adam. If you recall, your Aunt Iris is *still* married to Frank Fletcher. Think a second. This came as a complete surprise to Marianne Gardner, Frank's partner of ten years. Oh, and me? I fell in love with a woman who never bothered to tell me that she was still married, you know? Just a small bombshell in *my* life, if you consider it. Which you obviously haven't. But I would have guessed that you guys would have spent a *minute or two* thinking about your dad. He thought he had a nice, quiet life. He thought he had a handle on this dad business: you know, keeping the identity of the biological father of his beloved son a secret. To protect his wife that he loved so much. And Winnie? She's opened a can of worms that may just eat her up!" (No comment on *that* metaphor from me.) "This is a much bigger problem than what you three teens think it is. It isn't just about *you*. Why do you think I volunteered to drive up to Michigan, anyway?"

Oh my God. I nearly inhaled a chip.

Adam, the nitwit, asked, "Why did you?"

Don snorted. "Damn. You kids. I'm going to say this once more. Try to listen and let this sink in. This problem involves you, Adam, *yes*. But it also happens to be about the future of myself and a *few* other people. Hell, boy, your mom and dad might get divorced over this! Try to see the big picture beyond your own little self, kid, okay?"

We were shocked. I mean, shit. This whole thing was growing ever more enormous. We sat there, kind of reeling. Nobody made a move to say anything. Even Adam's freckles went pale.

"How will this get solved?" I was nearly crying. "I want things to go back to normal! Don, what can we do? I want my mom back..."

Barley looked as flummoxed as the rest of us. This was so uncharacteristic of her. I think it hit her hard, maybe harder than it did me, because Barley had always been the "solver." But sitting there at that scorching, grease-stained picnic table in the middle of the highway in northern nowhere Ohio, she must have realized that her teenage powers were not a match for this situation.

Adam sagged. "Should we go back home?"

I looked at Don for guidance. We all did.

"Here's what I think. Sometimes life grabs you by the balls and squeezes, pardon my French. There's nothing you can really do to overpower it. You have to give in to things sometimes, you know? You can't plan on what to do. You can't control stuff. You have to go with the flow. We have to go there, keep our emotions from exploding," (he looked at Adam) "and try our best to see this thing through. As I see it, we can't go back to the way things were, Mandy. Nope. But we can try to ease things as best we can. You know, communicate. Forgive."

Forgiveness. Now that was a concept that hadn't come up.

"But how?" Adam really looked as if he wanted the answer. His eyes got kind of soft, as if the irises were starting to dissolve. His freckles faded even further. He needed more sugar in his system. I motioned for him to take a sip of his Coke. He gulped the rest of it down and threw his can in the direction of the litter bin. It missed, but nobody even cared. "I feel so freakin' furious. At Mom. At Fletch. At Dad. Life is just a ball of suckiness right now! How am I supposed to forgive people? Or see the fucking 'big picture?' Shit!" Adam wrenched up from that pocked table and rocketed away, flinging himself against the scabby old tree beside us, wrapping his arms around it as if he needed that hug. For dear life.

√ The enormity of the situation clobbered us. Well, the three of us. Don had apparently been aware of it in his own adult way all along. I guess adults know that things like this happen in life. But the three of us? We'd been kind of floating on top of it the whole time, figuring that something we could do would make it all go away. I guess there comes a time in everybody's life when it suddenly becomes clear: some problems are huge. And life isn't like a movie—there isn't a way to manipulate the ending. Your parents can be really fucked up. They aren't in control of things, either. No kissing away the boo-boos.

Where did that leave us? Sitting at a rest stop in Cornfields, Ohio?

"Look. Kids. You live your life. You do your best. Got it, Adam? Your *best*. It's all any of us can do. Let's get back in the car, keep the peace, and spend the rest of the trip thinking about love, or the Good Book, or family, or whatever gets your mind straight. Because the way we act when we get there is very important. The way the rest of your lives come out may depend on this. Let's get our butts in gear and our minds right, okay?"

Don stood up and began gathering up our trash. Barley seemed to shake herself and began to pack up the cooler. Adam unwrapped himself from the tree and wandered over to the car. I followed him. Barley and Don brought up the rear. Whew.

The four of us set out. One wise man and the three stooges.

The highway was more crowded when we got back on it. Don had put the top up, and so between the buzzing of cars passing by and the whooshing of the wind coming in the windows, our thoughts were almost drowned out. But not completely. We rode in silence for a long time, maybe even an hour. Don at the wheel, chewing on a toothpick, Adam beside him, his earbuds forgotten, immersed in the storm swirling around inside his head. I was behind Don, my head against the window frame, pretending to be asleep, but actually repeating *ohmygodohmygodohmygod* to myself like some sort of prayer. Barley, her hands clasped tightly in her lap, looked out the window, staring hard at the cornfields as if she could somehow read a message in the rows. We were a pitiful, sad group, I can tell you.

As we got farther north, the cornfields and cows gave way to forests and hills. Maybe mountains—I don't really know the true definition of what a mountain actually is. But it got very Paul Bunyany all of a sudden. The temperature dropped, too. As if we drove right into Bambi's bailiwick. We even rolled up the windows halfway. It was, literally, *cool.* Tall pine trees and lots of them. Like a Christmas tree farm gone wild. Deep shadows between them, with fallen logs and deep, brown mulchy carpet underneath. I kept expecting to see wildlife, like at least one deer or a bear or something. I guess there aren't any bears around highways. But it was beautiful and very soothing. The traffic thinned out, also.

Between stops for gas and peeing (these old model cars are not known for their highway mileage), we mused. Still not much for conversation after Don's sermon at the picnic area. The word *love* rang in my head. I guess all I'd thought about love up to now was the kind I *got*, mostly. I'd been secure in love right up until this summer. Dad sure kept us safe, and he took care of us at all times with his pharmaceutical knowledge. I hardly ever got sick, and when I did, I had all the cough medicine and Tylenol I needed. Roy knew how to head off a lot of illness. He was certified to give flu shots and stuff. So our family was hale and hearty.

And Mom? With all of the sterility and good food? She kept us healthy at home, too. No dirty clothes. No forgotten backpacks. We never ran out of juice for our devices. Winnie even plugged everybody's phones in at night. I always had plenty of hugs and bedtime stories. Not a worry in the world. And Aunt Iris? She was the finest of the fine. She filled my life with beautiful lullabies and chopsticks on the piano. She had all the best board games and the patience to go with them. Sleepovers galore.

I had Barley for a best friend and practically sister. The more I thought about it, the less I was prepared for all of this bliss of kidhood to end. I wanted to stay securely wrapped in all of this naiveté.

Does everybody get slammed in the head with adulthood like this, I wondered? You waft along, humming and eating popsicles, and then one day the world just falls apart. Is this what growing up means—facing hulking, ragged problems? I remembered one time when I was looking through the bookshelves at Iris's house. She had all the usual stuff: the Bible, Danielle Steel, *Gone with the Wind*, and things. But there was a big, yellow book called *The Power of Positive Thinking*. I asked Aunt

Iris what it was, and she said something like, "Oh, that's the mother of all self-help books."

When I asked her what self-help was, she said, "You know. Sometimes we have problems that we can't figure out how to fix. This book helps people look at their problems in a different way. Not so much like problems. More like challenges."

Funny. As the pine trees flew by and the breezes got more shadowy, I thought about this. Challenges. Maybe this summer was our first challenge. Probably not the first one for Mom and the rest of them. But for Adam, Barley, and me.

I have to tell you right now, I am not a fan of challenges. I think life shouldn't be so jolting for people. This was why I loved movies and wanted to write them: most of the time, everything worked out in movies. Two hours, two and a half, tops—the loose ends got tied right up, people learned their lessons, and we heaved big sighs of relief. But shoot. What if this was why everybody loved movies? What if those were the only times when the loose ends got tied up right and stuff ended happily? Winnie tried to tie up her loose end and look what happened. A major debacle. Frank was one HELL of a loose end. If only Winnie had just kept her loose end *loose*...

I sat in the car and let the wind blow my hair into my eyes, and I hoped I could measure up to this unwelcome challenge. I crossed my fingers and said a few more *ohmygods* for Adam and my and Barley's sakes. Then I fell asleep from the exertion.

> *A red 1960-something Mustang convertible hurtles northward. Inside, the occupants wrestle with this huge life challenge: In the front seat is a strapping bald man with aviator sunglasses and thick fingers, clutching*

> the black leather-and-chrome steering wheel, chewing thoughtfully on a toothpick. Beside him, a muscular, rangy boy with ginger curls and a tortured look, jumpy, his earbuds in, then out, then in again. In the back seat, one gleaming but worried-looking teenage girl, picking at her pink manicure and looking for an out. Beside her, a tortured wrinkle of a girl, her armpits soaked and her mind in a whirl. Background music: something anguished, like Beethoven. Buffeted by the wind, they ride along toward their doom. (Mandy—a bit overwrought; fix this part later.)

After a while, Don got off the highway and started driving on country roads. We began to pass small towns on huge lakes. Towns with names like Cherrydown and Crown Lake. There were scenic outlooks you could park on to see the gorgeousness. We stopped at one, and the view from beside the road was of a shiny, navy blue lake, with speedboats and skiers. Lots of woods around the lake, dotted with houses where docks were festooned with a rainbow of beach towels hanging to dry on railings. Porches with comfortable furniture.

We stopped in a town called Locust Lake for a pee and to check the map. Don didn't trust Siri. "Are we almost there?" Adam asked. It was close to dinnertime, and although Adam was a bundle of nerves, it never affected his need for french fries and large portions of meat.

Don consulted the map. The town where Marianne had her cabin was called Aldrich, after some scion who made a fortune in Cleveland and came up here for years, bringing his rich friends who built woody mansions, and founded the town. It sprang up sometime in the 1900s, and now there were lots of vacation cabins around its lake, one of them being Marianne's.

"I think it will be in another half hour or so. It looks pretty close, but it's hard to tell how the local roads will be. It won't be that long. Let's check the cooler. If we're low on sandwiches, we may want to buy more. You know, just in case they don't invite us to stay for dinner."

Adam looked very alarmed. As if he hadn't even considered this. Like Winnie would just throw her arms around us and rush to fry up some chicken. Barley opened the cooler.

"One turkey sandwich, three Snickers, plenty of Cokes left, and let's see—in the snack bag we have an assortment of peanuts, pretzels, Twizzlers, and two packs of beef jerky—eew, I hate that stuff.

"Okay, we have to be practical here," Barley continued. "If we aren't welcome at Casa Marianne, what will we do? Stick around? Sleep in the car and come back in the morning? Are there hotels in fair Aldrich?"

Don was the adult for *sure*. He said, "There's a Motel 6 on the road outside Aldrich. We don't have to worry about rooms, because places like that are almost never full, even in the busy summer season. Plus, I bet most people coming up here already have a summer home. Anyway, if we have to stay someplace, we can stay there. But I'm not sure about restaurants, so let's get a few sandwiches or something. Just in case, 'cause this Aldrich doesn't look very big on the map."

So we went into the minimart at the gas station (since now in America, there is no such thing as just a plain old gas station; they all have markets, sell ghastly souvenirs and stuff like milk, baked beans, diapers, and beer) and got some of those cheese and cracker packs, a loaf of bread, some bologna, mayo, and more chips. Because Adam must have his chips. Barley picked up a pack of paper towels, Cheez-Its, of course, plastic forks and knives, and a jar of peanut butter. We were ready for anything. Don threw in a couple six packs of beer (we might really need that) and paid for everything.

We piled back into the car for the final leg of this ungodly journey. This time, Barley was in the front seat beside Don, and Adam folded his legs into the back beside me. He looked like origami. Before he started the car, Don made this pronouncement:

"Okay, guys. When we get there, let me do the talking at first."

As if any of *us* wanted to.

Barley took the words right out of my mouth: "Don, do you have a certain speech planned or something?"

Don looked solemn. "Not really. But I think I'll be able to gauge pretty quickly how Iris feels about seeing me. Us. As for Winnie and Marianne, I don't have a clue what they might do. I mean, Winnie will probably be so relieved to see Adam that I figure she'll be kind of happy. I don't know Marianne at all. I don't know if she's pissed off at Frank for still being married. I mean, I'm sure pissed off at Iris about that. But anyway, it's a mystery. Like I said before, we have to keep ourselves under control if we want this thing to have any kind of solution, you know what I mean?"

We all nodded.

"Here's what I'm thinking: Iris is probably worried about how mad I am at her. And she's as guilty as Winnie for keeping a secret for so long. I'm figuring that she and Winnie might have softened up up a little. Since Marianne offered this whole cabin idea, I'm thinking she's holding some hard feelings toward Frank. I guess she isn't too mad at Iris for still being married, and at Winnie for spilling the beans, or she wouldn't have carried them off up here with her. Maybe it's the three of them against the world. Or maybe it's the three of them needing to take a time-out to sort through things. Whatever it is, we have to be careful. I'm electing myself as the only adult in this car to be the one to do the talking. Got it?"

Nods all around. I think we were relieved to have the countertop king as our advocate. We buckled our seat belts and got started. Yeah. The old classic movie line about doing that, because the ride was going to get bumpy? Well, that.

First off, the town of Aldrich was *small*. It consisted of one main street, very picturesque. Pavers, not concrete. Those old-fashioned iron streetlamps with actual gas running in them. Flickery. One fudge shop, a bakery featuring "local cherry pies and tarts" (yum), and an ice cream parlor. There was one "restaurant," called Snowy's Grill. As we passed, I looked inside, where a lady at a table in the front window was eating what looked like a giant burger. I wondered about obesity around here.

It was all-Americana gone North Woods, with lots of hand-painted signs, big tubs of mixed flowers that shouted "lots of fertilizer," tons of places to eat high-fructose corn syrup, and it looked impeccably attractive. All on the edge of a large lake. You could see to the other side; it wasn't Lake Michigan, but it was big enough. The whole place looked like a set right out of the movie inside my head.

The entire town was maybe the dozen buildings on the main block, and then all the houses and cottages surrounding it, in a real Norman Rockwell way. I really liked it. No wonder the people from the clotted cities in Ohio came up here for some air. It was refreshing.

Don drove up a lane with what he said were cherry orchards on both sides. It was like a leafy heaven. At the end was a small cabin made out of stone and wood. The porch was wood, but there were stone pillars holding up the low roof. Don said this was a Craftsman bungalow. The sides were filled by burly, tall trees. Deciduous and evergreen both. I don't know my trees well enough to go any further.

The rear of the cabin and the other houses on that side of the road smacked right up to the lake in their backyards. The foundation and the porch were stone. The stones were big and round and looked very solid. (Ha. Like a rock.) The wooden boards on the rest of the house were vertical, instead of horizontal, and they were painted dark green. Under the porch overhang was a wide screen door painted dark brown, almost black. On either side of it were big, wide windows, also trimmed in that murky brown. Above the porch roof jutted a dormer with double windows in the same trim color.

Apparently Marianne loved flowers, because there were tubs and pots of pink geraniums, orangey marigolds, and some really frilly blue-and-white flowers that looked a tiny bit like bells. She had scads of them all over the place. The front walk was stone, too—but these stones were gray and flat. They looked as if people had been wearing them down for eons. And there was a porch swing with (you guessed it) floral Pottery Barn upholstery. I loved the cabin with all my heart right away. It looked as if it had jumped right out of my imagination—the kind you float around in right before you go to sleep, when you want to conjure up all the coziness you can.

I felt as if I were Goldilocks, and those three beds were in there just waiting for me. I envied my mom, getting to stay here. And I *really* envied Marianne and Frank, for having it anytime they wanted to come. Then I was literally dumbstruck. With the thought that this lovely dream place was kind of in *my* family now. The joy of it. Or the pain of it, depending on what happened up here.

We *scrambled* out of the car, mainly because, for once, it was Barley saying she needed to pee for the past half hour. But Don's words rang in our heads, and we let him take the lead toward the door. We marched single file past the pots and a rough-hewn bench in the front yard, past a concrete bunny sitting under the charmingly gnarly yew bushes against the steps and, when assembled, Don gave us the once over, nodded firmly, and knocked on the door. Actually, he used the pinecone door knocker.

We waited. I felt sweat dribble down my temple into my ear. Adam cleared his throat and shuffled nervously. Barley looked serene, but the vein in her neck was a little bulgy. Nothing. Don knocked again. We waited. Nada.

"Shit! They aren't home!" Adam did a twitchy frustration dance across the porch and banged his head on an asparagus fern hanging basket. "Shit! There are plants all over the fricking place!"

"Maybe they're around back. On the dock, or swimming or something. Let me go see." I wandered around the side of the house, and once again my heart leaped (okay—too much?). But it was even more gorgeous than the front. A screened-in porch. Hummingbird feeders. Beautiful, worn stone steps leading down from the screen door to the lawn. A grassy slope surrounded the house on both sides, like parentheses with flowering bushes. White flowering bushes that smelled like vanilla. Stepping stones in the soft grass swooped down gently to a small dock.

There were those comfortable L.L. Bean Adirondack chairs on the dock—three of them, worn and peeling white. One had an open book on the seat, the other had *my mom's* blue-and-green striped beach towel thrown casually over the back, and there were three pairs of flip-flops strewn around. I wanted to go bury my head in Winnie's towel. Instead, I looked around the back (more flowers in big concrete urns at each side of the porch steps, but these were white and yellow), scanned the lake, covering my eyes against the glare, and saw no one. I went back to the group.

"The back is to die for, by the way. We could swim right off the dock. But they aren't out there."

"I guess they aren't home, kids." Don shook his head. "It's early yet. Maybe they're at the store or something. Or maybe they went out to eat."

"What, *fudge*? It seems to me that the only thing you can get around here is that or cherry pie." I looked at Barley, who by this time had her legs crossed. "Don, we can't wait here. Barley needs a potty stop or else."

"Okay. I did notice a gas station outside of town, and down the road by the Motel 6 was a little diner kind of place. We can go there for some food and maybe see if we can reserve some rooms—you know, just in case."

"We'll get some actual food, not snacks, freshen up," (Barley, come *on*) "and come back?" Barley asked.

"Yup." So we followed Don back down the path of my dreams and squished back into the damn car. Adam claimed the front, and Barley and I resigned ourselves once again to the now snack-bestroon (I made that up; great word) backseat.

"Wait a minute. We may be overestimating the element of surprise. Don, should you call Iris on her cell and warn her we're here?" I said.

Don turned around to look at us, eyebrows high. "What if they don't want us here? They could refuse to see us."

"Yeah." Adam concurred. "If that happens, I guess I'll have to get used to the idea that I now have an extra father and no mother. This whole thing blows." His head hit the back of the seat heavily, and his lids fell. Nobody can look sadder than a distressed ginger kid in a Mustang. No one.

"Okay. I'll call. Come on, this may take a while." Don got out of the car and headed for the bench in the front yard. The one surrounded by blooms and lush grass. Barley and I got out, and Barley strongly suggested that we look for some bushes. Her bladder. There was a group of them at the side of the cabin. Not the best, but it would do. I covered for her, and Barley managed to take care of her business. Whew. Then we dropped down into the coolness of the grass and looked up into the Michigan clouds. If God was up there, we needed him or her. Adam stayed in the car in his freckled trance.

The clouds in Michigan seemed fluffier than the ones at home. Maybe we have too much particulate matter in northern Ohio or something. The clouds in Framington have some grit around the edges. The ones up here looked like marshmallow fluff. And were floatier. It was clean and cool up here, not so oveny, the way it is at home in late summer. It smelled like the color green. I wondered if it smelled like wood fires in the winter. Framington has ordinary odors. It smells grayish, like mud, in winter, and plain dust-dirty in summer. Or like french fries, if you get close to McDonald's.

After we finished in the bushes, we sat and eavesdropped on Don's side of the phone conversation while gazing at the sky. Don started with a very friendly greeting and statement of our whereabouts, and then he was silent for quite a while. Oh, no. Not a good sign. Then he said, "Okay. Time is fine, but we can't stay more than one night because we aren't packed for it, Roy is alone and worrying down there, and we aren't on vacation, you know." Then he said, "Bye, hon."

The "hon" was encouraging. Barley caught that, too, and she sat up, a piece of grass sticking out of her ear, and asked, "What did she say? We have to spend the night? Where are they? Are they coming home now? Are they fine with us? Mad, what?"

"Whoa, whoa! Too many questions! Wait a minute." Don motioned for us to wait up a sec, and then he shouted out to the man-child in the car: "HEY, ADAM—COME UP HERE! WE HAVE A PLAN!"

The car door opened, and Adam unfolded himself out of it, slammed the door with finality, and turned to face us, leaning against the hot, red paint, his arms folded on the black canvas top. Squinting! He was clearly tired, scared, and reluctant to join us. "WHAT? DO I HAVE TO COME UP THERE? JUST TELL ME HERE!"

"I'll get him." Barley rose in one fluid motion, all grace and glory, brushing off the Michigan lawn from her clothes. I watched her approach my brother, her calves flashing and her arms swinging. She seemed to be, right then, the woman she would become—a lovely, competent, golden thing, reliable and wise. A gift to all of us schmucks without a clue. She flowed beautifully down to the car, and walked around it to stand next to Adam. She gently turned him to face her, and they conversed, with Barley's arm resting soothingly on Adam's shoulders.

Watching the two of them, I thought about how many times Barley had told me she was completely certain that she would marry my brother. I considered how seamlessly Barley fit right into our lives. She was more than my best friend. Barley was a presence in our lives. She sat at the kitchen table at meals with the Heaths, and we always welcomed her. Heck, dinners without her were kind of tasteless.

Barley accompanied me everywhere, and Winnie always trusted the both of us, even though one of us clearly had the kind of looks that might invite trouble. But Barley always steered clear of trouble. She helped Dad at the store. She adored Iris's house and loved the nights we spent lying on the soft carpet at the cottage, listening to Iris play her piano. Barley was already a part of our family. I bet not one of us has ever considered what it would be like at the Heaths without her.

After what seemed like a half hour but was a few minutes, they walked toward the house holding hands. But it wasn't a "lover" hold, more like some nice Girl Scout leading an orphan back to the orphanage (great scene for the movie, but I didn't have time to frame it in my mind at the moment). They came up the walk and sank into the grass beside me. Don, looming over us on the bench, resembled the incarnation of our destruction (okay, I was just brainstorming the scene).

"Here's the situation," Don told us. "Iris and the girls" (inward groan on my part) "are at a neighbor's cabin for dinner. The Grouses, or the Grosses, or something. They don't feel it would be good manners to leave. Plus, Winnie apparently almost blew a gasket when she heard we're here. Iris feels that the wise thing would be for us to go get a hamburger at Snowy's Grill, which is on Main Street. Well, it's the main street, but it's actually called Front Street. Then we can check in at the motel. They'll expect us at around ten tomorrow morning. I guess that means there'll be some sort of confrontation or reunion but it won't keep us from getting back on the road home by noon."

"Don," Barley wondered. "Is this good news or bad news, do you think? How did Iris sound?"

"She was surprised, I'll give you that. When she covered the phone to tell the others, I didn't exactly hear screams, but they were definitely not laughs of joy in the background."

Adam rolled over onto his stomach in the grass. He buried his head in his arms and moaned.

I took this as my cue. "Well, guys, I for one have high hopes for Snowy's. From the sound of it, we can get cheeseburgers and ice cream. Let's concentrate on getting some decent calories into ourselves, shall we?"

Barley added, "Oooh. A cheeseburger sounds heavenly. With extra cheese on it."

Chapter Eleven

Dinner was great. Snowy's was as old school as Don's car. Black-and-white linoleum, knotty pine (Don said that's what it was; I just thought it was dirty yellow wood) paneling, waitresses in black dresses and white aprons and white sneakers. Of course, they called us all "sweetie." The food was greasy great. We all had cheeseburgers and fries, and Barley was in heaven because they even had cheese fries. Double cheese on the burger *and* cheese fries. How this girl stayed so pimple-free and skinny was beyond me.

We were stuffed beyond belief when we checked into our motel rooms. They apparently don't leave the light on for you at this one. Two double beds with bedspreads the color of rusty nails. Slightly lighter orange walls. A pitted desk with an old box TV (this road trip was turning out to be all over with the vintage). A sticky-looking wooden chair pulled up to the desk, blocking the view of the TV. A metal rack with four bent hangers. One picture hanging crookedly above the bed. I think it was supposed to be abstract art. It looked more like somebody swallowed a box of crayons and then vomited on the canvas.

Our room was clean. It smelled like vinegar and bleach. But that was about all the positive I could say about it. Barley immediately wanted to take a shower. She waltzed into the bathroom and screamed.

"OH, MY GOD! DO YOU CALL THESE PLACEMATS OR TOWELS?"

I was too busy moving the chair and trying to get a decent channel on the box TV. Barley exploded out of the bathroom, waving a washcloth. "This is what they call a towel. Feel it."

I felt it. "This is a little harsh. More like sandpaper. Barley, this can't be the towel. Did you look under the sink?"

She snorted. "There's *floor* under the sink. It's just a sink jutting out of the wall. There's a shelf above the toilet with exactly two of these rags on it. The washcloths are *these*." She held up a grayish cloth the size of a bar of soap. "So really, the question is, are you going to take a shower? Because if so, we each get one placemat and one rag. Impossible."

"Go over to Don and Adam's room and ask if they can spare a towel. Or go to the front desk for extras."

Barley sighed. "You know that woman at the front desk has missing teeth. I'm scared of her. Come with?" She gave me her most winning smile. Shit.

We put our shoes back on and wandered down to the office, where, sure enough, the lady with missing teeth was watching a similarly grainy version of *Jeopardy* on her box TV. Her name tag read "Loretta."

We politely asked Loretta if there were any extra towels. It was really hard for her to tear herself away from Alex Trebek, but she reluctantly turned to us and smiled graciously, baring her toothless gums. (How she got any kicks out of *Jeopardy* was intriguing. She couldn't possibly know the answer to any of the questions, could she?)

"Girls, we don't normally give out extras. We have just enough linens. The service don't come as often as they used to. But seeing as how you're both nice, I'll go look in the back. Keep your eye on the desk for me, okay?"

She turned to leave, and we watched her buttocks kind of follow the rest of her out the door.

Barley whispered, "This is the best argument for staying in school, right here." I had to nod in total agreement.

Loretta came back, beaming. She held out four placemats/towels. "Here you go, girls. You can take showers and wash your hair! Just don't let on I gave you these."

We promised. On the way back to our room, walking along the stained concrete corridor with the spotty green stucco walls, I tried not to brush against anything. Once inside our room, we both fell onto our beds (Winnie had taught me to remove the bedspreads immediately—God only knows what happens on top of motel bedspreads) laughing.

"Yes, we can wash our hair, and dry ourselves all over with these luxurious and plush towels! Then we can wrap ourselves in them when the room service arrives with our gourmet breakfast! I think I'm going to order eggs over easy, some croissants, and a latte—you?"

I nodded, not really listening. "I wonder what Don and Adam are doing. They can't be watching TV with this reception. I wonder if they have a deck of cards or anything. I really don't need to take a shower now. I can do it in the morning. Let's go over to their room."

Adam and Don's room was three doors down. We knocked, and Don answered the door. "Welcome to our suite, ladies! Come right in." He motioned for us to enter the way they do in those old English movies with butlers and footmen. Inside, Adam was lying on his bedspread, *ick*, arms behind his head, staring at the ceiling.

"Oh, my God, Adam! What has Mom always told us? GET UP AND TAKE OFF THE BEDSPREAD. You could get some kind of disease!"

Don laughed, but he folded his bedspread down and draped it over the desk chair. "Come, on, Adam— you heard the lady. She's probably right."

Adam looked at us witheringly, but he complied. Unlike Don, Adam got up, stripped the rusty old thing off his bed and shoved it between the bed and the wall. Then he sat down on the edge and asked, "Now what?"

"Do you have cards or anything? The TV reception in this place blows. What are we going to do all night?"

Adam looked glum. Barley sat down on Don's bed, facing Adam. She pulled the drawer in the bedside table out and peered in. "Nope. Just the Bible."

Don cleared his throat loudly. "I wasn't a Boy Scout for nothing. I planned ahead, just in case of this eventuality. I have my instrument in the car. Shall I go get it?"

Just what we needed up here in the wilds of Michigan. Accordion music in a seedy motel. In defense of the Motel 6 people, not actually seedy. Just a little worn around the edges and tired. With intermittent linen service and a toothless concierge.

Barley jumped up and clapped. "Yes, yes! We can have our own polka party!"

Don exited, grinning. Adam rolled his eyes. "Can this nightmare get any worse?"

"Oh, Adam. We need something fun. Don's really good. Plus, he brought us up here out of the goodness of his heart. To help you and your mom. So be polite and try to work up just a little enthusiasm, will you?" Barley punched his arm repeatedly as she said this.

I added, "You don't have to admit to anybody that we had a polka party in a Motel 6. It can be our guilty little secret."

A laugh kind of erupted out of Adam's inner depths. He threw himself backwards onto the bed and roared until tears spilled down from his eyes into his ears. Barley bounced on the bed beside him, so that Adam jounced around, his arms flailing. Ha! I heard Don's footsteps coming down the hall, and I opened the door. There he stood, with what we all thought was his black duffle bag. But it was his accordion case. "Come in, Mr. Welk, come in!" I stepped back with a flourish. "Let the concert begin!"

I took the bedspread off the desk chair and threw it over on top of Adam's, and Don put his case on the desk and took out his accordion. He slung the straps over his shoulders and sat down on the chair, settling the instrument in his lap. He pulled it open and closed a few times, playing some chords. They resounded off the walls. Like, I mean, a massive acoustical assault. You know, accordions are really loud.

"Let's start with a few classics, shall we? I always like the 'Beer Barrel' to begin. Oh, one more thing. Mandy, unzip the side pocket of my case. Yes, there. I always carry sheets of lyrics with me, just in case. Pass those out."

Sure enough, Don had copied sheets of a whole bunch of song titles and lyrics, all neatly stapled. Who was this guy?

"Don, where do you play that you have to carry around these handouts?" I asked, trying not to sound at all judgmental.

"I play for nursing homes and church socials. Some weddings. I get little gigs all the time. It's fun, and people seem to really enjoy it. I try to bring people out of their shells with this, you know? I play old standards that most people remember from when they were young. I engage the audience and try to get them to share their memories, sing along, and even dance."

Oh, man. I looked over at Adam, who may have looked more miserable than this the day he got his wisdom teeth out, but not much. Barley was beaming graciously, naturally. She reached over and pinched Adam in the side and hissed, "Sit *up*!"

"Okay, then, kids. Page one in your handouts. 'The Beer Barrel Polka.'"

And he ramped up and into:

> *Roll out the barrel*
> *We'll have a barrel of fun . . .*

We started out mumbling along, reluctantly. Cordially, so as not to hurt Don's feelings. But he played three choruses. I mean, really. What can you do after two choruses of "Beer Barrel" but get into it? Give in and go with the flow. By the end of the song, we all felt cheerier. Who knew the polka was fun and not all that embarrassing? I started to feel one with the fifties generation. Kind of.

"Don, what about 'Love Me Tender'? Do that!" I couldn't believe I was asking this. Me, *Elvis?*

We got really corny on that one. Then Adam requested, "Born in the USA." A classic. During the chorus of that, someone in the next room began to knock on the wall. Uh-oh. Don ignored it and kept right on going. We launched into "The Bitch is Back" from there (you can't expect old people to know current rock). We were really starting to, as Don remarked, "Groove!" Predictably, we were interrupted by a banging on our door. We stopped cold. Barley whispered, "Shit, now we're in trouble! What should we do?"

"For starters, answer the door." Don took off his accordion and set it reverently on the tatty beige carpet and walked over to the door and opened it. It was Loretta.

"Mister, that accordion you got is pretty damn loud, you know."

Don interrupted her with his palm. "I'm very sorry—"

Loretta interrupted Don right back. "If you're going to play it, you might as well come down to the lobby." (*euphemism*) "You might as well do a concert down there instead of up here. We have chairs and things. And Joe Tracewell is stayin' here tonight. He's a regular. A trucker, you know? He plays harmonica. Come on down." She smiled. I was beginning to like her smile, despite that big gap in the front. Her gums were friendly.

We trooped down to the lobby, Don toting his accordion and handouts, and, sure enough, Loretta had set up some folding chairs. Six people were milling around, drinking free coffee from the machine in the corner.

Loretta beamed her smile at all of us. "I guess I'm the MC here tonight. This is gonna be fun, you guys. This is Don. He's the one we've been hearing. These are his kids." (We didn't bother to correct her.) Loretta went around the group. "This here is Joe Tracewell. He plays harmonica. He stays here when he's on the road. I don't know the rest of you. Why don't you tell us your names and stuff?"

There was a great big guy named Ron. Curly black hair and lots of tattoos. He was also a trucker, but he didn't know Joe. Then there was Bill Sells, a very skinny and hesitant black man. He had a sweet smile and a grill. Well, a gold tooth, but kinda hip. He sat down in one of the folding chairs after telling us that he was going to visit his granddaughter up north. He sipped his coffee and made himself very small in his chair.

Then there were the Hulls, a middle-aged couple from Hanover, Pennsylvania. Flora and Ralph. They wore jeans and Penn State sweatshirts. They both had pot bellies and plump, pink cheeks. They said they traveled around the country in their RV but liked to stay in motels once in a while, to "get away." (Why in this place, I wondered.) And Loretta. The missing front teeth. She told us she lived on a farm outside Aldrich. Born and raised. Three children, all gone now. She worked part-time at the Motel 6 to help out her husband, Burt, who lost his job as a welder five years before this and now mostly did handyman jobs. I wondered about Burt, and if he had a few missing teeth.

"Grab a chair, and let's have some music!" Loretta was really workin' it.

The "lobby" wasn't very big. It was really just another motel room set up with a worn front counter. A card table in the corner was covered with a pink lace plastic tablecloth, coffee maker, cups, cereal bowls filled with packets of sugar and chemical creamer, the equally useless stick stirrers, and those cocktail napkins that are good for absolutely nothing, either.

Four black pleather chairs marched along one wall, like in a doctor's waiting room. Oh, and the fake ficus. All motels are apparently required to have at least one fake ficus. Loretta had pulled out a bunch of folding chairs from somewhere, and she set them up in front of the doctor's office ones. It was a veritable little auditorium.

What could we do? We sat down. Adam blushed with embarrassment, setting off his red hair and freckles flamingly, Barley flashed her million-dollar smile and sat down beside Bill Sells, and I sat on her other side. Adam sat between tattooed Ron and Flora Hull. He looked tortured. Ralph Hull remained standing, like a man who thought he might be leaving any second. I didn't blame him.

Joe Tracewell pulled up a chair beside Don in the front and pulled a big silver harmonica out of his plaid shirt pocket. "Well, now, Don. Do you know 'Pretty Woman'?"

"I do!" And so they started. It was pretty good. Joe Tracewell followed Don's lead and kind of filled in the background. He seemed to know just how to do that, like those studio musicians they hire to come in and somehow make the lead singer sound better. Don pointed to the handouts he'd put on the floor, and I jumped up and passed them around. "If you would like to sing along," Don said. Then they played "Too Fat Polka" and that nursing home favorite, "The Band Played On." Things were starting to get a little bit static. Adam was fidgeting.

They played "C. C. Rider," then Bill Sells raised his hand and half stood. "You boys know 'Frankie and Johnny Were Lovers'? 'Cause I can sing along on that one."

Don said, "I can fake it. Joe?" Joe nodded. They launched into it, and Bill Sells's voice just wailed into it like a man in pain. A man in pain who could sing the shit out of a song. Then Bill started in on "Bess, You Is My Woman Now," all by himself. He just grew in stature and coolness, right before our eyes. Bill had enough soul for ten men. It was like, yeah, a scene.

A cheap motel "lobby." Walls that were probably once tan, now a faded and smoky yellow. Assembled around the brown-and-white speckled linoleum floor are chairs filled with tonight's detritus of the road. A plump, sunburned couple wearing Penn State sweatshirts and a kind of hysterical friendliness. They seem to have been traveling the roads of America hoping for friendly faces and some fellowship—something that they obviously have not had much of in their lives. A thin, mellow black man with a brilliant, white smile, laced with gold—mysterious. A mountain of a trucker with sexy black curls and tattoos of Elvis. A plump woman with missing teeth and a name tag; she is smarter than she looks. (Here is a place to bust up a stereotype about women who have missing teeth and also women who have to work night jobs—cast somebody like Kathy Bates or maybe even Amy Adams; she'll get an Oscar nomination again.)

A massive man in plaid with a harmonica in his pocket and an easygoing manner. Two teenage girls, one beautiful and one completely aware of the contrast between her friend's beauty and her own ordinariness. A stunning red-haired boy on the brink of becoming a brooding and extremely desirable man. Finally, a countertop king with a gleaming accordion. A motley assemblage as the scene opens: stiff politeness, a lot of milling around and throat clearing. Certainly their faces reflect the strangeness of finding themselves all together on this particular night in this particular cardboard motel.

When the music starts, the transformation does, too. The accordionist gets more relaxed and easy with each song. His bald head goes from anxious beet red to a smooth, creative flush. He loosens up and plays with flourishes and improvisation. The plaid-shirted trucker is a real musician, and he blows that harmonica till it sounds like ten harmonicas and then some.

It's a party. It's friends. It's adults and children who really, really want to stop being children right now but still have a long way to go.

They take a break to get coffee and Cokes out of the vending machine. The couple from Pennsylvania disappear and come back bearing cookies, fresh baked. (There will be an important plot development in this scene from the movie. Background music—a segue from polka, gradually getting more steam-driven: think modified Zydeco. Or maybe some B. B. King. Research this, Mandy.)

Anyway, when Bill Sells started to sing, we got an education in music and R & B. That man requested songs I'd never even heard of. Like "One Room Country Shack," and "Lord, Lord, Lord." I bet Bill Sells was a preacher. His voice testified to the ceiling, out the windows, and into the tall trees of north Michigan. Here's the thing: Don Horley was a hell of a musician, too, because he just listened to Bill sing the song once, and he *had* it! Joe, who had to have been more than a trucker—maybe in some crazy cool band—just fell right in. It was cosmic, no other word for it.

Of course, Barley got up and started dancing. Ralph and Flora did, too. Nobody cared if they looked old, crooked, or totally cool, we just started grooving! Barley pulled Adam up. Bill Sells was busy singin' the blues. Loretta and I danced. That toothless woman knew how to lay it *down!* Ron the trucker was stompin' and rockin' those Elvis tattoos.

Before we knew it, it was very late. We were all pooped. Flora's chocolate chip cookies were gone. But it was the best party I think I've ever been to with old people. (Now I know that "you're as old as you feel" must be the truth.)

We helped Loretta straighten up. As I collected the empty Styrofoam cups and jammed them in a trash bag,

I saw Loretta put her arm around Adam's shoulder and whisper something to him. The chairs were folded up and stashed, the lobby restored to its usual tired orderliness. We reluctantly left to go back to our rooms. "Keep in touch!" "Yes, we'll leave our email address at the desk when we check out." and "Drive safe out there!"

In the corridor upstairs, we waited while Don put the accordion back in the Mustang. We hung over the railing, enjoying the cool Michigan night and the stars. We don't see many stars in Framington but we don't really look up into the sky much, either. I guess it's kind of like having a great big old stain on the ceiling—you notice it at first, and before long, you never even see it when you walk into the room.

"Hey, Adam, what were you and Loretta confabbing about during the cleanup, anyway?" Barley asked.

"Oh. See, I told her a little about Mom and Fletch while we were sitting and eating Flora's cookies. Loretta said that she'd been thinking about it afterwards, at the end of the party." (Adam called it a *party*; that made me so happy.) "When we were leaving, she said, 'Honey, give your mama the benefit of the doubt. That's all you need to do. Forgiving may be too much for a boy your age. But the benefit of the doubt, if you push it into a mess? It loosens it up just enough to let you fix things.' What do you think that means?"

I smiled and leaned back against the greasy stucco. "It means, bro, that Loretta is some kind of homespun genius. You better think about what she said."

Then Adam surprised the shit out of me, for one. He probably sent Barley to heaven because he smiled and said, "No shit, Mand. No shit." Then he leaned over, gathered Barley up in his arms, and kissed her on the lips like Ryan Gosling or something. Barley swooned, and I dropped the key twice before getting our door open and shoving Barley inside. Before I shut us in for the night,

I called out, "Goodnight, Don, see you at about nine in the morning! *Wake us up!*" I punched Adam in the shoulder, nearly knocking him down. Then I shut our door and locked it.

"I told you I was going to marry your brother."

A box of Frosted Flakes and a gallon of milk were on the card table in the lobby, and beside them some paper bowls and napkins along with plastic spoons. Not the best breakfast, not the worst. Adam had two bowls, I had one, and Barley had four flakes and three coffees. Don just had coffee. Loretta wasn't working. Instead, there was a man behind the counter with a nametag that said "Dan."

Apparently, Dan hated his job, because he scowled the entire time we were eating, and he kept his head down. I wondered if Dan and Loretta could possibly be related; then I realized that just because you had a missing tooth, it didn't make you somebody's son.

Don crumpled up his cup and glanced at his watch. "You all ready? It's nine thirty."

Adam shook his head. "I won't ever be ready for this. But let's get it over with."

I was worried, all right. I also thought that just maybe today would be the end of this garbage that we'd been going through all summer. Nobody's life could be a daytime drama forever, right? I was envisioning lots of hugging and crying, then a caravan back to Framington, with everyone involved heaving giant sighs of relief all the way back. But I also had my fingers crossed, literally and figuratively.

Nobody said much on the drive to Marianne's house. Instead, we let the cool air ruffle our hair and zoom around the windshield. There were a few plump clouds in the piercing blueness of the sky, and "crisp" was the only adjective for the weather up here.

When we stopped in the driveway, I immediately noticed that Marianne was standing on the porch, looking out for us. As soon as Don put on the brakes, Marianne hurtled down the steps and rushed the car.

"This can't be good," Adam said.

Whoa. Marianne nearly fell against the driver's side of the car. "Don't even bother to get out! There's been a crisis. I don't think now is the time for you to introduce your family drama."

We looked at each other in complete confusion. "What do you mean?" Don asked.

Marianne closed her eyes for a sec, as if she was trying to wish us away. When she opened them, there we four were, as big as life and about to self-combust.

"We just got a call from Mrs. Crowder. Apparently, Roy had a little heart attack this morning. He's going to be fine, but you need to turn this car around and go back home, pronto. We're packing up now, leaving just as soon as I can close things off here—I have to turn off the water and shut down the electricity and things."

"I need to see Mom!" Adam and I both said it simultaneously. I tried to get out of the car, but Marianne gestured wildly, "No, no! She doesn't want to see you! She's in a state of hysteria. If she sees Adam, I don't know what she will do! Go home, go home! Right now!" With that, Marianne bolted off and disappeared around the side of the house.

"Wait a minute. I'm going to call Iris." Don pulled out his cell phone. Adam looked as if he might vomit. I felt like fainting. Barley got out her phone to call her mom.

What seemed like a decade passed.

The first one to hang up was Don. "Okay." But Barley held up her hand to shush him. So we waited another decade while Barley finished listening to her mom. She finally ended the call.

"WHAT, WHAT?" Adam shouted.

"Okay, let's get moving. We can talk as we go," Don said as he backed down the drive. "Here's what Iris said: Roy apparently went out to the front yard to get the paper this morning, and he collapsed. Luckily, a person was walking by with her dog, and she saw it and called 911. The ambulance got there almost immediately, and they took him to Framington Memorial. He's in ICU as a precaution, but they think he'll be just fine. A small attack. He'll need a stent, and they're putting one in ASAP. This is why Winnie is hysterical, because she isn't going to be right there at his side. She wants to get the hell home."

I turned to Barley. "What else did your mom say?"

"The same. He'll be fine. My mom's at the hospital right now with my dad. They're going to stay all day, but they're not allowed in the ICU because they aren't family. So your dad is all alone."

"OH, MY FREAKING GOD! THIS IS ALL MY FAULT!" Adam was nearly bursting.

Luckily, he was in the back beside me, and I could grab his hand, hard. "Adam, we'll be home in about five or six hours. So will Mom. Dad will be okay. We have cell phones, and we can keep checking in."

Adam shrieked, "Oh, my God—let's call the hospital. Why haven't we CALLED THE HOSPITAL?"

"Calm down. I'll do it." I pulled out my cell and Googled Framington Memorial Hospital, Framington, Ohio. Then I pushed "call." Finally, ringing.

"Framington Memorial. How can I help you?"

"My dad, Roy Heath, had a heart attack this morning. I think he's in the ICU, or he's in surgery getting a stent. Oh. My name is Mandy Heath. We're on our way home from Michigan, and my mom is too. We're in separate cars. Anyway, is my dad okay? Can you give me some information?" She said to hold on, and it took *a million years*, but she finally connected me with the nurses' station in the ICU. By this time, I'd begun to stutter. "H-hello, I a-am Mandy Heath. My d-dad is in there? He's all alone; we're coming from Michigan, and so is m-my mom. How is my dad?"

It was very reassuring, thank God. As I listened, Adam proceeded to crawl out of his skin, Barley bit her nails (she *never* does this), and Don steered, but with his head craned as far back toward me in the rear as possible.

I guess they knew things were all fine, because I guess I began to grin like a fool. I ended the call and let out a cleansing breath. "You guys. It's okay. She says he's in good spirits, and he knows we're all coming. He says for us to drive carefully." (S*uch a dad.*) "It was mild, and only one artery was badly clogged. The stent, a better diet, and rehab should be all he needs. He can't talk to me, but he told this all to the nurse. He's kind of drugged right now, because he goes into surgery in a few minutes for the stent. Oh, yeah, and the nurse says not to worry. Oh, and that the Crowders are in the family waiting room, and Mr. Fletcher just arrived. Huh. Frank is there."

"But this doesn't mean that you have to comply with the speed limit, Don." Barley was a good person. She sat with the GPS system turned on, peering at her cell screen. With her and Siri up front navigating, I felt confident. "Don't they say you can go ten miles over the limit without getting stopped? And anyway, if we are, we have a medical excuse. Let's step on it!"

Don looked at Barley for a sec and pulled his shoulders up. Then I guess he realized that Barley is right 90 percent of the time. He leaned forward and blasted us into the seventy-five miles-an-hour zone—the hell with the cops.

It was silent for about fifteen minutes, as we each wandered around in our own heads. I pictured Mom nearly bursting a vein, stressing over how her one little confession mushroomed into this gigantic calamity. I worried about her feeling helpless and so far away from Dad.

From the congested red desperation on Adam's face, I knew he was reliving the entire Fourth of July party, and playing it over and over in his mind. How saying things like "I hate you" to your mom can unravel your family.

Barley. I bet she was figuring out some sort of strategy to save us, and I wondered if that was possible, even for her. And good old Don. He threw himself into the breach. Even though he was in love with a woman who never even told him that she was still married to a hunky saxophonist who turned out to be the actual baby daddy of her nephew. Apparently, Winnie and Iris attracted a certain kindness and loyalty in their men. As far as that goes, I considered Fletch; he was turning out to be a sterling guy as well. Somewhere behind us, probably going ninety miles an hour, medical excuse waving like a flag, was Aunt Iris's car, Iris flooring it like a NASCAR driver, Winnie and Marianne egging her on.

We stopped once to pee and refuel. Nobody wanted to eat much, so we passed around the last bags of peanuts. Don got a Coke from the vending machine at the rest stop. We were somewhere near the Ohio-Michigan border when we noticed the coolness of the North evaporating into the searing August of Ohio. When we scrambled back into the car, Don said, "Same positions. I need Barley up front. Only one Coke; we share. We can't afford too many more pee stops."

Chapter Twelve

I bet even people who work in hospitals hate them. They try to make them seem welcoming and soothing. There are plants everywhere, and when you go in to visit somebody, they station kindly old ladies at the information desk. When we rushed into the main lobby, a bluish-haired lady with "Abby" on her nametag smiled warmly and gave us coupons for free cups of coffee and ushered us toward the bank of elevators that would carry us up to the Intensive Care Unit.

It doesn't matter whether you get free coffee, sit in a fake jungle, or listen to the classical music piped in to the waiting area—it's still a hospital where people are terribly sick, and a lot of them die. And today, Roy Heath, the dearest man in the world, was *not* going to be one of them.

The ICU was a weird, otherworldly place. This one was kind of like a dark pod, with a cockpit in the center where the nurses worked. Blinking computer screens and phones and lots of charts and papers were scattered all over the workspace. It was the only illuminated area. All around it was purple darkness with blinking green, red, white, and blue lights. Encircling the nurse's station like a satellite were rooms with the patients in them, but they weren't like normal hospital rooms: they had glass walls.

When you're sick enough to be in the ICU, the docs and nurses need to see you all the time. So can family members, and it was frightening. Every single patient looked like a science experiment, all tubed up and pale. Since the only two people they let go up to the ICU were me and Adam, we clutched each other.

"You are the Heaths? Oh, good news. Your father isn't here anymore. He had his stent put in at three this afternoon, and he stayed in recovery for about an hour; then he was put in a standard room. Let me check. Yes. He's in room 2008 on the second floor. You can go down there now. Maybe you can have dinner with him."

Dinner? I looked at my cell. It was six o'clock. I'd lost track of time completely. I wondered if Mom was here yet. They won't let you use your cell phone inside the hospital, so none of us could call her.

As we rode down in the elevator, Adam said, "I'm scared."

"Me, too. But they say Dad will be okay. This wasn't a big heart attack."

Adam shut his eyes. "No. I'm scared Mom will blame me for this. First, I hate her, and now she probably hates me."

"We don't have time to think about all of that now. Adam, you don't hate Mom. I know she doesn't hate you. And blame? Blaming people for stuff doesn't get any of us anywhere. Let's both shut up about the whole family dynamic thing and just be with Dad. Okay, Adam?" I nudged him.

> *Two despondent kids in an elevator. Hospital linoleum and stainless steel. Baroque music (Muzak) piped in, the strains of a harpsichord plunk mildly. The teens are disheveled after a long drive in the heat, their hair knotted from the wind of the convertible,*

> their underarms stained with sweat. The girl, who knows that the next twenty-four hours will be crucial to the entire family, looks at her tight-wound brother, his eyes ringed with dark purple circles, his lips taut with fear. They are without their mother and maybe going to lose their dad. The girl, who has no experience with this kind of emergency, her black eyes deep with concern and her head aching, leans against the elevator wall, hearing the music but not listening to it. The elevator doors glide open to their fate. (This might be a bit overdramatic—Mandy will work on it, perhaps adding comic relief somehow.)

When we got out of the elevator, we saw the three Crowders, Don, and Frank in the waiting area. No worried looks or furrowed brows, thank God.

Barley stood up and smiled. "Your dad is just fine. He's sleeping right now. Your mom just called the nurses' station. She and Iris will be here in about a half hour."

Mrs. Crowder, her blonde hair only a little less golden than her daughter's, gave me a hug that was almost as good as Mom's. Don put his arm around Adam's shoulders. Mr. Crowder asked if any of us wanted anything, "A coffee, or a sandwich? I can run down to the vending machines. Or if you want something from the cafeteria, I can get it. Or you can go in with your dad if you want to."

"The nurse in the ICU said we could eat dinner with Dad. I want to wait until he wakes up and Mom gets here. But thanks." Adam smiled, but it was one of those tight ones that looked as if it hurt his cheeks. You know the kind—the smile you put on when you're waiting to see if you made the softball team right before they post the list outside the gym.

So we all sat down. The waiting area was a little bit homier than the lobby. There was that industrial carpeting that they try to make look like the carpet at home, but fail: you know what I mean—beige, flat, but with little pink flecks. Pink (why do hospitals choose pink, I wonder?) pleather loveseats with wooden arms that were stiff and totally not comfortable. Chairs with that same industrial/home-hopeful upholstery, green with dark brown stripes. To camouflage the coffee stains, probably. A flat screen TV playing an endless loop of Dr. Oz telling us how to keep fit by eating avocados and doing lots of cardio. Plants, of course. A coffee table here and there, with leaflets about mammograms, daily dietary guidelines, and surprisingly, one about infant car seats. They probably wanted to cover a lot of bases while you waited.

Barley pulled up a couple of chairs so Adam and I could put our feet up. "Try to get a little nap or something." So we shut our eyes. Don and the Crowders murmured, and Frank paced. I bet he felt like a fish out of water.

Wait. It dawned on me that Adam had one father who was in medical jeopardy (well, I hoped that was overly dramatic), so his other father jumped right in. Fletch's attendance was totally voluntary, involving a long drive from Dayton to Framington. He must have run to his car the minute he got word about Roy. Oh, man—I wondered who told him. Iris? Mom? Oh yeah, probably Marianne. No matter. He was an upright guy, Fletch. As a matter of fact, as I watched him pacing in his Eagles T-shirt and red-and-blue plaid flannel pants, wearing what looked like Ugg slide-ons, it hit me that he must have *rolled out of bed and into his car and just started driving*. He certainly hadn't shaved. And red stubble isn't all that sexy, I can tell you. So Fletch was really family. Huh.

About forty minutes went by, extremely slowly. We drank way too much caffeine. There were paper cups on all the surfaces. Luckily, there were no other groups in the waiting room, or they might have been annoyed at our complete takeover. Barley sprawled out on one of the couches, reading about colonoscopies. She'd studied the other brochures and this one was apparently horrifying, judging by the look on her face.

Adam and Frank sat side by side on the opposite sofa, staring blankly at Dr. Oz and his special guest, some botoxed starlet who was discussing the benefits of juicing and raw food.

The Crowders sat in the armchairs, looking out the window at the scorching landscape. I think they sighed a few times, and then they both kind of nodded off. Chair naps. Save me from getting old, dear God.

Don kept disappearing. I think he was periodically checking the main lobby and parking area for Mom and the other women. I alternated between biting my cuticles and fidgeting in my chair. I counted the coffee stains and noticed that somebody had probably either had a peanut butter and jelly sandwich that leaked on the corner of the upholstery, or a bloody nose. Maybe worse. Ugh.

Suddenly, Don burst into the waiting area, his arm around Aunt Iris. We reacted as if lightning had struck the waiting area and shocked the hell out of us. Then there was a group hug of massive proportions. We all talked at once. Iris stepped back after kissing me and Adam, patting Fletch on the cheek, and bestowing, "Bless you, bless you's" on the Crowders.

"Marianne is getting a parking pass. She'll be here in a minute." (Fletch relaxed visibly.) "Winnie's in with Roy, and the nurse told me that Roy is awake and can have visitors. Family only. Adam and Mandy, you can go in. Kids, he's going to be fine." She smiled beatifically. I loved Aunt Iris to death.

Don grinned. "Go on, you two. Through those double doors and to the right. Room 2008."

Adam and I went through the double doors. I turned right then noticed he wasn't beside me.

"Mand. Wait."

I turned. Adam stood with one arm against the wall, underneath the No Smoking sign. He looked like a patient himself, rigid, pale, set lips, and *grayish*. "This is it, Mand. If I blow this, both Mom and Dad will hate me. Because I probably caused his heart attack. What will I do when I get in there?"

"Adam, you know what? We have to stop trying to plan things. You can't plan for this. We have to go in there and see Dad and face Mom. This isn't something you can rehearse. We have to stop all this ruminating. Come *on*."

This was what screenwriters probably call a *turning point*. I would have to write that pivotal scene. It would require lots of pale makeup and atonal background music. I'd have to spend time thinking about that one later on. But I had to *live* it first. I grabbed Adam by the elbow and wrenched him forward, and I *dragged* him down the hall to room 2008.

The door was open and I saw Winnie first, leaning over the bed, stroking Roy's forehead solicitously. To say I was shocked would be an understatement. Mom was disheveled, sure. She radiated energy, of course. But here's the thing: she was *gorgeous*. She'd been gone for not even a month but up there in Michigan she'd gotten her hair colored light brown. It was short and curly. Shiny. She was thinner. She had *a French manicure*.

They were murmuring to one another. My attention shifted to Dad, who looked very small under the rumple of hospital sheets. He had horrible tubes in his nose and coming out of his arm. An IV pole was beside his bed, and that scary beepy dashboard suspended above the head of the bed, green lights and numbers flashing. He had a catheter and urine bag. I could hardly bear it.

Dad turned his head to look at us, and I felt a rush of relief because it was Roy Heath, the magical pharmacist, after all. His face was nice and rosy, despite the tubes in his nose, and he looked his usual chipper self, and he still had that eye twinkle, thank the Lord. He motioned for us to come in.

"Mandy, Adam! Pull up those chairs over there and sit down! I'm going to be fine! Especially since all of you are here now! Come on and tell me how you are!"

Mom kept smiling at us, although her face was just a little rigid as she looked at Adam. Probably because Adam seemed like the walking dead. We pulled up the chairs and sat down. Adam was an automaton.

Nothing. It was sixty seconds that seemed like a year. Dad broke the ice. "Anybody want to know what happened to me or how I am? Because we're in a hospital, you know? And I am in this bed right here, hooked up to monitors. You wanna hear the story?"

Mom sat on the side of Dad's bed, stroking his arm. "Of course, Roy. Tell us."

He did. We knew the story, since we'd heard it from the nurse and the Crowders and had been turning it over in our heads all day. But we listened as Dad said things like, "I was just knocked right out," and, "The first thing I remember is being in the ambulance," and, "The docs say that I'll be just fine."

We nodded and sighed and smiled and nodded. Even Adam. When Dad finished, he seemed worn out, and he closed his eyes. "Let me rest a little. They're bringing supper in a few minutes. I bet it will be applesauce and Jell-O. Ugh." Then he drifted off. No wonder.

Mom, her hand on Roy's arm, looked up at us. Well, at Adam. I gulped.

"Mom. Mom," Adam whispered.

Winnie took her hand off Dad's arm and pointed her finger at Adam. "Sssh! We have things to say to one another, Adam Heath. But not right now. Not in front of your father. Do you understand?"

She must have realized how frightening that manicured finger was, because she looked at it as if it were attached to somebody else's wrist, then dropped her hand into her lap. She shook her new fashionable curls and looked a little less formidable. "Let's be cheerful and supportive right now. Okay?"

We said nothing.

A nurse's aide trundled in with a tray. "Mr. Heath, are you awake? I have your dinner here!" Dad stirred and opened his eyes.

"Let's adjust your bed so you can eat." She pushed a button, and Dad gradually rose up into a sitting position (those beds looked so fun). She rolled the tray table thing in front of Roy and placed the "dinner" on it. It had one of those metal covers. Denise (I read her name tag) uncovered the plate with a flourish. "Enjoy! Do you need anything else right now?" Dad shook his head. "Hit the call button if you need anything. Enjoy your meal!" As quickly as she appeared in her pink uniform, running shoes, greasy smile, and dead eyes, she left.

Dad chuckled. "Just what I thought. Blandy-bland."

Why is it that hospitals, where you're supposed to get healthy, serve such sickening food? On the green melamine plate was a dab of cottage cheese, a small plastic cup of green Jell-O, and what looked like a bowl of pee. Apparently, it was chicken broth.

Mom looked horrified. "Are you on some kind of special menu? This looks terrible. I don't know how they expect you to eat any of this!"

Dad, ever the glass-half-full guy, picked up the cocktail-sized napkin and tried to spread it over his chest. Then he took the plastic spoon and dug into the Jell-O. "It isn't bad. They have to start me slowly, because I haven't eaten since dinner last night. They don't want me to be sick. And the anesthesia, you know." He seemed to savor the Jell-O. A big act, but no one does chipper better than Roy Heath.

"Winnie, have you eaten? Kids? You know you can order something from the cafeteria; they'll deliver it up here. That's what the nurse told me. Want me to push the call button and ask for a menu?"

"That sounds like a good idea." I said. I was starving. Even the cottage cheese on Dad's plate looked kind of good.

Adam agreed. "I can go. Tell me what you two want. I have money."

Mom smiled. "Get me a sandwich and a drink. I don't care what. While you're gone, Mandy can tell the ones in the waiting room that they don't have to stay. Iris can come in if she wants to, since she's family. Mandy, I'll be staying here tonight with Dad. Tell Frank and Marianne that they can stay at our house if they want to. I'm not sure if they're going back to Dayton tonight or not."

"Mand, what do you want?" I wanted to go back in time and have things the way they were before this summer happened. But I knew that wasn't what Adam was asking. So I told him I wanted a burger if they had them, and a Coke. He left, and I stood to go and deliver Mom's message to the others, but she said, "Mandy, wait." Oh, no.

"How is Adam?" Dad, in mid-bite of cottage cheese, also looked at me expectantly.

This was not how I'd envisioned things. It was supposed to be Mom and Adam talking about this, not me and Mom. With Dad lying right there, listening.

I tried to evade. "Well, I don't really know."

"That's nonsense. You've been with Adam every minute of every day since I left. You took a trip with him to Michigan and back. I know you and Adam talk. And certainly Barley Crowder talks to both of you. She isn't afraid to ask questions. Come on, Mandy. Simple question. How is Adam?"

I sat back down. Fidgeted. Stalled for as long as I could. The wheels were turning. What to say?

"Well. You know that Adam isn't exactly the spill-your-guts type. But I know he was torn up about having two fathers, and he thinks about that all the time. And he has said he feels responsible for Dad's heart attack. You can both tell from looking at Adam that he isn't exactly the happiest camper. But I haven't a clue what he's thinking right now. About Frank. About you, Mom. Or about the family or anything else. I'm not sure that Adam really knows what he feels. I mean, he loves us. That's for sure. But you know, he's mixed up."

"You know what? This is probably not the best time to dissect the situation with Adam." Dad. The master of the understatement.

Here's the thing about parents: you think they're stupid, but at the same time you expect them to be wise. I mean, Roy Heath wouldn't know a rap song if he fell on one, but then again, he was the king of kindness and optimism. I always expected him to make a fool of himself when discussing anything pop culture, but I knew he wouldn't let me down when it came to the wisdom of the ages. And Winnie? I kind of thought she was canny like no other.

"Yes. Mom. Let's table this whole subject for a while."

Mom misted over. But she nodded agreement just as Adam walked back in with Aunt Iris, a sack of food, and a weak smile.

"Iris sent everybody home. She said Dad needs rest, we need food, and we can keep in touch. Dad. Frank Fletcher is here. Iris said he and Marianne could stay over at her house. So I think they'll be here tomorrow."

"Very good, very nice." Dad took a few sips of broth and grimaced. "This stuff is awful. Do you have anything in there I can eat?"

And we passed a very companionable evening—Iris, Mom, Dad, Adam, and I. Sharing ham sandwiches, cheeseburgers, popsicles, and watching *American Idol* reruns. Mom was nervous, but she seemed to slow down to a minor hum, and Adam actually talked. Not to Mom, but to the room in general. He made a few comments about the talent, asked Dad if he had any bruises from when he fell in the yard—that kind of thing. It was pretty eventless. If a fraught and tense situation that is eventless was a good thing.

Adam and I left with Iris at around ten thirty. Mom, of course, was staying, as she had made clear to every nurse and aide who walked in and looked at Mom funny. Dad seemed tired. It had been a long, long day.

We drove home with Iris, since Don had left earlier. He'd moved our stuff into her car. The house was dark, and it kind of loomed as we drove up. Dark houses are discouraging.

"Do you want me to come in with you?" Iris asked. "You know, to get you settled in or something?"

We both declined. I wished we hadn't. Because as soon as we got into the kitchen and switched on the light, we saw Dad's cold cup of coffee on the table. The coffee pot was still on, and Dad's reading glasses were on the table, next to a plate with the remains of his toast on it. The sight of that made my throat kind of close up. Adam looked around, too. Then he said, "This is fucked up." But ol' Adam picked up the glasses, looked at them wistfully, folded them up, put them on the counter, and set the plate in the sink.

We went upstairs to bed. I'm willing to bet money that neither one of us closed our eyes the entire night.

My cell woke me up. I guess I did close my eyes. It was nine o'clock.

I gasped a greeting—kind of a combo between "Hello?" and "Whassup?"

It was Winnie. "Mandy, Dad gets to come home later on today. Isn't that great? The doctor said he'll have to go to some rehab and change his diet. He has to start exercising. But he'll be okay! Isn't that great news?" She panted this out like she had been running up stairs.

"Mom. Calm down. You may be the next one to have heart failure if you don't. Great news! Do you want us to come over?"

I didn't really want to go back there. It smelled of sterilized puke. And I hated seeing Roy down like that.

"No, you kids stay home. Can you clean up? I'm sure things are a mess. Have Adam take you to the store. Get fruit and yogurt and healthy things. Maybe some brown rice?"

"Mom. My God. Don't worry. Dinner of brown rice and yogurt won't cut it. You can trust me to get something well balanced. Just chill."

She gave me another five minutes of dietary suggestions, including Metamucil, wheat sprouts, cottage cheese, and green tea. I think she'd been doing a lot of phone Googling. I promised to vacuum and use bleach liberally in the bathrooms, and she let me go.

I went upstairs to begin my purge and met Adam in the hall, toothbrush in hand.

"Mom on the phone?"

I nodded. "I'm supposed to clean and sterilize. You're supposed to keep a civil tongue in your head and oh, yeah—take me to the grocery store. Have you ever heard of kombucha?"

"Huh?"

"Yeah, me either. Prepare yourself for a whole new world of health food around here. They'll be home later this afternoon. You have to be here."

"I know. I'm going out to shoot some hoops for a while. I need to stop my head, you know? But I'll be back. I'll take you to the store after lunch. I know I have to. Don't worry."

Here's the thing about Adam. He was confused. I knew that he was a quality person, despite all the sickening things he did. He was eighteen, for God's sake; all boys that age were funky. This situation had forced Adam to face things none of his friends could even contemplate. This stuff was propelling him toward adulthood like a rocket, with me right beside him. So our heads rang and throbbed. Our minds . . . reeled . . . you know?

I was confident that I'd end up okay, because I was going to write this movie, get famous, and stuff. And I was once removed from the actual two-dads situation. Plus, I had Barley to talk with. And Iris. But Adam was not the type to cry on someone's shoulder, and so he was all alone.

I got out the cleaning bucket. I started with the kitchen. It wasn't bad. Dad had kept up with things. All I had to do was general swabbing and dishwasher filling. There weren't even any crumbs on the floor. Mom would be okay with it. I put the coffee grounds in the trash and washed the pot, put his breakfast dish and knife in the dishwasher, moved Dad's glasses to the windowsill above the sink, and wiped down the counters with the sponge. I loaded his cup into the dishwasher as well and hit "quick wash."

I walked around the rest of the downstairs and gave it a thumbs-up. I turned my attention to the upstairs bathroom, where I knew that the gray scum on the bottom of the tub would make Winnie hurl. So I began to work on it with Comet. As I was scrubbing, feeling kind of satisfied at how well the Comet was bleaching the foot crud, I had a thought that stopped me cold.

Adam wasn't alone. He had *me.*

Chapter Thirteen

Thank God we had Mom's charge card, because Adam and I really got into the health food. We grabbed spinach salad (washed, the bag said), oranges, some kind of melon that looked good, green tea that is apparently full of antioxidants, brown rice, and some tilapia. The guy at the fish counter said we should get fresh dill to sprinkle on the fish. He told us to cover it with olive oil, the dill, and lemon juice, and bake it. But if we wanted to make things easy, to microwave it for three minutes. Sounded great to us. So we got the dill and a couple of lemons. Then we went to the produce section and looked at the veggies. We agreed that even though we both hated broccoli, we should get some of that.

Adam surprised the hell out of me and suggested we get some blueberries, too, because "they help prevent cancer." Who knew Adam was up on blueberries?

We cheated and got some Fritos and salsa. We figured we were still young enough to eat that and, if we had to, we could hide them in our rooms if Winnie frowned on them.

We took the long way home. We needed to postpone the inevitable.

"Adam, are you still totally anxious about talking to Mom?" I asked, idly watching a lady in extremely tight Bermuda shorts cross in front of the car at a light. She looked as if she was trying not to notice that the shorts were riding way up on the inside of her thighs. I felt a fleeting pang for her. Do fat people hate themselves?

"Shit; that's one obese female." Apparently, this woman needed to get bigger shorts.

"Adam. Forget her. What about Mom?"

"Mom isn't fat; she's chubby."

I sighed. "Adam, don't be purposely dense. How are you going to handle the Mom situation?"

Adam, who smashed down on the accelerator a little too emphatically after observing the woman chugging by, peeled a little rubber, refocused on the street in front of us, and slowed down. "I'm sick of planning. Like you said, I'm not in control of anything. We drove all the way to Michigan for nothing, so now I'm just going with the flow."

"Speaking of going with the flow, what about school? You know, it starts again in a few weeks. You don't seem to have applied to any colleges. What are you going to do about that? I thought you wanted to get out of here. Especially now."

Adam nodded slowly. "I know. You think I haven't been thinking about that? I'm going to get a job. Save some bucks. Then go to school. Or maybe get an apartment, then save, then school."

"What kind of a job? You can work for Dad. But I guess that doesn't count as 'getting out of here,' does it?"

"I've been looking in the paper."

I looked at my brother. My stupid brother. "Adam, what can you get for a job, really? You don't have skills or anything. That is why people go to *college*. So what, you think you can get an apartment and pay bills and stuff by working in the fascinating and upwardly mobile world of fast food? Or washing cars?"

He banged his palm on the steering wheel. "Shit, Mand, I don't know! There has got to be something! Or I can go into the service. And then they'll pay for college."

I about aspirated my own saliva on that one. "Adam. If you enlist, you become a *soldier*. You know what they do with *soldiers*? They train them and get them all *killer*, then they send them to Afghanistan or some other hellhole, and they either get killed or come back with PTSD. But I guess you can go to college after that—you can get one of those *service dogs* to help you from freaking out and having flashbacks."

By then, Adam was getting worked up. His neck was flushed, and the mottled pinkness was creeping up into his face. His nostrils flared. Ugh. Bigger nostrils are not a good look for Adam.

"Mandy, can you cut me a little slack here? Can you let me work through one disaster before you force me to choose my lifelong path? Okay? Can you let me get a shit job and have a little time to *think*, for God's sake? Shit, Mand, fuck, you are the perfect practice for dealing with Mom right now!"

We had reached the old homestead. Adam pulled up the driveway, turned off the car, and shot out of it and right into the house. Yep. Ol' Mand would have to make three trips to lug in all the healthy food. As I unpacked the greens, the fish, and the rest of it, not bothering to wash anything because I knew Mom would do that multiple times, I thought about Adam. I tried to picture him in camo, with a helmet and an M16, or 14, or whatever the soldiers used to annihilate jihadists and hapless villagers. Shit.

Just as I was imagining Adam and his platoon surrounding a grainy compound, aiming their guns over the razor wire at a group of swarthy terrorists with equally terrifying weapons, goats, and cowering women and children, Mom and Iris walked into the kitchen, one on each side of Dad, who looked pretty grayish.

Mom smiled tightly at me. "We just have to get him upstairs and into bed. He needs to rest. Then we need to make a plan." I nodded, relieved that I'd been mature enough to think ahead and decide that along with a germ-free bathroom, dear Roy might enjoy clean sheets on their bed.

Adam slunk into the kitchen after they shut the bedroom door.

"So. What's going to happen?" He sat down at the table and began picking at a pimple that apparently had just sprung full grown out of his chin.

"Mom and Iris are getting Dad settled, and then there's going to be a planning meeting. You need to stick around. You know, we may need to tell Mom what acai tea is."

Adam continued to pick. Disgusto. But I gave him a pass and didn't say anything.

"I'm going to volunteer to work at the store until Dad can get back. I bet Mom has already arranged for Mr. Clark to come in." (This was a retired pharmacist that Dad had asked to fill in before, when we went on that one vacation that one time.) "I bet Mom won't be able to work much, 'cause she'll be here with Dad. And you'll be starting school soon. This solves the crap-job dilemma, I guess."

Adam was beginning to scare me. I'd never equated Adam and "rising to the occasion" as being in the same bandwidth. "Adam, I'm sorry I yelled at you about working. I guess I was trying to help you see straight. But you seem to be doing that just fine yourself."

He shot me what I'd have to call a rueful smile. "Mand, I'm a fully functioning human being. Much to your surprise."

"Adam, I said I'm sorry. You know, you and I haven't exactly been soul mates up to this point." I reached into the fridge and got us each a raspberry yogurt "with active cultures," and fished around in the silverware drawer for two spoons. "Here. We might as well start by eating this stuff. I am sure this is just the beginning. We may have to learn to like kale." I sat down across from him at Mom's place. Thank God Mom was back.

Adam took a bite and made a sour lemon face. "This stuff is gross." He turned and aimed the yogurt container at the sink, and it crashed in, pink splatting everywhere, including on Mom's curtains.

"Good one, oh massive human being of adult stature. Now you can explain that one to Mom—maturely."

"Okay, smugface. Anything else?" He leered at me.

"Geez. Sorry. I think that your working at the store is great. Really. And Mom and Dad will appreciate it."

I took another bite of the yogurt. It had a sort of fruity flavor at first, kind of nice. But then, after swallowing, there was a lingering bitterness. I hated it, too. How was this stuff so popular? I smiled at Adam and lobbed mine into the sink. "Mr. Heath, I have to concede your point on the yogurt. It's vile. We'll have to get sherbet or something for Dad."

"But it won't have 'active cultures.' No worries, though, Mand. Down at the store, I'm sure there are *active culture pills*. Since I'll be the interim store *manager*, I'll make it my goal to familiarize myself with the inventory in the heart health category. I'll bring home the appropriate medications in pill form. Fuck the yogurt."

We both died. It was cockle-warming, I can tell you. Sibling bonding of the highest order. Hey, it wasn't much, but it was a beginning.

We had the tilapia for dinner. Mom didn't do the microwave thing. Of course not. Winnie Heath was a gourmet cook. A matter that I overlooked at the market.

She made the fish with caper sauce that had the dill in it. She transformed the triple-washed spinach into a salad with the blueberries and a tangy dressing. The woman was a kitchen wizard. She took a tray up for Dad, and Adam and I carried our plates up to the bedroom, too. So he and Mom would have company. The whole family thingy.

Dad was wearing his favorite limp, short-sleeved *Bayer Aspirin Low Dose* T-shirt, which had been washed a zillion times and had frayed edges. Cozy. He was propped up, and Mom had put his dinner on the yellow wicker bed tray that we'd used for sick people ever since I could remember. I pulled over the sky blue velvet bench from the front of their bed so that Adam and I could sit on it and be closer to Mom and Dad. We balanced our plates on our knees and began eating. Rickety lap thing but delishmo food.

Dad picked at the food. But he was very cheery and tried to make small talk. It was obvious, though, that he was really tired.

"Dad, you don't have to eat much. But at least drink some of the tea. It's green. It's very good for your heart. We put honey in it. For energy." I didn't add that both Adam and I had tasted the green tea, and it was pretty awful.

Mom didn't seem to be eating much, either. She'd pulled their comfy blue-and-beige plaid armchair close to the bed, and her plate was pretty much untouched in her lap. But she was beaming away at Dad. And not looking at me and Adam. At all.

Of course, it was the four of us in the bedroom, along with *The Elephant.* You could cut the tension with a knife. I took another bite of the fish. It melted in my mouth. "Mom. This fish is delicious. Really."

"Okay. Let's cut the crap." Adam might as well have hit a gong. He stood, plate in hand. We all started, and

Dad dropped his fork. It slid off the wicker and disappeared into the sheets. Mom looked alarmed and started to say something.

"No. Mom. Just everybody be quiet for a minute. Let me say what I have to say."

Mom nodded, her face taut. I put my plate on the floor beside me.

"A lot has happened this summer. It's been kind of like a tidal wave of stuff, you know? First it was the Fletch thing, then the party when I exploded, then Mom left, then Dad got sick, and a whole bunch of other stuff that I probably can't even remember. Let's just say those were the high points, okay?"

This was going to be epic. Mom looked stricken. Dad leaned back against his pillows, his face, if possible, getting even grayer. I said a quick prayer that whatever Adam was going to say, we would all survive it. *Please, God, don't let Adam give Dad another heart attack or Mom a stroke...*

Adam put his plate down on the bench beside me and continued. "I find out that the man that I have always called my dad isn't. Instead, some musician from Dayton who I always thought was my long-lost uncle is my actual dad."

Adam paused to collect his thoughts. He straightened up, his spine like a plank. I could almost see sparks flying out of his clotted red curls. He paced up and down at the foot of the bed. Intense, focused.

"I hated you, Mom." He thrust out his palm at her. "I hated you, yeah. Can you blame me? You even gave me permission to hate you, remember? Then you and Iris left. I was glad, at first. Me and Mandy and Dad. I thought it would be a relief, and fun, sort of."

I realized I wasn't breathing. So I took a jaggedy breath. Adam stopped pacing and faced Mom and Dad.

You know about the pin dropping? It's true. You could actually have heard one in there.

"It wasn't fun. It was weird. Mandy did her best. But she isn't supposed to be a housekeeper. Shit, she's a teenager, and she should be hanging around with Barley and shopping for school clothes and stuff, not grocery shopping and vacuuming! And you, Dad? You knew all about the Frank thing all along, and you kept it to yourself, being my dad, loving our family and everything. You stepped right up to the plate when Mom left, and just kept on loving her and taking care of me and Mand.

"I couldn't wrap my head around *that*. Things were fucked up. Sorry, Mom. But they were. Add to this the fact that I wasn't going to college in the fall in spite of all of Mom's pushing me to, whether or not I really wanted to." Adam's head dropped to his chest.

He sat on the bottom of the bed. "Oh, yeah. And then throw into all of this Aunt Iris and Don, and why the hell Frank and Iris are still *married*? And while you're gone, Frank the Fletch comes over, and he's a *nice guy*. Then Don Horley offers to drive us up to Michigan to get you. Shit, man! Too much. Too many men in the family all of a sudden."

"Oh, honey." This from Mom.

"Wait. Just wait. I have to finish. So. What was there to do but think about stuff? I mean, while you weren't here, Mom, and then on the whole trip to Michigan, which, by the way, was like something out of a Wes Anderson movie."

Again. Shock. Adam knew who Wes Anderson was? *My* thing was movies...

"I've been thinking about this whole sucky situation. Nonstop. First of all, Mom. You screwed *up*. I don't know how any person could screw up so royally."

Winnie stirred. Like majorly. I thought she might erupt.

"*Wait. Just wait.* Like I said, you screwed up, Mom. But then I thought about how old you were when all of that went down. You were my age, like. I asked myself how smart *I* am at making decisions. College. A job. My future and stuff. I realized that I don't have a *clue* right now about my life. I'm just a kid." He paused to take a breath. "I was wrong to blow up in your face at the Fourth of July party. I give you that. But even so, there was still a huge bunch of crap tangling everything up." (He sliced his hands back and forth like Edward Scissorhands.) "Mom: gone. Me and Mand: confused as shit. Then the road trip from hell. Then Dad drops. Jesus."

Adam looked down at his lap. He'd dropped his hands into his lap, knuckles white, just like in the movies. (This will surely be the scene that wins me the Oscar. But it will be hell to write.)

"I want to go back. Start over. But I can't. We can't. So the best I can come up with is this: Mom, we have to have time. We both need to live and let live. I won't say that I can forgive and forget. Not right this minute. But you don't have to do anything, either. We have to go on as best we can.

"Dad. *You* are my dad. Frank Fletcher is a nice man, but *you* are my dad. I guess I can let Fletch be in my life, in a way. But that will take time, too. As far as he and Aunt Iris are concerned, it's none of my business if they are married or not."

Dad actually grinned.

"That's all that I have to say about the whole family situation. Time. I want time. No talking or analyzing, okay? In the meantime, Mandy needs to get ready for school. Mom needs to take care of you, Dad. And you need to do your rehab and get better. So. Since all of you will be busy and I'm not, I'll go to work at the store. You know, manage things. We'll get by with Mr. Clark until you can come back. 'Cause you will focus on your rehab big time, and you *will* be back. That's it. That is all. What we need to do, and what we need to remember: time and space and the benefit of the doubt. Okay. I am done." And Adam flung himself backward onto the bed, so that he was beside Dad, on the other pillow. An old, wrung-out male, and a young, strung-out one. Roy and Adam Heath, both bushed.

Father and son. Down but never out.

Chapter Fourteen

Our family was pretty clean cut, actually. No drugs or alcoholism. Winnie was a typical germaholic housekeeper. Roy was the endearing breadwinner, dependable and stoic, yet cheery. Adam, albeit hormonal and musky, actually had deep thoughts and feelings, as it turned out. I remained fifteen and never been kissed, not actually ashamed of my virginal status *yet* because, thank God, I had Barley as the buffer for all that. Like I said, I figured she was probably a virgin, too, but I wasn't going to go there. Because, you know, *Adam*.

When you put a bunch of decent people in a hairy situation like we were in that summer, maybe it turns out better than it would have if it were to happen to a less "normal" family. Of course, if something scars you *for life*, the scars may not show up right away. But so far, the Heaths seemed to be dealing like champs. Cue Dr. Phil.

After about a week, Dad felt much stronger. He could walk around the house just fine. His rehab was due to start in another week, and the doc told us to encourage Dad to do the stairs five times a day, drink a lot of water, sleep well, and concentrate on getting well.

Here's the weird thing of it: Who went up and down the steps five times a day right behind Dad, to encourage him and make sure he did it? *Adam*. He did it with Dad every morning before Adam went into the store.

While they went up and down, they talked shop. Dad filled Adam in on things he needed to know, like stocking and inventory management and stuff. I would hear them from my bed. It sounded like healing to me.

Meanwhile, Adam and Mom gave each other a wide berth. It wasn't as if they were furious or anything. More like they'd forgotten they knew one another. They just exchanged polite nods, the way you do when you run into an acquaintance whose name is on the tip of your tongue.

Yesterday, after she made Dad a lunch and put it into the fridge for him, Mom and I went school shopping. School started in exactly one week, and I had nothing to wear but sweats, a few stained T-shirts, flip-flops, and jeans that had seen much, much better days.

I have always despised shopping. Not the shopping, exactly. It's the constant trying on: Take your clothes off. Put on this new stuff. Look in the mirror. No. Put your clothes back on. Repeat. So I wasn't in the best of moods. In the car, there wasn't a lot of chatting.

Then Mom said, "I know I said that it was okay for Adam to hate me. And he does. But it isn't okay. It's breaking my heart in two."

Oh, man.

"Mom, remember what Roy the Pharmacist always says: 'Tincture of time heals most things. Tincture of time.'" My God, I was really grasping at straws.

She heaved a sigh, gripping the wheel with her stubby fingers, now a little chipped around the French manicured edges. The old Winnie was slowly returning. At least physically.

"I never should have said anything. Never. I should have just kept on carrying that around inside. Stupid. I thought it would clear the air and help things. What an idiot I am."

This was going downhill fast. I really didn't know what to say. So I added my own stupidness into the mix. "Do you think Aunt Iris and Fletch will get a divorce?"

Mom nearly ran a stop sign. "How should I know? God, I have enough awfulness going on in my own house without worrying about them. Of course, their situation and poor Marianne—that's my fault, too. They were all fine before I raked up everything."

"Mom, why don't you pull over? The park is right there. We might as well sit on a nice shady bench and talk this over. Driving and family crisis don't mix." I pointed to the leafy greenness of Framington City Park, where there were lots of beautiful plants and tall trees. The grass was lush, and there were plenty of late summer flowers. They obviously have a sprinkler system. "Mom. Let's take a break. Plenty of time for bargains today."

Winnie parked the car by a meter that still had twenty minutes on it. I discouraged her from putting in a quarter. I wanted to get this over with. Twenty minutes seemed like an eternity, actually.

We wandered over to a park bench under a giant maple tree. This tree was one of my favorites. In the fall, it was the first tree in town to turn gold. It was the kind of maple with leaves that remain dark orange along the edges and turn bright yellowy on the inside, almost as if the sun had caught them on fire. When I was little, I made Mom take me there every fall, so I could search for the perfect leaf. Then I'd take it home and put it inside the huge Webster's dictionary we have in the living room bookcase. There were at least six of them still in there.

Anyway, Mom plumped herself down on the bench, and I sat beside her and patted her on the arm. It was very cool under that champion maple. We sat there for a minute, lost in our own thoughts. Then Mom started in again.

"So you think things will work themselves out in time?"

You know, kids are *not* supposed to die before their parents do. I think the same goes for kids giving their own parents advice. But here we were, sitting in a park in mid-August, in a dumpy little city in northern Ohio, my mom looking beseechingly at me.

> *Strains of the Low Anthem's "To Ohio." A large, leafy park. Birds tweeting. Dogs woofing. A fountain in the background spraying cool mist. Children wading in. Camera glides over the scene. We see two females on a bench. Zoom in. A competent-looking woman, her wiry hair obviously in stages of growing out, her face a smudge of anxiety, leans earnestly toward a young girl with similarly unkempt brown hair. They share some facial features: the nose, the strong chin. Obviously mother and daughter.*
>
> *The dialogue concerns the issues that drive the entire motion picture: a family rife with conflict, and the hope that love can somehow conquer it. As the daughter casts around in her head for just the right thing to say to her mother (Mandy: pivotal speech—spend a lot of time on this one), we see the lines ease in the mother's face. She listens to her daughter with a mixture of admiration and relief. The scene fades into the next scene in the mall; we see the mother take her daughter's hand.*

If only.

"I know you've talked about this a lot with Dad. What does he say?"

Mom smiled slightly. Roy had that effect on us. "He says it took him a long time to figure things out—you know, all those years ago, right before Adam was born. He said that it always came back to one thing: his love for me. He said he put his faith in that."

See? This is why you don't ask your teenage daughter for advice. Teenagers have nothing to go on. They haven't lived long enough. But then, of course, when Roy figured out to put his faith in love, he was what? Twenty? I had a lot of wising up to do in a few short years. Whoa.

"Mom, that sounds like just the thing. Trust that you love Adam, and you know that, deep inside, he loves you back. It seems to me that all of us just have to hang on to that fact. Right?"

Winnie gave me another half-smile and a knowing nod. "Yep, honey. I guess this is what we all have to do." She slapped her lap with both palms. "Let's get this shopping thing over with, and maybe afterwards we can have an ice cream cone or something."

I got three new pairs of jeans, five polos in assorted colors, a new pair of running shoes, a totally cool hoodie that was waterproof, and Mom insisted on body wash, shampoo, and matching spritz at Bath & Body Works. A new fragrance that smelled like a rainy day. Romantic. Not really what I needed, but you know, *high school.* I had to start being girly.

Our lovely philosophical discussion on the park bench was tried to its limit the minute we got home and Dad reported that Adam had forgotten to come home to take Dad to his one o'clock rehab appointment, as agreed previously. Winnie was pissed at her son all over again. Dad was fine with it. He simply called the rehab center and rescheduled. But Mom said something about "never forgiving Adam" under her breath. You know, this family thing—it sucks. I would have to think long and hard about having children, for *sure*.

It is obvious that my movie will be "based on a true story," because nobody would be the slightest bit interested in the actual ins and outs of this one right here.

Guess what? Aunt Iris filed for divorce! Yep. But that wasn't the real shocker: She didn't do it so that she could marry Don Horley. Because Don broke up with Iris. I know, *what?*

Iris came over the next morning to have lunch with me and Mom before school started. We always did this. Mom made homemade soup, and Aunt Iris always brought something delectable like egg salad sandwiches and her world-famous fudgy brownies. After lunch I would do a fashion show with my new school clothes, and we'd gossip and giggle. But this day was different.

First of all, Aunt Iris was a half hour late. This was a complete shock, because the woman was punctuality incarnate. Mom and I called her twice on her cell, but it went to voice mail. We were concerned. We sat at the kitchen table and speculated about her fate. Dad, who was in the den watching golf on TV, wandered in and told us not to worry. "Maybe she stopped at the bakery for some cookies."

"*Bakery?* Roy, you know Iris wouldn't eat store-bought baked goods! Heavens!"

Dad sat down with us. His cheeks were much rosier, and he looked almost like his old self. He was raring to go back to work, but the doctor said he had to be off for six weeks. For Roy Heath, it was not a welcome vacation, I can tell you. "I'm sure she's fine. Maybe she overslept or something."

"Roy, these are the weakest attempts at excuses I have ever heard. Do you *know* Iris Fletcher? Has she ever been late a day in her life? Has she ever slept past sunrise? You know my sister!"

Luckily, we heard Aunt Iris's car pulling into the driveway, or Mom would have hauled off and called the authorities. Dad gave us a "told you so" look and disappeared back into the den to watch the most boring sport on television.

Iris came in, carrying nothing. Not a box or a bag. She was all caved in on herself, like a hundred-year-old woman. Her usually lovely, flowing, coffee ice cream-colored hair was a little greasy, and there was a large snarl above her left ear. Total bed head. To top it off, she was wearing her pajamas and a pair of Dearfoams. Jesus.

"Iris. Honey. Sit down. Let me get you some coffee." Mom leaped up.

I didn't know what to do. It was the worst I'd ever seen Aunt Iris look. I couldn't believe this. We thought the family shit storm was over. Apparently, it was now swirling around Iris. Crummy metaphor. But totally apt, judging from the way Iris looked. And smelled. My God, she still had morning breath. Unbrushed teeth? This was way serious. Iris slid into a chair. Her head drooped; she had to prop it up with the palm of her hand. Silent. Eerie. When Mom put the mug of coffee in front of her, she took a drag on it that I swear made me worry she'd get serious mouth burns.

"Did something happen?" This from me, the master of dialogue. Obviously, I will need a lot of work in this area before I become a screenwriter.

Iris looked down into her coffee. As if maybe there was an answer in there. Then—oh, my God—she started to cry. That hiccup kind of sobbing. Mom leaned over her and hugged Iris. "Oh, honey. Honey."

Finally, it came out. In between sobs, Iris told us what happened. "Don called me this morning, like he always does, to say hi and start out my day. Today he said he's been thinking things over. He is 'uncomfortable' with the fact that I never 'bothered' to divorce Frank. He thinks that Frank is now a part of the family." More sobs, more hugs from Winnie. I sat there like a lump.

"He says he needs 'time to think,' and he wants to 'go our separate ways' for a while." (Louder sobs, nose running freely, ugh.) "Oh, what will I do?" (*Torrents of sobs.*)

If ever there were a time for a plot-turning, climactic speech, this was it. I had nothing. I was so shocked that the countertop king would do this. He'd seemed so rock-solid all the way to Michigan and back. I mean, he'd been the voice of reason the whole time. I was mute with disbelief.

Mom, on the other hand, terrier that she is, jumped into the breach. Thank God.

"Now Iris. Don has had a lot to deal with, just like the rest of us. You know what? Maybe he does need time. We all need time, for heaven's sake. But life goes on. One foot in front of the other."

Iris looked up from the depths. "Time? That's all you can come up with? *Time?*"

Winnie wasn't daunted, not one bit. "There is no magic wand. No perfect saying that will make everything right again. You can go to the library and check out every single self-help book on the shelves, but they won't tell you anything different. When terrible things happen, we just have to go on. That's the truth of the matter. Iris, we both know this. Everybody does. When times are tough, we wish and hope for a magical abracadabra solution." (Mom waved her arms like a swami.) "There aren't any of those." She quoted the pharmacist: "Tincture of time, dearie, tincture of time."

I sat there wondering if it was better to have all of life's bitter lessons drummed into you when you were fifteen, or whether it would be much nicer to learn the tough stuff gradually. You know, like during your twenties, when you have your own apartment and a job. And a driver's license. We sat, limp and downtrodden. Well, Iris and I. Mom was vibrating around with her usual zeal. At least there was one silver lining. Winnie was *Back Atcha.*

Iris downed her coffee and held the cup up for more.

An hour later, Mom had managed to get Iris to calm down, eat some toast, and go upstairs to freshen up. Iris came back down with her hair combed and wearing Mom's pink chenille robe, which looked kind of cute on Winnie, but ridiculous on lanky Iris. It looked like she was in drag or something. Anyway, Iris was calmer, and I guess she agreed to take it one day at a time. She left to take the rest of this one day at a time, driving slowly down the street. We watched her from the front porch. As she turned the corner, she stuck her arm out and gave us a pink chenille salute.

So far this summer, two phrases: "Benefit of the doubt," and "Tincture of time." I was really hoping for one more, one I could sink my teeth into. Wait. Okay. This one: *"Life is tragedy when seen in close up. Comedy in long-shot."* Charlie Chaplin.

Thank God for Google.

Fast Forward

Barley and I can't wait for school to start. First off, it will get us both out of the house. This is just what I need, and Barley says that she's getting sick of going in to the store, hoping to catch a glimpse of Adam. She says he's really busy all the time, and the one time they had a conversation, he told her that right now he has to "focus." Barley says that makes complete sense. So she is going to "live in the high school moment."

We are sitting on my bed, putting outfits together, trying to decide what I should wear on the first day of school. It's down to studded jeans, a yellow Ralph Lauren polo, and a string belt, or black jeans with a hot pink Lauren and black Reeboks. I'm leaning toward the black. More chic. Or something. Barley is forcing me to start wearing nail polish. I have three bottles so far: Zuzu's Petals, Heavy Metal, and Barcelona. On my right hand at the moment was one pink nail, one brown one, and a navy one with sparkles.

"I think we should go ahead this year and have a lot of boyfriends."

"Barley, this is easy for you to say. I'm not exactly a boy magnet."

Barley looks at me, appraisingly. "But, see, this is what we're doing right now. Transforming you into a boy magnet."

I look at my nails. I prefer them plain. Winnie is like that. She went and had them take her French manicure off. She says it made her nails ache. I think mine are kind of aching right now. "Can't we just let things alone? I can tag along with you in school, you know—like being popular. On the weekends when you have dates, I can stay home and write movies and make sure Adam knows how many boyfriends you're having instead of him."

"No, Mand. We have to experience things. High school is for that. You don't want to go to college all virginal and unworldly, do you? How can you write a screenplay if you haven't really *done* anything?"

I could see her point. It wasn't that I didn't have hormones or anything. I still have a crush on Bill Winthrop from the basketball team. But he graduated last year. Plus, I doubt he ever even knew I was alive. This is the way things have always gone with me and boys.

"So, what—you can somehow turn me into a man magnet this year? With nail polish and the right wardrobe? Barley, you're powerful, but come *on*."

"Mand, I think part of it is your attitude. You have to get more confidence. And make up your mind that you can get a boyfriend. Really." OMG. Winnie. She knew this when she was my age. Winnie knew about the *attitude*.

"But wait, Barley. What about Adam? I mean, you've always been in love with him."

Barley, the wise and powerful, looks at me with those aquatic blue eyes. Arrayed on my bed, her legs long and tan, her blonde hair spiking in all the right places, she smiles.

"Mandy, Adam is for later. We both know that."

Wow. I wonder how many fifteen-year-olds have their lives figured out. I don't. I have had a summer full of events that have proved that my life is just beginning, really. I am neither old nor wise, not yet.

Here's the plan: I am going to stick with Barley. I am going to give Mom, Adam, Dad, Don, Fletch, Marianne, and everybody else in my life the benefit of the doubt. I am going to go to high school and have crushes, defeats, and I hope some triumphs. Fear of sex or not, the virginity may have to go. I have mixed feelings still. I will just keep an open mind. Oh, and I'm going to keep a notebook for movie ideas. Sometime soon, Adam and Mom will make up—I mean completely, no lasting hard feelings. There will be lots of dinners in the kitchen, full of laughter and low-fat foods. Dad will go back to work, I hope. Mom will admire the shit out of Adam for keeping things going at the store. Maybe Adam will go to college and be a forest ranger after all. Aunt Iris will get her divorce, and Fletch and Marianne will get married. I hope. Maybe the countertop king will come back and carry Aunt Iris off. And she'll get a whole new bathroom with Italian marble around the sink.

And maybe I *will* read that book about the cookie that made Marcel Proust famous.

Acknowledgments

I never thought I could write a story, much less a novel. But Lou Aronica somehow knew I could. He read my first attempt and kindly suggested that it needed a plot. After a lot of his kind and patient mentoring, I was able to produce this one. Thank you so much for your years of support and encouragement, Lou and The Story Plant.

I have great friends. I want to thank Beth Hoffman, Sheryl Kammer, Suzanne-Kelly Garrison, David Lee Garrison, Robin Black, the women of Creative Alliance, Jane and Dave Reeder, my sister Lynne, and all of my blog readers who make me feel talented. What a gift.

I would not have been able to do this project without my crack editor, Hazel Dawkins. And I never would have found her without Dennis Fairchild. Bless you both.

Speaking of editors with amazing skills, I also want to give tremendous thanks to Nora Tamada, copyeditor extraordinaire, whose skills amaze me.

I began my writing career after winning The Erma Bombeck Writing Award two wonderful times. Thank you to the University of Dayton for sponsoring it, and Terri Rizvi and Debe Dockins for making it possible. The Erma Bombeck Writer's Workshop is an event that no writer should miss.

My family is the best, and my husband Charlie, the *real* accordionist, is my cheerleader and best friend. My two girls, Annie and Marion, inspire me, and I hope they are proud.

I only wish my father were alive to read this book.

About the Author

Molly D. Campbell is the winner of two Erma Bombeck writing awards. A long-time blogger and lover of quirky characters, she wrote her first book, *Characters in Search of a Novel,* with illustrator Randy Palmer.

Molly lives in Dayton, Ohio, with her accordionist husband and five cats.